The Nutcrackers

B.S.

The Nutcrackers

Olympia Publishers
London

www.olympiapublishers.com
OLYMPIA PAPERBACK EDITION

Copyright © B. S. 2024

The right of B.S. to be identified as author of
this work has been asserted in accordance with sections 77 and 78 of
the Copyright, Designs and Patents Act 1988.

All Rights Reserved

No reproduction, copy or transmission of this publication
may be made without written permission.
No paragraph of this publication may be reproduced,
copied or transmitted save with the written permission of the publisher,
or in accordance with the provisions
of the Copyright Act 1956 (as amended).

Any person who commits any unauthorised act in relation to
this publication may be liable to criminal
prosecution and civil claims for damage.

A CIP catalogue record for this title is
available from the British Library.

ISBN: 978-1-80439-211-9

This is a work of fiction.
Names, characters, places and incidents originate from the writer's
imagination. Any resemblance to actual persons, living or dead, is
purely coincidental.

First Published in 2024

Olympia Publishers
Tallis House
2 Tallis Street
London
EC4Y 0AB

Printed in Great Britain

1

"His name should be Purple," said Oak to Hazel when Purple was born.

"Purple," said Hazel, surprised. "Why?"

"Because I can't call him Yellow, Red or Orange."

"Why does he need a colour name?"

"Because he is born with the energy from the sun."

"He is what?" said Hazel, astonished.

"Never mind," said Oak, angry.

"Can't he have a name that shows he's your son?"

"Like Acorn," said Oak dryly.

"That's a great name," said Hazel, excited.

I have to find her a new boyfriend, thought Oak, *preferably one who lives on the mainland.*

2

Dian went to play with her best friends Purple and Angus, she had just lost her mother. Purple patted her on the hair the same way he patted his horse.

Angus said she could move in with him and his mother, Flora had always wanted a daughter. Dian was happy, mostly because it meant that she would have a big brother. Angus was seven, Purple six and Dian five.

Angus and Purple had found an old Viking sword in a hollow tree, they decided to try it on Dian.

"Close your eyes and lay your head on the tree stump," said Purple. Angus roared long and wildly before he cut off her hair. Purple and Angus looked like two gambolling fawns afterwards.

Dian took the sword from Angus and said, "Your turn!"

Angus objected strongly. He had long almost white hair that went like a waterfall down his back.

"You look like an angel," said Dian, "but everyone knows you're not." Angus had to agree, he lay his head on the stump. He looked much nicer with shorter hair. Then it was Purple's turn.

"Do you want a fringe?" asked Dian.

"No," answered Purple.

They hid the sword in the hollow tree again. Angus had something to do, so he left.

"What do you reckon he's up to?" asked Purple.

"Don't know," replied Dian.

Dian and Purple tiptoed behind Angus, and hid behind the

tree trunks. Angus went to a meadow and started picking dandelion flowers in a large sack. When the sack was full, he strolled home to Blairmore.

Flora was stirring a large cauldron. Angus emptied the sack in the cauldron and took over the stirring. After a while, he pulled out some yellow clothes and threw them up in a large oak tree.

"So, that's the secret," said Purple, "that's how Angus gets the nice yellow colour on his clothes."

"What are you using?" asked Dian.

"I'm using the roots from the cranberries and a few blueberries. What about you?"

"I'm throwing my clothes in the water you have used."

"And you get the nice pink colour?" asked Purple, astonished.

"Yes, it's a weaker version of your red colour."

3

Frøya looked at Angus, Purple and Dian who climbed a solid oak tree. Dian jumped down from the tree and took a stick and wrote 2015 and 0314.

"What are you doing?" asked Angus.

"I'm writing down some numbers."

"I can see that, but why?"

"It was only some numbers that fell into my head, but I can see why."

"Why?"

"The numbers can be expanded or contracted. Number 15 is related to number 14 and is one more, and number 2 is related to number 3 and is one less."

"Why isn't number 3 one more than 2?" asked Purple. Angus just shook his head and looked up into the sky.

"It's obvious," said Dian, "number 2 stands first."

She wrote down the numbers so they stood aligned. 00112345-7.

"They are good numbers," said Dian, satisfied.

Frøya was satisfied too, Dian had picked up the numbers she had sent her. Dian was on her way to become the greatest nutcracker the world had ever seen.

Frøya decided to go ahead to Catacol, it was the annual market for the druids, they gathered by the Water of Life every midsummer. It was her task to guard the rare rowan that stood by the ford. Frøya liked Catacol, she had made sure the place was named after her two black cats.

Flora stood on the plain, and waved at Frøya who sat on the nearest mountain top, Frøya waved back. Flora was so sure that nobody else could see her, but she was wrong. Dian and Purple were already on their way up the mountainside. It didn't take long before Dian and Purple reached the top. They said hi to Frøya and lay down on the side and rolled down the hill.

Flora looked at all the girls with braided hair and brown clothes doing different chores. She grabbed Dian when she ran past her and combed her long, sand-coloured hair. Dian was glad when Purple came and dragged her with him. They ran to the river which came from the mountains and continued into the fjord. Purple jumped from rock to rock at full speed across the river. Dian bent down to drink the clear river water.

4

Oak stood on top of the hill in Blairmore. Purple had come to help him roll some large stones into place.

"Nice circle," said Purple, "but it's a bit small."

"We don't want to draw too much attention to it. When hundreds of years have passed, Dian will sit in the middle of it. Then we can give her the information she needs."

Oak thought how unlikely it was that Dian would sit in the stone circle in 2015, but he had to do his utmost.

"Whose stone is that?" said Purple and pointed to a rock which stood alone behind the three stones.

"It belongs to the two daughters you and Dian will have."

"Now I understand why she sneaks into my bed every time she thinks I'm asleep."

"I don't think that's why Dian sneaks into your bed," said Oak and laughed. "She doesn't like to lay awake, so she crawls into your bed to get some sleep."

"What do you think we will name them?"

"I think Dian will suggest Flora, and you will suggest Hazel."

"Maybe," said Purple.

5

Oak was born in the middle of a large oak forest which lay by the road that went across the island. He and Flora had taken the trip to see where he was born.

"Look what they have done," said Oak sad.

"The worst part is that it will take hundreds of years before they realise they shouldn't have planted spruce trees in straight rows," said Flora.

"Do you think they will realise?"

"One day they will."

Oak looked at the three large oak trees that remained. There had been thousands of large and old oaks, it had been a healthy forest with a bustling wildlife. The forest was a sight early in spring when the wood anemones covered the ground. The dark spruce forest was so depressing that Oak couldn't stay there anymore.

The next morning, Oak was himself again. He bent over Flora while she was still asleep.

"Would you marry me?" he asked.

Flora opened her eyes and whispered yes into his ear. "Let's have a small wedding, just us and some animals."

"Who can get married without animals?" whispered Oak back.

"How do you feel about me getting married?" Oak asked Purple.

"It's fine!" replied Purple.

"You don't think I should be with your mother?"

"You are. Don't you remember when I was a baby and Flora gave me food and comforted me while I howled like a stung pig?"

Oak said he had a vague memory. Purple had howled so loudly that he had escaped every time. It hadn't stopped until Angus had sung to him. In the end, it was by Purple's side Angus spent all his time. He roared and sang, day in and day out. At night, Purple would strangely enough sleep.

Purple remembered what it had been like to be a baby. He cried every time the sun rays hit him. Flora thought the sun rays were life-giving, but for Purple the energy from the sun had been way too strong. The reason he stopped crying when Angus sang wasn't because he liked listening to Angus for hours every day, it was because Angus stood so he shaded him from the sun.

Purple could still remember all the horrible sounds he had to listen to. Angus was only one year and a half, he couldn't talk yet, only make strange, really strange, noises.

Dian crawled up on Oak's lap, she had never done that before.

"Is it true that you will marry Flora?"

Oak nodded and said, "Then you have heard correctly."

Oak felt that Dian looked straight through him. Dian saw what she wanted to see. She wanted to see what true love looked like. She went down from Oak's lap.

"What was that?" said Oak quietly to Flora.

"Dian wants to recognise what she saw when she sees it again," said Flora.

"And what did she see?"

"What do you think?"

Oak thought for a long time, he had absolutely no idea.

Dian looked at Flora. "You are gonna marry Oak?" she asked.

Flora blushed like a kid. "Yes," she replied.

"Come," said Dian. "Let's go to the burn, the wood anemones are in bud." Flora took Dian's small hand in hers; she still thought it was nice to hold hands.

Dian went down the steep slope to the burn, while Flora watched her from the path above. Dian picked a large bouquet of wood anemones and gave them to Flora.

Flora got dumbed. Dian had always been her daughter, both she and Dian knew it. Sofia was Dian's biological mother, but her real mother was Flora. Flora knew that Purple felt the same.

"You know you are my daughter?" she asked Dian.

"I know," said Dian. "Now, always and for all eternity,"

A man was watching them, he came out from the shadows and introduced himself.

"Haug," he said. "I'm named after a mound that lays on the other side of the sea. It contains a green stone that originally came from here, at least that's what I have been told. If you need a Viking ship at any point, I'm your man. My ship lays in the bay, it's not hard to find, since it's the only one."

Dian looked at him with an arch on her eyebrow.

"What?" said Haug.

Dian laughed and said, "You talk a lot for someone we meet for the first time." She saw the glances Haug and Flora exchanged.

"Not easy to fool," said Haug. "I know Flora, but it must be kept secret how well I know her, can you keep a secret?"

"If it's worth keeping," said Dian.

"You're a well-spoken bairn," said Haug, "I have a feeling you're gonna need it."

"What she needs more, is to understand what secrets to keep

or not," said Flora and laughed. "Let's go and find the others," she said to Dian.

Flora and Oak decided to get married late at night on the island Ailsa Craig. They rode on the ridges to Kildonan and set sail from there. Haug had arrived at Kildonan fairly early on, with his black Viking ship with red and golden sails. The ship set sail towards Ailsa Craig as soon as they were on board.
"Which animals have you brought with you?" Oak asked Flora.
"I brought some white moths; in case we need to transform one of them. And you?"
"I brought some silver trout in case we got hungry."
"It was some stately animals we took with us to the wedding," said Flora and laughed.
"I have a wedding gift for you," said Haug. "It's Hugin and Munin, originally they were Frøya's ravens."
He gave Hugin to Oak and Munin to Flora. Soon after the ravens lifted and flew towards a huge oak which was full of lit candles, the branches were adorned with light yellow roses. Flora and Oak went ashore and followed the ravens.
"My favourite tree and your favourite flowers," said Oak, touched.
"Do you know who decorated the tree?" asked Flora.
"I have my suspicions," said Oak. He had seen Angus and Purple dragging one large sack each. Haug had obviously sailed them out to the island.

6

Oak looked at Purple. He stood trying to hang his wet clothes in the huge oak tree outside the house. Purple threw them up into the air again and again.

Oak asked Flora if Purple usually had so much trouble hitting a branch.

"I don't think Purple looks up when he throws, his thoughts are elsewhere," replied Flora.

Oak looked at Purple. He looked far beyond when he threw.

"I wonder what's on his mind," said Oak.

"Why don't you ask him?" said Flora.

Oak went outside and asked him. Purple looked at Oak and replied, Blackbird.

"Who's Blackbird?"

"He is my unicorn."

Poor boy, thought Oak, *that will never happen, the unicorns are always owned by females.*

"You know that you are a boy, and you will grow up to be a man?" Oak asked worriedly.

Purple didn't answer and Oak went inside. Flora asked what Purple had said.

"Purple thinks he will own a unicorn one day."

"Maybe there will be born two unicorns," said Flora thoughtful.

"What about the name?" asked Oak. "It's quite unusual for a unicorn."

"It suggests that it's a stallion Purple will have, they are always born black. Purple Black and Blackbird," said Flora slowly. "I think he's on to something."

"How is it possible that Purple already knows that Blackbird will be born?"

"He knows because he comes from the middle star of Orion's belt. Just like me and Dian."

"It looks like Purple finally managed to hang his clothes," said Oak and looked at the tree where the red clothes hung.

Purple knew very well that Oak didn't believe him. Suddenly a mass of snow fell from a dark grey sky. *Snowflake,* thought Purple, *that is what Dian's next unicorn will be called.* Purple ran to tell Dian that he had found a name for her next unicorn. Angus and Dian were on top of Goat Fell.

"Forgot your horse?" Angus asked, when Purple came running.

"I thought about something else," said Purple and breathed heavily.

"What?" asked Dian.

"My unicorn," replied Purple. Angus just rolled his eyes.

"What is it called?" asked Dian.

"Blackbird."

"Blackbird and Snowflake," said Dian and looked up at the black sky where the snowflakes fell slowly to the ground.

"How did you know?" asked Purple surprised.

Dian just looked at him. Purple could read the same in her eyes as he felt himself. She knew, but not how she knew. Angus pulled Purple up on his horse.

"Time for supper," he said.

It snowed all the way back to Blairmore. Both Dian and Purple looked at the two foals that walked in front of them, one white and the other black.

7

Flora stood and looked out of the window, at the heavy white snow, slowly falling to the ground. She worried about Purple, Dian and Angus always landed on their feet. Purple was different, he believed that it was how it should be if he felt miserable. Flora saw that he couldn't find his way, Purple expected someone to drag him out, but he would still refuse.

"Do you think it has something to do with Hazel leaving him when he was a baby?" she asked Oak.

"Some people think they don't deserve to have a good life," said Oak.

"In the future he will struggle much more than today, who will help him then?"

"I have a feeling it will be Blackbird."

"Let's hope so. Now it's up to you, Blackbird," she said.

Oak was glad Hazel had left straight after Purple was born, it had always been Flora for him. Angus's father had just travelled through, no one had seen him before or since. Oak saw the strong chemistry that was between Purple, Dian and Angus from the beginning.

He had been so shocked when Purple had been born on the day the druids had talked about in infinite times, the fourteenth of March. He had been even more shocked when Dian was born on the same day the year after. Oak decided to conceal their birthdays, they celebrated with Angus instead. Flora used to bake a tall cake with cream, it was decorated with dandelions, pink cornflowers and red poppies.

8

Oak looked at Dian's father. He was sitting on a stone looking out over the firth. Oak was on his way to the meadow in Catacol.

"Will you join me?" he asked.

Dian's father just smiled and shook his head.

"Thanks for taking care of Diandra by the way."

"No worries," said Oak, "she is funny."

"I know, I just don't want to have fun anymore."

"What about your other chores, any chance you want to resume them?"

"I just want to sit here and think about my deceased wife and do nothing."

Oak said he had to go; he was already late.

"How was it possible that Dian has such a self-absorbed father?" he mumbled to himself.

It was an emergency meeting, only those with the highest thinking power were summoned. Flora should have been there, but they couldn't find anyone to watch the bairns, on such short notice. Toralf was the leader of the meeting. Oak felt a little out of place, he was the one to be questioned, even though it was him who had the future underneath his roof.

The others were sitting solemnly in their white dresses. Oak sat there with his tousled hair in his pink shirt and green trousers. He was glad Flora didn't have time to sew a yellow rose on his shirt.

Toralf began solemnly, "We are gathered here today because

we know that the solar energy and the lunar energy is born and live under the same roof as Oak and Flora. All we want to know is how we can secure the future. We want to hear what you have to say, Oak Black."

"They are still bairns," began Oak. "Flora is teaching them that things can happen quickly, but beyond that I don't know what to say. Neither Dian nor Purple knows that they have enormous powers. They are messing with the clan, but it's mostly harmless pranks, the same as we did when we were bairns."

Oak looked at the assembly, everyone looked back at him with a serious gaze. Oak didn't know what else to say, he just wanted to go home to Flora.

"It is said that they come from the middle star in Orion's belt," said one of them. "How is it possible when they have earthly parents?"

"Imagine two seeds coming from space, then they grow up on earth instead of in space."

It became quiet. *Let me go home,* thought Oak. His prayers were answered, suddenly a torrential rain appeared, and everyone ran to their horses. Oak galloped back to Blairmore and Flora.

9

Flora rowed out to the island, Inis Shroin, and went straight to the top to see Frøya.

Frøya asked if Flora was all right. Flora looked a moment at the pink and yellow sunrise above the firth of Clyde, before she replied that everything was fine. It wasn't completely true, Flora was scared.

"Al right then," said Frøya lightly, "then we can enjoy the sunrise." Flora writhed for a long time, she was famous for not being scared, it was an unknown feeling for her.

"I'm scared," she finally said.

"I know," said Frøya, "try to put into words what you are afraid of, then it will be easier."

"What we are preparing for is impossible."

Frøya looked at Flora, their green eyes met. In Flora's eyes there was discouragement. In Frøya's it was the will to fight. Flora felt that Frøya changed what was in their eyes, now it was Flora who had the will to fight and Frøya who had despair.

"You need the will to fight more than me," said Frøya, "after all it's you who has the nutcracker under your roof."

Flora turned her gaze to the sunrise; the discouragement had disappeared like dew to the sun.

"There is one plant that can keep the dew in the sun," said Frøya.

"Frøya's Mantle," said Flora and laughed.

"On the first leaves in the spring you can see the waterways

I have created in order for the droplets to gather in the middle when the leaves are fully grown. It's ingenious if I must say it myself. There's a pattern, how the droplets gather and become one, Dian will recognise it."

"Angus told me that she had written down some numbers, do you know what they mean?"

"2015 is the year and 0314 is the date and month."

"Why do you want Dian to know now?"

"She needs to collect the threads during the remaining nine hundred and ninety nine years." Flora still didn't understand why Dian had to start so early.

"Dian is five now, the numbers I am giving her will lay in the brain like a memory until the day she needs it. Nobody will understand how she can pick up the patterns and recognise the numbers so fast."

Flora just nodded and looked at the sun, it had managed to get up in the sky, the blur around the sun was silver and the sunbeams shone in gold.

10

Angus was on a raid. He walked silently into the field and began picking the vegetables in the sack; he usually picked dandelions. The cabbage was for the horses, the carrots and potatoes for Flora. Angus envisioned a steak with potatoes and carrots, but he knew it was too dangerous to steal an ox, it was certain death.

Stealing vegetables on the other hand, thought Angus when an arrow suddenly hit one of the carrots. Angus looked up; it was at least thirty members of the Hamilton clan on the edge of the field. Suddenly there was a storm, the clan no longer stood, they blew away. Angus knew what Dian and Purple were capable of.

"Do you need any help?" asked Dian shortly after.

"If they return," said Angus.

"They won't, we blew them out on the firth."

They could all hear Flora shouting their full names in their inner ear, but for once they had managed to escape Flora.

"Maybe she is occupied with Oak?" said Dian.

"Hope so," said Angus, "we are old enough to look after ourselves now."

Dian nodded, but Purple was disheartened.

"What is it?" asked Angus.

"It's Oak and Flora. I don't exist anymore, they only have eyes for each other."

Angus and Dian didn't bother to answer, they were both satisfied that they could torment the Hamilton clan without Flora roaring at them.

They delivered the vegetables to Flora, she hardly noticed. Flora and Oak fell in love once a year, and often it happened during the summer.

It looked like Purple was thinking about something.

"Do you remember the closed copper cauldron with the long neck? Some celts gave it to Oak a while back, a gift because he helped them with something?"

"I remember," said Angus, "what were they using it for?"

"They fired up underneath and put herbs and water into it, then they got different oils."

"What's on your mind?" asked Angus.

"We have ale," said Purple.

"You're thinking of making a fluid stronger," said Dian.

"Exactly!" said Purple excited.

"Evaporation!" said Angus slowly. "Oak and Flora won't even notice if we borrow it."

Purple tied it to the wagon with a solid rope, and Dian harnessed two of the horses with collars. It was unusually heavy, but the horses had no trouble pulling the wagon. They went to Catacol and followed the river for a while until they came to an open space where they could see the mountains far beyond.

They dug a pit in the ground and made a bonfire with enough room on both sides, so they could continue putting on more dry twigs once it was in place.

"They have a cave where they store the ale until the next market," said Angus.

They loaded all the oak barrels they could fit in the wagon. Purple's squirrel ran in front, it didn't believe for a second that the horses could find the way better than itself.

"It's made from copper with a long neck, and none of us have ever seen anything like it before," said Dian. "We can't keep on saying it, we need a name."

"It's not going anywhere," said Purple, "so we have time."

"No, it is still," said Dian, "it's quiet, calm and not going anywhere."

"Still it is then," said Angus.

The still held all the barrels of ale, and Purple could finally light the fire.

"How long do you think it should boil?" asked Dian.

"As long as we bother, afterwards we hide it in one of the caves," said Angus.

"Let's drink it at the first wedding we attend to," said Purple.

"Wonder whose that will be?" Angus said dryly.

"We have to come up with a good name," said Dian.

"The Water of Life, after the river that flows here," said Purple.

"In Gaelic Water of Life is Uisge Beatha," said Angus.

"That works too," said Purple.

They stood looking at the ale that looked like water when it came out of the long copper neck, it ran with a thin jet. Dian placed a new empty barrel under the neck as soon as it was full.

"Now it needs to get even stronger," said Angus.

"First we have to get rid of the sediment at the bottom of the still," said Purple.

They drew the still into the river and let the river clean it.

"It will be a magical drink," said Dian.

"How come?" asked Angus.

"Don't you see the clarity of what comes out?"

"You're right," Angus said astonished. "We begin with the clearest water from the Water of Life, then we put in grains and let the elements rule for a while before it starts to bubble. It could have ended there, but then there were some rascals who wanted to make something stronger, and suddenly the ale became shiny and clear as the Water of Life again."

Angus put some dandelions into the still when Dian and Purple had their backs to it.

"Should we add some water?" asked Dian.

"More the merrier," said Angus. Purple just nodded.

Dian threw away the first that came running from the neck, it didn't have a nice smell to it. She had done the same the first time also, she knew Angus and Purple would have kept everything.

"I think we have cracked it," said Angus when all the barrels had a stronger liquid inside.

They rolled them to the cave nearby and stacked them on top of each other.

"When are you getting married?" asked Angus.

"When we are twenty-one and twenty-two," replied Purple.

"The Water of Life or famously called Uisge Beatha, made by Angus, Dian and Purple, will lay here and rest for at least six years then," said Angus solemnly.

"Why famously called?" asked Dian.

"I have a feeling it's not gonna be called the Water of Life in the future."

They hid the entrance to the cave with some stones they rolled in front.

11

Dian was on her way to her grandmother Ailsa, she lived between Bredvik and Sandvik. She tethered her black mare Silver to the fence. There were Angelica archangelica on both sides of the path that led up to the house.

On the right side of the front door stood a rowan, it was almost extinct, it was the last specimen. Ailsa had set the table in the small grove which was surrounded by five old oak trees. The branches filtered the light from the sun and made a pattern inside the grove.

Ailsa poured Dian a glass of ale.

"White heather," said Dian satisfied when she had taken a sip.

"I thought you needed it," said Ailsa seriously.

"Tell me what's going on," said Dian.

"You and Purple will have two daughters, which in itself is good news, but not quite. You have to give them away as soon as they are born. The Hamilton clan is not to be joked about any more. Before you say anything, you should know that there is nothing you can say or do which can stop what is predetermined, that ship has sailed.

The druids will be exterminated, the date has been set. In the end it will only be four druids left, but that's all we need for what will happen next."

"And what's that?" asked Dian.

"You have been given a task that is the most difficult ever

given to a druid. You have to control what happens at a given time, in a given place using numbers. Purple will not be with you, but he will help you mentally from a distance, that's how it must be in order to keep you both safe."

"Have you found a family for our daughters?" asked Dian.

"There is a fishing family living in Pirnmill, they have sworn that they will never reveal the bairns druid blood."

"You're sure it's the only solution?"

"It's just one solution," Ailsa said seriously. "Once the cards are laid, there is nothing that can change them."

Dian said she had to find Purple. She found him in Lochranza, he was trying to get a thin flat stone to jump several times in a line on the water.

"Two daughters, that's not bad," said Purple when Dian told him what Ailsa had said.

"You are aware we must give them away immediately?" Purple nodded.

"Ailsa said one more thing. The first is already on the way." Purple went down on one knee.

"Dian Rowan. Do you want Purple Black?"

"Yes," said Dian.

Silver and Golden lifted their heads and neighed, a huge flock of crows lifted nearby and made a terrible noise.

"I'm not sure the crows agree," said Purple and laughed. Dian didn't care, she just kissed Purple.

Raven stood behind a tree and watched them.

They both knew they were going to die soon, but it didn't stop them. Raven wondered why.

Lusifer came and stood beside him.

"Dian and Purple are happy," said Raven. "They know they can't keep their daughters, and they know they will die within a few years, it doesn't add up."

Lusifer understood why Dian and Purple hastened the wedding, but there was more to it, he decided to find out what it was. He went inside Dian's thoughts. It was supposed to look like Dian and Purple died, but they didn't.

"What did you find out?" asked Raven.

"Dian and Purple do die, but that's not all. They take up residence in two Vikings who live on the other side of the fjord from Orkdal."

"That makes sense," said Raven. "Noralf, Angus' father came from Orkdal."

Lusifer thought of the green stone that had moved from Scotland to Norway billions of years ago, the place it finally landed was the same place Dian and Purple had intended to go.

"I didn't even know the druids could resurrect," said Raven.

"Neither did I," said Lusifer. He entered Dian's mind again.

"You don't like waiting," said Raven laughing.

Dian wondered if she should invite Flora and Oak over for supper. Lusifer influenced her thinking, so she started thinking about the resurrection instead. A long line of numbers appeared.

"You know we don't stand a chance," said Raven. Lusifer went inside Dian's thoughts again.

"Number nine is the decisive number, no one knows that it's number six, that's all you need to know," said Dian.

"How do you protect the numbers?" asked Lusifer.

"I don't need to, it's only the four of us who know that the nine is a six."

Lusifer wasn't sure, but he said nothing.

"It doesn't matter," said Raven, "no one understands the rest of the numbers anyway."

Sus came without them noticing. Lusifer told him what Dian had planned to do. Sus thought for a long time, he was a man of action, he didn't fall into thoughts. Raven and Lusifer stood with their arms crossed looking at him.

"It isn't just the green stone that is the link, it's the colours of the landscape and the shape of the mountains as well, they have the same chain."

"You are talking about the mountains DNA-chain," said Raven impressed.

Sus nodded and said, "The mountain ranges are like the spinal cord."

12

Angus gave Dian a bouquet of dandelions, he had picked it on Dian and Purple's wedding day.

"Shouldn't we go and change?" asked Angus.

"We should," said Dian and started walking towards Blairmore. She could see smoke coming from the chimney. Angus saw it too. He took Dian's arm and held her back.

"Be cautious," he said.

They hid behind the trees as they approached the house. Flora came out and looked directly at them, she wanted them to stay away. Soon after, three men from the Hamilton clan left the house.

"What do you think they were up to?" asked Dian.

"Same old," said Angus, "they can't understand why their oxen are tame all of a sudden."

Dian knew he was wrong, but she didn't say any more.

Flora was gazing at the flames when they entered the kitchen. Her eyes seemed to see things far away, but then the turn seemed to pass.

"There you are," she said. "About time, the dresses are ready, all we are missing now is Oak and Purple, they went up to the stone circle."

"What's going on?" asked Dian.

"I'm just sick of having to relate to so many idiots all the time."

"The famous Hamilton clan," said Angus.

"Let's not make them famous. Let's make them infamous," said Flora.

"How?" asked Angus.

"We're letting all that is happening get lost. We won't write down anything."

"You want our history to be lost because you want the Hamilton clan to have no history as well?"

"We are invisible because we have to hide from the clan, we will do the same to them."

Oak and Purple came back, and Flora gave them a dress each. She gave Dian a pink long dress, Purple a red and Angus a yellow, Oak went outside to get their horses ready. They were going to the beach with the best view of Ailsa Craig.

Purple and Angus began to whisper when they reached the beach. Finally, Angus said to Dian, "We were wondering if we should fix your hair?"

Dian knew she would never figure out what they were up to if she said no, so she said yes.

Angus looked surprised at her. Purple asked her to close her eyes. He made a sign to his squirrel; it jumped on top of Dian's head and lay its tail nicely backwards.

"And now you sit completely still until the ceremony is over," said Purple.

"And how long will that be?" asked the squirrel.

"When the sun's position is directly above Ailsa Craig."

"So, half the day then," said the squirrel.

"Something like that!"

Purple asked if Dian noticed that she had a squirrel on top of her head.

"No! It could have been anything."

Oak and Flora arrived, and the ceremony could begin.

It was Oak who was giving them their blessing. He looked at the squirrel on Dian's head, and said dryly while he looked at Purple, "Who can get married without an animal?"

Angus stood by Purple's side and the unicorn by Dian's. Oak talked about all the stars in the sky. At one point there would be a special moment, when Orion's belt and the Plough stood with an exact equal distance from the full moon.

After the ceremony the druids rode to the next beach. Ailsa Craig was covered with sunbeams. The beach was white and silky soft. Everyone's eyes were fixed upon Ailsa, she was a magnet laying in the fjord floating between Ireland and Scotland.

"You know that Ailsa is a portal in time and space?" asked Oak.

"No," said Purple, "but we do now."

"It's the blue granite Ailsa consists of that makes it possible. She's from the middle star of Orion's belt."

Dian and Purple weren't surprised, they had often talked about how it looked like Ailsa Craig came from another planet.

A long table stood on the beach, decorated with a tablecloth in the colours of the moon, and flowers in the colours of the sun.

Flora and Angus put ale, wine and Uisge Beatha on the table. Fried rabbits lay on a large wooden plate with a new light green vegetable Oak had made. It looked like it came from out of space, it was a cross between cauliflower and broccoli.

Angus got up after everyone had been seated, they were looking forward to a nice meal. Everyone knew it had to wait, Angus was known for dragging things out in the long run.

"I will make it short," began Angus, and everyone roared with laughter. "Well, maybe not, just drink and eat while I talk, as long as you don't speak." He paused and drew his breath.

"I have been preparing this talk for more than ten years. I

know it's a long time, but everyone who has seen Purple and Dian knows that they belong together. Dian is Purple's moon and Purple is Dian's sun. I'm just Angus Moon who is present to deceive evil, so they don't realise that it's Dian who has the lunar energy and Purple who has the solar energy. Fortunately, evil is stupid and will always be.

Am I jealous of the bride and groom? Of course I am. Everyone here is, whether they want to admit it or not. I have had the pleasure of spending almost as much time with Dian and Purple, as I have with the oxen."

"You're an ox, Angus!" shouted one.

Angus just looked at him and continued, "I have written a poem; it is called "Wandering Aengus".

"I went out to the hazel wood,
Because a fire was in my head,
And cut and peeled a hazel wand,
And hooked a berry to a thread;
And when white moths were on the wing,
And moth-like stars were flickering out,
I dropped the berry in a stream
And caught a little silver trout.
When I had laid it on the floor
I went to blow the fire aflame,
But something rustled on the floor,
And someone called me by my name:
It had become a glimmering girl
With apple blossom in her hair
Who called me by my name and ran
And faded through the brightening air.
Though I am old with wandering

Through hollow land and hilly lands,
I will find out where she has gone,
And kiss her lips and take her hands;
And walk among long dappled grass,
And pluck till time and times are done,
The silver apples of the moon,
The golden apples of the sun."

The sun stood low in the sky, it had almost disappeared, Dian and Purple's wedding day drew close to an end. They planned to spend the wedding night in between the mountains that lay by the Water of Life, the river that wound up from the firth of Clyde and Catacol.

Angus left beforehand to light up the hut, it was getting cold. Dian and Purple left soon after.

They saw the smoke from the hut a long way away, the thin grey smoke went north with the wind.

"Have you noticed that Orion is completely orange?" Angus stood in the midst of the mountains, looking up at the sky.

"Orion and the Plough stands at exactly the same distance from the moon. Oak talked about it during the ceremony, I thought it lay in the future," said Dian.

"You two get to find out," said Angus. "I will continue to annoy the clan for as long as I can, they have a new ox. If I interpret the stars correctly, this is a perfect night to tame it."

"What will you do when you have tamed all the oxen on the island?" asked Purple.

"I think Orion has the answer," said Angus and mounted his horse. He galloped out of the glen and back to the foot of Goat Fell where the ox was waiting for him.

Purple stood looking after Angus, wondering how much

time they had left, he couldn't go inside yet, a black jealousy threatened to devour him. *Who can resist someone, when they get a unicorn as well*, he thought. Purple wondered how he was going to calm down.

The squirrel came out to him.

"How long are you going to let the bride wait?"

"I have to get over my jealousy first."

"Haven't you seen Orion? You can find out how to deal with your jealousy when you're dead."

Purple smiled. The squirrel always got him back on the right path. He went inside, Dian lay on her back with her head against the wall and slept.

Purple felt paralysed. He meant so little to her that she fell asleep on their wedding night.

The squirrel jumped on his head and scratched him with its front claws.

"Stop it!" said Purple furious.

"You need to stop believing that Dian doesn't care about you. Get some sleep, maybe you'll wake up normal."

Purple knew the squirrel was right, he wasn't much of a man when he was jealous. He lay down next to Dian and fell asleep as soon as his head hit the pillow.

Dian awoke by the moonbeams shining through the open door, the fire was still burning. She went outside and saw the beams from the full moon reflected in the river. The moonbeams hit her in her chest and took all the water in the river with it at the same time, it went through her, up to the full moon, and back again.

Dian went inside and lay down next to Purple, this time she put her head on his shoulder and one arm around him. The squirrel sat on its hind legs looking at her. The unicorn and the white deer grazed outside, and it was peaceful for a wee while.

Purple woke up to the sun rising, he went out and bathed in the river, Dian came out shortly afterwards.

"This is the best," said Dian and kissed him.

"What?" asked Purple.

"To swim naked with you."

Purple kissed her back and said, "I will stop time now."

"Agreed!" said Dian.

They knew they could stop time for all posterity only once.

13

Angus looked inside the palms his hands, then he turned them back and forth.

"What's the problem?" asked Dian.

Angus was pale, but now he was almost light blue.

"What happened?" asked Dian.

"I just moved that tree; I used my hands."

Angus took his hands up and lifted them as he looked at the large oak tree. The tree rose slowly from the ground and shook its roots on the way up. Angus took his hands down again and the tree followed, it hit the ground as the soil lay over the roots again.

"Not bad, we can use it against the clan."

"That's not the only thing. Watch!"

Angus took a wee white moth from Dian's hair and blew on it. It turned into a big eagle.

"Wow!" said Dian. "You'll surpass Purple soon, but don't tell him."

It amazed Angus how similar and different Dian and Purple were. Dian was the one who knew most of all the druids, but she never talked about what she could do.

Evil searched high and low for the lunar and solar energy they knew existed, they saw the energy every time Dian or Purple used it, but they didn't think to look for one that was visible and one that was invisible.

Evil had long believed that Angus had the lunar energy since his name was Moon, but they got tired of watching him taming the oxen all the time. They also thought he had the solar energy for a while, since he wore yellow clothes.

Angus Moon played his role as a misleader perfectly, that's why Oak had given him a stone in the circle, without Angus, evil would have found them long ago.

"What is it with you and the dandelion?" asked Dian.

"The seedpods are just as pale as me."

"It's like the flowers and the seedpods don't belong together," said Dian.

"If you count the petals on the dandelion, you get different numbers every time you count."

"How do you know?"

"I have picked dandelions in bags since I was a wee boy. At night I have counted hundreds of petals and seedlings, I've seen the pattern.

The root system is completely unique, it won't move from the ground. There's no use dragging it, you have to dig until you get all of the root, otherwise it will come back. The flower belongs to the sun, but the seedpod belongs to the moon. You are the only one I know who has used dandelions as the only flower in a wedding bouquet."

"I wonder why?" said Dian and laughed.

14

Angus slipped out into the night on one of his many nocturnal expeditions, he was followed by the golden eagles. Angus walked the hidden paths that no one else walked.

Angus rowed the boat to Inis Shroin, the gannedruids were up to something.

"What are they doing?" Angus asked the eagles.

"They collect rounds and squares."

"Why?"

"They are formatting."

"How?"

"They put a round then a square into an infinite line, they can put it into whatever form they like. It's a lot of information hidden in a small space. They are trying to get the sun and the moon to cooperate, if they succeed, they will have the greatest power in the world."

"What are they going to use it for?"

"To fight evil of course. It's on Inis Shroin the control of the elements is happening. If you are wondering what's going on, just look at how the sun and moon behave above the island. If you notice the changes from day to day you will see the patterns eventually, like you did with the numbers hiding in the dandelion. Everyone believes that a plant must be rare in order to be unique, but the best place to hide is in plain sight."

"And walk among long dappled grass."

"Exactly! When you wrote Wandering Aengus to Dian and

Purple on their wedding day, it was we who gave you a secret in every line. One day, Dian will crack the code, she will recognise the landscape: through hollow lands and hilly lands.

Purple will recognise the part where he is looking for her in the future: I will find out where she has gone, and kiss her lips and hold her hands. In the end, the island will be both: the Silver apples of the moon and the Golden apples of the sun."

"I don't understand the part with the apples," said Angus.

"The apples are the symbol of temptation, it's heaven or hell. It's the balance between good and evil. The sun and the moon need to be one in order for the balance to be reinstalled."

"Where do I come into the song?"

"You know what we called it?"

They may be right, thought Angus. He wondered if his father Noralf also had been a wanderer. Angus already knew the answer. The four golden eagles that followed him sat in the boat waiting for him.

"You know Dian. We need to know what signs she notices."

"No worries! Dian notices the smallest things."

"The hardest part will be to get Dian where we want her to be. You are so easy to lead, Angus. We give you a dream where you can find the biggest dandelion, and there you are. We never show you where it is, but you always arrive."

"Dandelions aren't my only interest, I like being with you too," said Angus.

The eagles looked down into the boat. They didn't know how to deal with Angus' nice words. None of them said any more on the way back to Lamlash Bay.

Angus smiled and looked at the eagles who were about to go out of their good skin when he praised them.

He dragged the boat up on the beach and walked slowly up

to the house. He was surprised when he saw Dian sitting in the dark in the kitchen.

"You are worried," he said, "I thought you were like Flora, and she is never worried."

"There is too much at stake, I'm not sure I can handle it."

"Of course you can, if anyone can handle it, it's you."

Dian didn't say anything, so Angus asked what was really bothering her.

"In the future it will be difficult, I know that, and I'm prepared. The only thing I'm not prepared for is if I meet too many idiots and evildoers. What if I don't have anyone who understands me, like you, Purple, Oak, Flora, Ailsa and Haug, what if there's no one, and I'm all alone?"

"You know who will always be with you?"

"You mean Frøya and God?"

"No, I mean the three that are your rock."

Dian wrinkled her eyebrow and said, "I thought I was the only one who knew about them."

Angus smiled and said, "I have been outdoors many a night, more nights than days, they hide in the dark, but I have a feeling they have been watching me too."

"We have," said Raven. "He sat down by the table and took one of Dian's hands in his. You will never walk alone, not as long as there's a breath still inside of me, Lusifer and Sus."

Dian took a deep breath and relaxed, Raven was right, she would never walk alone.

15

Dian looked up at the sky and cursed the full moon, she couldn't move.

"What is it?" asked Purple.

"The full moon," replied Dian.

My God what a drama every time, thought the squirrel.

"What is it this time?" asked Purple.

"I don't know, but it's like I'm swimming inside my brain."

"What can I do?"

"Nothing. You never feel that way, do you?"

"No, the sun is all right, it's because the moon controls the tides."

"I know, I'm just sick of it."

Angus asked if they would like to see something strange.

"Anything that can take my mind off the full moon," said Dian. They went to Sliabh Fada.

"This is where all the animals go when there's something going on," said Angus.

Purple asked the red deer what was going on.

"It's the gannedruids."

"What about them?"

"They are digging a deep hole in the ground."

"Is that where they will continue their formatting?"

"They think all the answers are hidden in the ground."

"It seems like they think the future is buried," said Angus.

"That's not so stupid," said Purple.

"I think they are preparing the ground for future times," said Dian.

"Should we do the same?" asked Purple.

"I don't think we need to," said Dian, "we can continue doing what we always do."

"Being rascals," said Angus and smiled.

"Why don't I have a girlfriend?" Angus asked the eagles.

"We need your full attention."

"You will get it when I have a girlfriend," Angus said angrily.

The eagles knew Angus well enough to know that he was serious.

"We have found a perfect girlfriend for you," they said soon after. Angus understood what they meant the minute he saw her. She stood by the fence feeding the oxen, her orange clothes could be seen a long way away. Angus went to her and asked if she liked oxen. She smiled and nodded.

"What kind of plants are you using to get the nice orange colour on your clothes?" he asked.

"Marigolds, and you?"

"Dandelions," Angus replied and smiled. "I haven't seen you before, or have I?"

"It's only recently I've started wearing orange clothes. I saw you on the market once, but then I wore brown clothes and braids." Angus thought of all the girls in brown clothes and braids, he couldn't tell them apart.

"I thought I had to change the colours on my clothes if I should have a chance to get your attention."

You're absolutely right, thought Angus. He asked her if she liked eagles. "My favourite birds," she replied.

"I want to show you the meadow where I pick dandelions," he said. The wind blew his long white hair backwards and Angus was ready for new adventures.

16

"So, you were born on Sola?" Purple asked Erik the Red.
"I was."
"How was it?"
"Windy, I couldn't stay there so I ended up in Greenland."
"Was it green?"
"It was, but I'm not much on land, the sea is where I thrive."

Purple nodded and thought he looked more like a pirate than a Viking. Erik the Red had long black hair and a red shirt with wide sleeves, his shirt was tucked inside his green trousers. Around his waist he wore a black belt. The long black leather boots were folded down just below the knee. The sword hung in the belt and made it asymmetric.

Purple thought Erik the Red looked magnificent.
"Where are you headed?" asked Purple.

They stood on top of the hill in Blairmore and looked down on the fjord.

"You see the ship lying there?"

Purple nodded and looked at the ship. It had three masts with black sails fluttering in the wind.

"I go where it goes."
"What are you doing here?"
"I wanted to see my relative."
"Who is?" asked Purple.

Erik the Red looked at him with his green eyes wide open and met Purple's green eyes. They stood watching the sun rise in their red shirts.

17

Flora and Hazel played on the beach.

"The riders are here again," said Flora to Hazel.

They looked up at the two horses which stood on top of the cliff.

"They don't think we can see them," said Hazel. "Who do you think they are?"

"They behave like they are our parents," Flora replied. Dian asked if Purple survived.

"If they're all right, I'm all right."

"Who do you think Flora takes after?"

Flora jumped from stone to stone at full speed, she almost fell multiple times, but she kept on going.

"I don't know, me maybe."

Hazel picked some stones on the beach; the swans were never far away.

"Flora MacDonald! Stop that immediately and come and eat!"

They could see their foster mother standing in the doorway, she couldn't see them. Flora ran to the house, but Hazel stopped and looked straight at them. Purple could see she knew who they were. Purple smiled and waved at her.

Hazel waved back and gazed at Dian.

"Smile and wave," said Purple. Dian did, and Hazel went inside.

"Do you think she will say something?" asked Purple.

"I don't think so, she doesn't say things lightly."

"I wonder where she gets that from?" said Purply dryly.

They turned the horses around and went to Glen Rosa. A pink bow of clouds stood above the valley, it hit the mountains on both sides. It was the fourteenth of March, Oak wanted to gather his family on that date every year in Glen Rosa.

"What do you think the bow means?" asked Dian.

Purple looked at the bright red and orange sunset that appeared shortly afterwards.

"The bow of clouds should have arrived after the red sunset."

"I think you're right," said Dian. "The next time the pink cloud bow appears, it means the danger is over."

"Then maybe we are on the other side of the dangerous sunset." Dian looked at Purple for a long time, they both knew it wasn't sure they would be together, even though the pink bow of clouds appeared once more.

18

Purple rode on the unicorn, he was on his way to Goat Fell. He didn't know what was about to happen, only that he had to get to Goat Fell and it was urgent. The unicorn galloped at maximum speed; Purple could no longer hear the hooves on the ground.

"Do you think I can be inside your sweater?" asked the squirrel thinly. It had great difficulties holding on to the unicorn's horn with the wild speed. Purple leaned forward and took hold of the squirrel and dropped it inside his sweater. The squirrel put its claws on his stomach, Purple slapped it on the outside of the sweater.

"Stop it!" he said. "The belt holds you in place, you can't fall further down."

The squirrel moaned but let go of its claws.

They had reached the top of Goat Fell. The unicorn breathed wildly and hefty. Purple looked around slowly, he didn't want to miss anything.

The squirrel shouted, "Let me out!"

Purple lifted his sweater and the squirrel jumped on top of his head. The squirrel began to scout around while the unicorn lifted the left front hoof high in the air.

So that's where it's going to happen, Purple thought, and looked in the same direction as the unicorn. The horizon became red orange in a small sharp stripe. The sun was setting, the rays hit a large spruce tree that looked like an old deciduous tree. Hundreds of druids came riding, and the Hamilton clan came walking from the other side towards the spruce tree.

I have to find Dian, thought Purple, *maybe she knows what's going on.* The unicorn galloped down the path from Goat Fell, on the way they met Angus.

"What's going on?" asked Purple.

"You remember Milly, she who always tries to mediate and sort things out between people?"

Purple knew who she was, he thought she was dangerous, but he didn't understand how dangerous until Angus told him the rest.

"We are to meet by the big spruce tree," said Angus.

"Why?"

"The unicorn knows why." The unicorn shook its head.

"You don't?" asked Angus, he sounded timid. "Milly said that you had said that everyone had to gather by the big spruce tree."

"We have to find Dian quickly," said the unicorn.

"You didn't summon a meeting?" asked Angus.

"Of course not, everyone knows how dangerous the Hamilton clan are. I believe in faith, hope and love, but I'm not as stupid and naive as Milly."

"Just wait until I get hold of Milly," Purple said, "then I will kill her with my bare hands."

"It's too late," said Angus. "She went to the mainland to celebrate in advance."

"We have to find Dian," said Purple.

They found Dian at the foot of a tree, she held a small blue and yellow bird in her hand.

"The bird told me danger lay ahead," said Dian.

"Milly," said Purple, he didn't have to say anything else, Dian knew what she was like.

Purple stretched out his hand and pulled her up on the

48

unicorn. Dian held on to his waist while he made the unicorn go faster. The sun had almost set when they reached the spruce tree. Angus threw himself off the horse and started running towards the river, Purple and Dian followed head over heels.

It was too late, Angus, Dian and Purple fell heavily to the ground with arrows in their backs.

"Get us out of here," said the squirrel to the unicorn.

19

Ailsa knew the time the druids were going to die had come, she had one last conversation with Myrt and Mort.

"You have to drag Purple and Dian out of the river where the two waterfalls meet. They are to be buried in the meadow between the mountains where the three rivers meet.

Dian shall have the highest stone, while Purple shall have the lower one. The stones will disappear for hundreds of years, but they will show up again when Dian comes back.

I had a dream last night, there will arrive two men in a ship with two ravens. You will take them to the rocks at Sliabh Fada when the moon is at its thinnest. There you will teach them how to make the circle of light."

"You want us to teach two strangers our best kept secret?" Mort asked petrified.

"Dian is the only one who can get the circles of light started. I will leave behind two circles of light. The second will be waiting for her on a small mountain in Norway with a fort on top.

We don't have a ship that can cross the North Sea; therefore we will give the second circle to the men with the two ravens. The gannedruids are preparing the third on Inis Shroin, and that's the most difficult to start."

"Why are they called gannedruids?" asked Mort.

"It's from gandr that means stick, it's the original wand. The gannedruids can infiltrate your dreams, visions and your thoughts, and reach far beyond to the outer bulwark.

Another thing," said Ailsa. "Håkon and Haug can sail through the centuries. They are not the only ones, later on you will meet two more who know how too."

20

Håkon and Haug were not on a raid. They had sailed inside a thick fog just before the island appeared.

"What do you think," said Håkon to Haug, "should we go ashore?"

"No doubt in my mind," said Haug and laughed.

Håkon took a deep breath, he wished he could stay on the island where he felt so strangely at home, even though he had never set his foot there. The two ravens followed them ashore. Mort had to rub his eyes; he didn't believe what he saw.

"Myrt!" he shouted.

Myrt arrived immediately. Her brother never shouted at her; he was the calmest person she knew. She had to rub her eyes too. When she opened them, she started laughing.

"I didn't believe a word Ailsa said," she said.

"You better believe it now," said Mort dryly, "they are headed this way, you better put the kettle on."

Mort went outside to greet them.

"Welcome," he said, "what brings you here?"

"I have absolutely no clue," said Håkon and laughed.

"Why don't you come inside? My sister has just put the kettle on."

"Love to," said Haug, "I'm thirsty as all the mounds."

"He means he could drink anything," said Håkon. "Haug means mound where we are from."

That explains everything, thought Mort.

They went inside, Myrt shook their hands, and said how pleased she was to see them.

"Do you by any chance know something we don't?" asked Haug.

"We are the last of the druids on the island. If the clan finds out, we are dead."

"Do you want us to kill the clan?" asked Håkon seriously.

Myrt laughed and said she would love to see them gone, but it wasn't up to her.

Håkon sat down comfortably by the fireplace and looked into the flames. The two ravens sat on the long wooden mantelpiece.

"When my ship came out of the fog and I saw this island, then I knew it was the hidden island of the druids. You have something to tell me."

Håkon didn't ask, he just concluded that they had something to tell him.

Myrt looked at him in surprise and said, "There was a druid called Dian, Ailsa was her grandmother, she could see into the future. Ailsa told us that there would come two men from the North with two ravens in a ship.

Ailsa wanted us to show you the druids best kept secret. She said you had to bring it back with you to a small mountain with a fort on top. It's a circle made from moonbeams; it can only be made when the moon is almost gone."

Haug went outside, he came back shortly after and said, "If the moon gets any thinner it will disappear for sure."

It was time to go to the rocks at Sliabh Fada.

"Do you see that the thinnest moonbeam spins a thread?" Mort asked when they stood in the middle of the stones.

Håkon and Haug gasped.

"It's the moonbeam you have to bring back with you to the wee mountain," said Myrt. "It will lie like an invisible worm until the right time comes. Then it will extend its entire length until it hits Dian in the chest, and the circle of light will start."

"Start," said Haug.

"To go around the mountain."

"Do you know anyone who can be there and protect it?" asked Mort.

"I know someone who is perfect for the task," said Håkon. "His name is Heimdal. He's the guardian of the rainbow bridge that goes over to the gods' realm."

The ravens were most concerned with the moonbeam lying on the ground shaped like a worm. They couldn't decide if they wanted to eat it or not.

Håkon picked up the moonbeam, put it in a small leather bag, and laced it with a leather cord.

21

Oscar was only eight years old when he died. He was on a holiday with his family when he disappeared. Oscar had been looking forward to the holiday, he had planned to swim every day.

They stayed in a hotel called Ormidale. It was located at the edge of a forest and had a great view to Goat Fell, the highest peak on the island and Brodick Castle.

Oscar had been given room number one. He immediately felt that there was something special about the room, but he dared not tell his parents, they were both scientists.

Oscar felt a deep restlessness in his body when he went to bed that evening. There was something going on by the river that flowed past the hotel. Oscar went to the window, he rubbed his eyes and thought he saw visions, but after a while he realised that it was real.

There was a little man with black clothes and a cloak standing by the river. On his head he wore a wizard's hat. In one hand he held a long pointed stick, which he drove down into the river with great force. Oscar gasped when he saw what the wizard had impaled, it was a seal pup. The wizard didn't give up until he had five seal pups on the stick. Afterwards he licked his mouth while making a fire.

Suddenly he turned his head and looked straight up at Oscar who stood looking out of the window. Oscar backed inside the room; it was pure evil he had seen in the wizard's eyes. He crawled over to the bed and hid underneath the duvet.

When morning came, Oscar was still scared, he shivered as he sat down at the breakfast table. As usual his parents didn't notice anything. They ordered a Full Scottish Breakfast and made plans for the day.

Oscar felt stupid being so scared, it was so nice at the hotel. There were white damask tablecloths on the old wooden tables, covered with silver cutlery and white porcelain plates. On the walls hung pictures of the island in golden frames. On both sides of the old oak and broad windowsills hung long grey linen curtains. The house was built of stone, it looked like it was several hundred years old. Oscar's parents asked the nice hotel hostess what Ormidale meant.

"It means a worm in a glen. The name comes from the Norse, that's all we know," she replied.

Oscar thought it was a strange name.

After breakfast they were going to Rosaburn where the historical museum on the island lay. Oscar walked behind his parents. As usual they didn't notice him, they were too occupied with each other.

There was a lot to see at the museum, but nothing caught Oscar's interest before he suddenly saw the word Ormidale on a map. It was the name of a road that twisted like a worm towards Machrie Moor.

He decided to sneak out while his parents had their nap. They said it was because they thought so many thoughts during the day. Their brain needed extra sleep since they did so much good for humanity with their research. Oscar never understood his parents, and he realised in a split of a second that he never would.

When they went up to their room, they didn't bother to ask Oscar what he was going to do while they slept. Oscar looked at them and decided to try and find a living being on Arran, so he wouldn't feel so alone.

The weather was hot, Oscar put on white shorts and a white shirt. He felt light-hearted when he left the hotel. It wasn't difficult to find the road he had seen at Rosaburn.

The day was glorious, the clouds played lightly around Goat Fell, and Oscar jumped happily on the road. What he didn't see was the small creatures hiding in the ditch. Once upon a time they had been good, but that was before the black wizard got his claws into them. Now they were on a mission, to get hold of the little boy the wizard had seen the day before. They envisioned an easy prey; they licked their mouths as they watched Oscar jumping on the road.

They didn't need much time to overpower him. Oscar felt a hand around his mouth and somebody that lifted his legs. An icy fear went all the way into his core, he closed his eyes and lay still while they carried his body between them.

Oscar knew he wouldn't survive, he had understood that much the night before, when he looked into the eyes of the wizard. Oscar cursed his parents who didn't let him believe in danger until it was too late, and he was mad at himself for not believing what he had seen.

Oscar had heard of the good and evil forces on the island, now he folded his hands and prayed to the good forces, that they had to save his soul.

He envisioned swimming in the firth of Clyde while they killed him. Fortunately, the pain was short lived. Oscar hovered while they fried his body. What they did further he didn't want to see; he went on into the unknown. Oscar was glad he still existed on some level.

Suddenly he was pulled back. He knew what had happened, it was the wizard who wanted his soul. Oscar knew he had lost, he folded his hands and prayed to the good forces again. They said Oscar should let the wizard take his soul, but they would protect his mind.

Oscar knew what that meant. He wouldn't feel anything, but he would be present. The good forces said that they had long tried to gain insight into the evil forces on the island, but it had been closed to them, the wizard's powers were too strong. Oscar didn't want to think of them as the good forces, he asked who they were.

"Heard about druids?"

"Yes!"

"This used to be our secret island, we ruled the island a long time ago."

"What happened?"

"We will tell you another time, now there are other things that are more important. It's important that you keep track of what they are planning and try to deprive them of their secrets."

"I will do my best," said Oscar.

The druids had tried to leave different souls to gain the wizard's secrets many times, but it had never worked, the wizard had cast a curse on the souls as soon as he discovered them. This was the first time they had tried to leave the mind behind. The wizard didn't understand how bright Oscar was, his parents had talked about the different building blocks in the universe from the day he was born.

Oscar had a mission, he just wished he had someone with him.

"You have us," said the druids, they obviously heard what he was thinking. "Before a hundred years have passed, a change will take place."

Oscar had some difficulty imagining the time aspect. He lay down comfortably on some soft moss underneath a tree. The next day he would see into the water, to see what was left of him. He didn't have to; Oscar already knew the answer. He was invisible that's why the wizard couldn't find him. Oscar sighed and lay down to sleep. It wasn't long before he felt calm and almost happy. He lay thinking of all the benefits of being invisible, at the same time he had all the druids to talk to. They said it was an animal he could communicate with, but he had to wait until the next day, now he needed some rest.

The next day when Oscar woke up, someone was sniffing him. He wasn't surprised when he saw who it was. It was the white deer that was so legendary on the island.

The white deer said Oscar could be with him if he wanted to, they could explore the island together. Oscar wondered why the white deer couldn't snatch the secrets from the goblins and the wizard if he was protected.

The white deer said he was protected, but they kept quiet every time he came near. That's why Oscar was so important, he could get close to the goblins and the wizard.

They went to Machrie Moor. The white deer said this was the place where the heart of Arran lay hidden in the moor. Oscar asked if the druids executed rituals there during the different phases of the sun, moon and stars.

"They are not the real druids; the real druids are changing the rituals they are doing all the time. Only those who have great thinking power can capture it. The fake druids take the attention away from what is really going on.

It's a little strange to use the word really, for those who don't have high thinking power it's just adventures and hoax. The real druids today don't even have a stone around their necks. Their smokescreen is that they look ordinary, they wear plain clothes. The day the person arrives who is going to change everything, I bet with you, Oscar, that it's not a person who is concerned about money."

"When will this mysterious person arrive?" asked Oscar.

"When you see the middle star in Orion's belt flash. How many scientists do you think it will take, to prove that we have had this conversation?"

"It will never happen," Oscar said and sighed heavily.

"No, I know," said the deer.

"Look," said Oscar, "the fake druids are here."

The torches they held in their hands lit up their white and long linen dresses, some of them wore light grey mantles, they were walking in a line towards the three Standing Stones.

"The druids keep an eye on them, but they gave up a long time ago, they are still using the mistletoe which has outplayed its role hundreds of years ago. When things are recharging fast, then great things will happen."

"What will happen?"

"Wait and see. When the middle star in Orion's belt flashes, that's the big sign. I think it will be in 2013."

"Why?"

"Don't you see, all the numbers are present?"

"I do."

"Exactly!"

Oscar thought of all the number opportunities before that time, from 1920 which was the year they were in right now.

"The years ahead of us until the year 2013, can pass just as fast as a dream, you know that right?"

Oscar shook his head.

"When you wake up the next time, it will feel like you have slept one night, but almost a hundred years will have passed by. It means that all the ailments you have seen the goblins and the wizard perform disappears, just as fast as a dream. It's the druids gift to you, they wouldn't expose you to so many years of suffering. Goodbye, Oscar, I have to go now."

Oscar began to cry for the first time since he was killed, but it helped that the white deer promised to stay with him until he had fallen asleep.

The next time Oscar woke up, he knew everything was different. He looked straight up at the starry sky. He wasn't surprised when he saw Orion's belt, the middle star was flashing. The druids said he was in the year 2013, but his story wasn't yet to begin.

They wanted him to be present because the mysterious person was on the island.

"Do you mean in the dark on Machrie Moor?" asked Oscar.

"It's the place where Arran's heart is buried, hopefully it will start to beat again. It has been dormant for a long while, hiding until the right time arrived, and that time is now."

Shortly afterwards, Oscar saw it was flashing and shining brightly on the moor. It was as if it was a light show to the rhythm of a heartbeat. It shone over a large area, occasionally it lit up parts of the sky as well.

Oscar was amazed. *My parents should have been here,* he thought. Before the next thought was that he was pleased they weren't. They had probably said it was the lights from a train, even though there were no trains on Arran. Oscar didn't bother to think about them anymore, he enjoyed the light show instead.

"Next time something important happens on the island, it will be the year 2014. The person who is here now and will return in 2014 knows about number magic. Now you need to rest, the next time you wake up, you will be back in room number one at the Ormidale hotel."

Oscar felt he became stiff with fear, *do they really think I can sleep now?* he thought, *I wish they hadn't said that.* Suddenly a lot of dust flew through the air. *Of course, they have magic dust,* Oscar thought just before he fell asleep.

22

Dian had booked a room at the Acorn hotel which was located on Elderslie street. When she got the key to the room, she saw that it was to room number thirteen. Everything in the room was brown, the beds, cabinets, curtains and even the carpet.

Dian felt she wasn't alone in the room; someone was hiding in one of the closets. She didn't bother to listen to the ghost, she just sent it straight up, the ghost disappeared within a second. After Dian decided to walk along the Great Western Road, she wanted to see if she could find the Timorous Beasties shop.

On the left side of Elderslie Street stood old stone houses black with soot. There were ghosts in all the buildings looking out of the windows, the whole block was full of ghosts.

They disappeared up in a grey spiral, as soon as Dian walked past the building. Dian didn't think it was strange that she could send hundreds of ghosts to the Milky Way, it was the first time she used her powers.

God wasn't the only one who saw what Dian did, all the evildoers saw it too. God summoned the black angels and assigned Lusifer, Sus and Raven to look after Dian.

The next day she went to the train station in Glasgow and bought a ticket to Arran. The lady in the hatch said, "Many?"

Dian said one and thought, if she had been in England, the woman would have bothered to say a whole sentence.

The train took an hour to reach Ardrossan and the corresponding ferry took an hour to reach Arran. Dian stood on deck and watched the mountain range that ran along the island, it looked like a sleeping warrior.

Brodick consisted of a long street with brick houses in front of the bay with different colours. Dian hadn't booked a hotel, so she followed the street until she came to a sign which said: Ormidale. It was located not far from the beach with a view to the mountains and the castle.

Inside the hotel was a bar with a large whisky selection. As far as Dian could see it was all single malts. A thistle wallpaper continued up the stairs. The room contained a large black metal bed and a chair, the curtains were white with black roses.

Dian decided to go to Machrie Moor to see the Standing Stones, it was late, on a cold November afternoon. The bus went from Rosaburn which was right down the road next to Brodick Bay.

The bus driver just looked amazed at Dian when she said where she was going. It was just before it got dark, and it had started to rain. When the bus stopped Dian wondered what she was doing, she would be alone on the moor in the dark, but something urged her to go on.

"Do you have boots with you and rainwear?" asked the bus driver. "It's very wet on the moor, it has been raining for days."

"Yes," Dian replied.

"Do you have a flashlight?" asked the bus driver, it was completely black outside now.

Dian said yes again. The bus driver nodded and said the bus would return in about four hours.

Dian watched the bus until it disappeared, she felt completely nuts, she had no boots, rainwear or a flashlight, she had a couple of small bottles of whisky from the Arran distillery she had bought while waiting for the bus. *I'll better take a sip before I start walking,* she thought to herself.

Without the puddles that lay evenly on the narrow black road, she wouldn't have seen anything. Eventually it stopped raining and Dian could enjoy the silence. She moved forward very slowly, the puddles were no longer present.

Dian drank all the bottles while she continued walking. After a while the bottles were empty, and Dian arrived at a fence. *Is this where the journey ends?* Dian thought to herself.

Sus appeared next to her.

"It's not just the fence that stops you," he said.

Dian turned and looked to the right of the fence. There was something white laying on the ground, she sent a beam of light in the middle of it.

"Do you know what it is?" she asked.

"That is Arran's heart," Sus replied.

They started going back again, Dian was amazed how easy it was to walk back again.

"There were a lot of creatures on the moor trying to stop you," said Sus. "They forgot to drain the puddles, without the shine in the puddles you wouldn't have seen anything."

When they sat down to wait for the bus, a strong white light came from the moor where the heart of Arran lay. The light on the moor was so strong that Dian didn't notice how wet she was.

The moon had appeared, it was at its thinnest. The stars shone and flashed and moved occasionally, it looked like they were swopping places with each other, while the bright light swept across the starry sky.

Sus could see how calm Dian was, she looked like she thought everything that was happening was completely normal, she didn't even ask what was going on. Sus asked Lusifer why Dian didn't ask any questions. Dian was busy taking off her wet shoes and socks, she put her mittens on her feet instead.

"She knows it's dangerous," said Lusifer.

After an hour the bus arrived, and Dian put on her wet converse shoes again. She took a different route back to the hotel, through a dark forest. The evildoers watched the normal route back to the hotel.

After a change of clothes, she went down to the bar and ordered a steak with mushroom stew and oven-roasted potatoes, a bottle of dark, with the Standing Stones on the label, and a smoky whisky called Machrie Moor.

The next morning, she drank coffee and ate kippers while she looked at the view. At the foot of the mountain lay Brodick castle, there was no doubt where she was going today. Dian put on her wet shoes and went down to the bus stop. It was no surprise that it was the same bus driver as the day before. He stopped the bus between two stops and said she should follow the path to the castle.

The path passed a garden close to the river. The garden was full of ducks, some were large and white, while others were small and brown. There was a box you could put money into if you wanted to feed the birds with breadcrumbs packed in a small paper bag. Dian stopped on the bridge and looked at all the ducks swimming up and down the river.

The path went past the cheese shop, the fish shop, Arran Aromatics and a cafe. A little further down the street was a large pink brick house, behind lay an outdoor shop. Dian couldn't believe her luck, an outdoor shop located close to the brewery and the castle was amazing. She went in and bought a pair of winter boots and wool socks.

The sun shone between the leaves of the large deciduous trees; a table stood on the border of the forest that stretched up towards the blue mountains. Dian went inside the brewery shop and bought a beer with a red squirrel on the label, she wondered if it was an amber or a mild. After she had drunk the beer, she went up the stairs that led up to the castle.

Dian walked around the castle, it lay where most of the druids had lived, then she continued on the path towards Goat Fell. Shortly after she stood completely still, she saw herself from another era. She was sitting on a fence while a young man called Purple was standing in front of her, Dian could only see his back. Suddenly they started running. Dian followed; they ran down to the river. It was steep, Dian crawled under a tree that had overturned.

A white deer was drinking from the river. A unicorn came walking slowly down the steep slope, it looked around uneasy before it turned and ran up the slope, the white deer followed. The trees surrounding the river set all the leaves in motion, they warned of danger. The spruces stood completely still; they had no leaves to rattle.

There was a hiss through the air, before all the air was sucked out of the atmosphere. On the other side of the river, the Hamilton clan had gathered, they had their arches ready. The arrows flew through the air at the same time and hit all the druids, they fell into the river one by one.

After a while the river turned red, and the clan withdrew. Dian followed them to Glen Rosa. Beside a small waterfall a long table was set, around the table torches were attached to long poles. The colours were amazing, the water was turquoise, the mountains blue and the heather purple. The full moon shone down on the table where five white swans lay.

The chieftain raised his glass and toasted for a successful mission. He cut the first swan in two from the head to the tail. The swan fell with a part on each side of the table. Clan members threw themselves at the meat, one by one the swans were consumed. Dian started going back. The squirrels in the trees jumped from branch to branch and the little birds flew around the trees while everything calmed down.

On her way back to the castle she passed a small, fenced area.

She opened the gate and looked at the stones, there were two members of the Hamilton clan lying there. Dian left the graveyard without closing the gate behind her.

23

In July 2014 Dian booked a room at the same hotel. The owner Laura said she was going to stay in room number eight. They went up to the room together. When Dian was about to unlock, the key didn't work, the door refused to open. Laura tried the other key she had, but it didn't work either.

Laura said Dian could sit in the garden until she found a new room for her. Dian bought a whisky at the bar and sat outside in the sun.

She could see Goat Fell and Brodick castle. After a while Laura showed up with a new key, it was the key to room one. This time there were no problems with the key, however there were plenty of problems inside the room.

The computer crashed as soon she opened the lid. Dian knew something was going on, the computer was only an indicator. She walked across the floor to close the open window, but before she could reach it, a snake had made its way through the window. Dian couldn't breathe, the snake pushed her against the wall, it was so enormous that it filled the whole room. Dian asked the snake to go outside. The snake went outside, and Dian could breathe again. It looked at her with its little black eyes.

"I just wanted to see if you were tough enough to handle what lay ahead of you."

"I don't mind that you're here, but it would be nice if you lay outside the window, the room is too small for you."

The moment Dian closed the window she saw a wizard

sitting by the burn eating seal pups. The snake crept up behind him, the wizard didn't see it, he was looking at Dian. The snake swallowed him before the wizard could swallow the seal pup.

Dian could feel how heavy and black it was in the room. She opened the window again and let out the black air. In the middle of the floor stood a small boy with blond hair and blue eyes, he was wearing white shorts and a white shirt. He had been set free when the snake devoured the wizard.

"I've waited a long time for you," he said and yawned.

Dian folded up the duvet and the little boy went to bed and fell asleep right away.

The next day Dian decided to take a trip to the distillery. It was located in a village called Lochranza, on the north end of the island. It was a short walk to the bus stop which lay cross the street from the historical museum in Rosaburn. Oscar walked beside her and held her hand.

Dian looked up towards Goat Fell, the mountain wanted her to stand at a small point close to the bus stop. Suddenly she felt a force. A powerful white beam came from the mountain and hit her in the middle of the chest, Dian sent the beam back. Oscar could see the moon beam attached to the mountain's core starting to move, it would probably take an hour before it had completed a round around the mountain.

Early the next morning Dian took the ferry to Ardrossan, where the corresponding train to Glasgow waited at the station. Oscar was still with her occasionally, Dian didn't mind, they didn't say much, any of them.

On the way to the hotel, she passed Glasgow School of Art. The school had just had a fire, it had started in the basement and continued up to the library. The school's tower looked like a burnt out chimney.

The hotel was located next to the school in a cramped Victorian row of houses. The strong smell of perfume hit Dian as soon as she opened the door to the hotel.

She held her breath in the hallway, and longed to open a window in her room, but of course there was no window, just a noisy and dirty fan. It was dirty under the bed and the mattress was rock hard. On top lay a thin hard duvet and under the sheet was a plastic sheet. The roof was high and narrow like a chimney. It was impossible to stay inside the room, Dian went to a cinema down the road. The cinema was old, with brown elaborate woodwork throughout, chandeliers and red plush seats.

After the movie, Dian went back to the room, she was prepared to stay awake. A large yellow sheet was taped on the door: If you feel danger, run to the reception. *Run from the perfume, more likely,* thought Dian.

She knew something was going to happen at 04.58 a.m. All week while she was on Arran the clock had shown 58 every time, she looked at it. At 04.58 she knew what to do. She opened the portal that was in the ceiling of the room.

The high ceiling was an opening in time and space. As soon as Dian opened it, creatures flew up from the underground all over Glasgow and further up into the universe.

Dian understood that she shouldn't try to stop anything, the roof would be open until the underground was cleansed, and it would probably take some time.

The next morning, she passed Glasgow School of Art on her way to Buchanan Bus Station. The creatures from the underground in Glasgow flew out from the tower where the fire had been as well. There were two places with a tremendous force with only a couple of houses in between.

24

Dian didn't stay long in Norway, she rented a house in Lamlash at the foot of Tighvein, the mountain was 458 metres high. On the way back to Arran, Dian and her cat named Lucy, had a strenuous trip, but also a nice trip.

She struggled to find a place to sleep, most of the hotels and inns accepted dogs, but not cats. After asking around various hotels and inns, Dian started to get bored.

She drove until she came to a small village called Aikton, it was almost dark outside. A pub lay on the other side of the river. It was called The Aikton Arms. Dian was tired after a strenuous day, so she left Lucy in the car, and went to look for a place to sleep.

She met a guy on the bridge, he was on his way to the pub, he said the landlord only accepted dogs. As they approached the other side of the river, hundreds of ghosts appeared.

The guy hurried on to the pub. Dian suspected it wasn't the first time he had seen them. The ghosts said that she shouldn't send them over to the other side, they had never had so much fun before. Most of them had a bottle dangling from their hand, Dian could see the label on one of the bottles, it was beige and grey and full of dust and cobwebs. It was as if Aikton was England's Valhalla.

Dian left them and walked past the pub to St Andrews church which lay close by, it was from the twelfth century. It was completely dark outside now, the full moon lit up the floor inside through the stained glass windows. The church was full of ghosts, it was packed, Dian stumbled upon them everywhere. It was impossible to stay, so she went outside.

The ghosts had left the streets. Dian looked through a window in the house by the church, an old couple sat in armchairs by the fire drinking tea from white and blue porcelain cups, the house was strangely enough ghost free.

She went to the pub cross the street and convinced the pub owner that her cat was a dog, she said it had four legs and a hairy body. The pub owner saw straight through her, but he saw how desperate she was. Dian got the last room; she crossed the bridge again to get Lucy.

After she had let Lucy loose in the room, she went to the pub, they had real ale. Dian wondered why the ghosts had been only on one side of the river. She asked the landlord. He was not surprised by her question, he just answered firmly that they were afraid of water.

The next morning Lucy sat ready in her cage, she was scared Dian would leave her there, with all the ghosts.

They drove on the small and winding roads from Aikton towards Scotland, they passed rolling fields and stone fences. After a while they arrived at an old castle. In the yard was a small cafe with homemade cheesecake and good coffee.

Dian sat on the steps of the castle overlooking Wigtown Bay with Lucy by her side and ate the best cheesecake she had ever had; the view was not to be despised either.

The landlord said the castle had belonged to the Brown clan; they had come to Scotland at the same time as the Vikings. Dian thought to herself that they were most likely called Brun which meant brown in Norwegian and was a surname too.

They passed Ailsa Craig later on, the island was tall and

shaped like a triangle, it looked like a sugar loaf floating between Ireland and Scotland.

Of course, the last ferry had just left when Dian reached Ardrossan. She gave up finding a hotel that accepted cats, the last room was always the largest and most expensive, Dian got a whole suite to herself. The rain was torrential, but Dian could see that Lucy was happy, she closed her eyes and fell asleep immediately in the rear window of the car.

The last ferry had just left when Dian arrived in Rotterdam as well. She had driven like Cruella de Vil to reach the ferry, but the signage was lousy. Before she found out she had to drive to the back of town to get to the ferry in front, the ferry had left. Dian sat on a bench with Lucy on her lap all day and looked at all the ships that went back and forth.

Now she was finally so close to Arran that she could see the island. The next day the navy had a large-scale naval exercise on the CalMac ferry, the soldiers capsized from small rubber boats that came up on the side of the ferry at full speed.

It was the morning of the seventh of October and Dian had arrived on time. She parked close to the well of happiness and went to get the key to the house from the landlord who worked nearby.

"You made it," said the landlord happy, "I never thought you would." *Neither did I,* thought Dian.

Her only neighbour came as soon as she arrived and gave her a bottle of white wine and a hug. She talked about the robin who lived in the garden and all the bright stars. The best place to see them was in the shared yard.

The next day Dian went for a walk, she drove to Arran Aromatics and parked the car. Soon after she found a path that lay in plain sight but was hidden at the same time. It went along a field with trees growing on a slope on the other side.

The trees were home to many of the red squirrels that lived on Arran. In the middle of the path stood a deciduous tree, it had seven trunks that twisted together upwards towards the crown. Usually, Dian had no problem seeing what kind of tree it was, whether it had leaves or not, she could tell by looking at the buds.

The tree gave no information whatsoever, other than it was a deciduous tree.

Before Dian had found this forest, she had walked in a forest that was sick and full of moss. It was a bewitched forest, the work of the black wizard. The forest was so waterlogged that Dian didn't understand how it had survived.

One night she dreamed three words: *Baig An Eigal.* Dian had never heard the words before, they sounded Gaelic. In English, she intuitively knew they meant: Raise the Earth.

The next time she walked in the sick forest she said the words. The forest transformed instantly. The trees rose from the ground and shook their roots a little before covering them with soil again. Dian had also dreamed that the squirrels lit candles in all the oak trees. The trees were small but fully grown and the leaves were light green. In front of the trees was a row of black grass and one with green grass.

25

Oak stood by the small stone circle he and Purple had made back in the druid era, he watched Dian driving by towards Brodick. Oak breathed a sigh of relief when Dian returned soon after. The stone circle lay at the top of the hill in Blairmore.

Dian looked up at the sky when she got out of the car. Orion's belt and the Plough stood at exactly the same distance from the full moon, there were no other stars to be seen.

She walked towards the stone circle. The snow lay like a white carpet with scattered black trees and a black mountain range ahead.

Dian looked at Goat Fell while she was standing in the middle of the three stones. The Water of Life arose from behind Goat Fell in its full length like a geyser. It looked majestic on the black sky with its invisible water, but at the same time visible.

The Water of Life moved like a snake over the sky, through the full moon between Orion's belt and the Plough, then through Dian and the stone circle, before it disappeared behind the mountains, back to Catacol.

Finally, the star people get clean water, thought Oak relieved. It was 7.33 p.m. 01.20 in the year of 2015.

26

Raven had shown Dian the gravestones of Dian and Purple. They stood in plain sight from her favourite path on a field, with the road leading up to the castle between them. He said she had to follow all the signs from now on, it would be signs from both sides, evil would try to deceive her constantly, the only one she could trust, was herself.

She went to the river the druids had been thrown into after they had been killed, there were two burns higher up that looked like small waterfalls, finding their way into the river.

Dian went to the bridge and looked at the gravestones, then she sent the lunar energy up and down the river. Afterwards she went back on the path and stopped when she stood in the middle of the gravestones. Purple came running on the path, he stopped in front of her.

Purple was only mentally present, but it was enough. Dian sent the lunar energy to the left and Purple sent the solar energy to the right through the gravestones and back again, the energies intertwined and united past and present.

Dian took a wooden stick lying on the ground and wrote the date, month, year and time in the sand.

012320151400-19
000011122345-19-10
432111-12-3
1113-6

31-4
11-2
10-3-6-4-2-25-7

27

Purple asked Angus if he wanted to go to Edinburgh, a big fight was brewing, it would be the toughest fight so far. Angus showed up the very next day.

They went straight to the pub the World's End and ordered two Caesar Augustus from William Brothers. Angus said it tasted a bit like dandelion. Purple tasted fresh crisp grass.

"What happens now?" asked Angus.

"Now we reconnoitre, I want to find out what awaits us."

"The evildoers are gathering; they call on all who are stupid enough to come."

"Evil is stupid," said Purple, "but that doesn't mean they don't know their stuff. Are the eagles ready?"

"The eagles are top trained. Have you thought about the fact that you got the deer and the squirrels because you wore red clothes?"

"And you got the golden eagles because you wore yellow. You are missing a white animal though, because you are so pale. The unicorn is white, but it can only be owned by Dian."

"I know," said Angus, "but there's another white animal."

"The white deer?" asked Purple astonished.

"You remember the wedding when you and Dian forgot about him? It came to me and asked so nicely if I had room for him. There is always room for a white deer in my heart, I replied."

"It makes sense, since you always lacked one animal."

"I'm training him."

"The way you tamed the oxen?"

"Not exactly the same, but not far off. What about Flora and Oak, have you heard anything from them?"

"They are not exactly born fighters."

"Remember how frightening Flora was when she yelled at us?"

"She yelled all our names every time we did something wrong," said Purple and smiled. "What about the gannedruids?"

"They are formatting, to get maximum strength for the fight."

"We should be well equipped then, especially since Oscar is coming. I'm wondering what he's up to."

"Ask him," said Angus, "he's right behind you."

Purple turned and looked straight into Oscar's eyes.

"What's up?" asked Purple.

"Evil has intensified the search for Dian, but they can't find her. Sus has made a protection around the house. Remember you had to be transformed into a horse because you couldn't get in?"

"It's not easy forgetting what it was like being a horse," said Purple dryly.

"You turned into a horse," said Angus, bursting out laughing.

"You haven't met Sus yet, have you?" asked Purple angrily.

Angus didn't answer, he wondered if he could be a black angel one day since he was so pale. He remembered when Dian was five years old, and he didn't want to cut his hair. His hair was long, white and went all the way down to his waist. You're not exactly an angel, Dian had said. Angus had agreed and let Dian cut his hair with the Viking sword. Purple thought about how much he eventually remembered from the druid era, he wondered if it had anything to do with the great battle approaching.

Oscar wondered if he should order a beer.

"Heard of the Water of Life?" asked Angus.

"Yes, it's a holy river belonging to the druids. I used the river in the first fight in Edinburgh. The one you weren't attending."

"We weren't good enough," said Angus.

Oscar was about to die from pride when he heard what Angus said, he looked down.

Just like my eagles do when they are praised, thought Angus.

"What is the Water of Life?" Oscar asked lightly.

"It's Uisge Beatha, popularly called whisky," answered Angus.

"Want to taste one?" asked Purple.

"I must be twenty then."

"Eighteen is enough, but you can be twenty if you want to be."

"Want to be twenty years old?" asked Angus.

Oscar nodded. Angus put a hand on his shoulder and looked around so no one could see what was happening. There was no danger, everyone sat and looked deep into their glasses. Angus performed the transformation and Oscar was ready for a glass of Water of Life.

"Who made whisky first?" asked Oscar.

Purple and Angus looked at each other and smiled.

"We did," said Angus.

"And Dian," said Purple, "we were the famous three-leaf clover."

"Heard about the four-leaf clover?" asked Oscar.

"You want to be the fourth leaf," said Purple smiling.

"What about whisky to celebrate?" asked Angus. Oscar just nodded.

Purple ordered a bottle of bourbon cask from Arran. "It's a bit weird that they make the whisky close to where we first made it."

"How did the whisky taste back then?" asked Oscar.

"Firstly, it had been made from the purest water that could be found. Secondly, it was stored for six years in oak barrels before we drank it, and thirdly it had a secret ingredient."

"You didn't?" said Purple, looking at Angus.

"Did what?" asked Oscar.

"He put dandelions in the whisky," said Purple cracking with laughter.

Angus just smiled his secret smile.

"How did it taste then?" asked Oscar.

"What do you think?" asked Angus.

"Divine!"

"Correct!" said Purple.

They raised their glasses and toasted the four-leaf clover.

"What actually happened in the first battle in Edinburgh?" Angus asked Oscar.

Oscar suggested that they sat down at a table, it wasn't for everyone's ears what he was about to tell them.

Purple found a table hidden away in the dark corner of the pub.

"What do you want to know?" asked Oscar.

"Everything really," said Angus.

"It was a test for Dian. She had only met Sus at that time. Lusifer, Sus and Raven wanted to find out how much danger she was willing to expose herself to. Not only was Dian unexperienced, but she was all alone. The only experience she had at that time was from the streets of Glasgow where she sent hundreds of ghosts all the way up to the Milky Way. Beyond that, she had strangely enough no experience at all."

"Do you know why?" asked Purple.

"Evil has a counter-formula for everything that has been

used before, therefore no one has taught her anything, she would have been exposed a long time ago if they had. Dian uses hidden formulas that appears just before she's using them, if she doesn't use any of the powers she's got."

"You have to explain more detailed," said Angus.

"Dian's powers are enormous, that's no secret, but in order for her to accomplish anything, she must be invisible too. Evil intensifies their search for her all the time.

The black angels have given Dian a strong protection, that's why evil can't find her, but that's not enough. Dian is using her intuition at all times, if something feels off, she's gone within seconds. Sus, Lusifer and Raven knew about the powers Dian possessed, but the rest of the black angels didn't.

They didn't even know that Dian was in the closed city below Edinburgh."

"But you knew," said Angus, "were you present?"

"No, Dian picks up what I'm thinking. The gate down to the city was opened, and Dian was let inside. Sus closed the door after her and Dian fell into a black darkness, she could barely make out the walls that ran in a long tunnel with rooms on both sides. It didn't take long before she was thrown to the ground. Evil had fragmented into billions of small black bits which attacked her all the time. In the end, she couldn't breathe."

"And that's where you come in, right?" said Angus, smiling wryly. Oscar took a sip from the glass. He felt a bit shy about what he had done.

"Tell us the rest," said Purple.

"Dian asked for help, she was almost dead. I told her to send in the Water of Life. Dian did, and the holy druid river cleansed the closed city beneath Edinburgh, and all the fragmented evildoers were destroyed."

"That simple?" asked Angus.

"The rest must remain a secret, strict instructions from Sus, it's too dangerous to share anymore."

"Cheers for the Water of Life!" said Purple.

They clicked the glasses together and felt perfectly happy for a wee while.

They were in a different landscape where a river flowed with the clearest water in the world.

28

Medusa and Sus stood on top of Goat Fell.

"Nice?" Sus asked Medusa.

"Very nice," she replied.

Sus looked at the island Inis Shroin. He had asked Dian if she had started the circle of light around the island yet. She answered that the gannedruids would give her the signs when the circle was ready to be started.

Dian saw every single sunrise over the island, she said the sun moved further and further to the left for each day it rose, she didn't understand why it moved the wrong way.

Sus knew why, but Dian had to find out everything herself, otherwise the circle wouldn't start. The sun moved to the left, because at some point Dian needed to go backwards in order to pick up lost time. The sun would help her move time forward again.

It had been calm and grey for a long time. The gannedruids had been giving Dian signs for weeks, she had flown like a whipped skin all over the island doing everything they asked of her, she couldn't miss a single sunrise, there were signs all the time. The gannedruids wanted to see if Dian picked up all the messages, they gave her.

They needed to be completely sure that she understood the slightest message, until now she had been listening to them. They had daily arguments about how far they should push her. Some walks Dian went on, she had to pick up a small stone and throw it into the water at a given point or say a number when she passed a tree. The gannedruids were scared it would be too much for her, but they were so close, the third circle of light was almost ready to be started.

"It's suspiciously calm on the island," said Sus, "I think we should fly up to the top of Inis Shroin and see what they are up to."

"They're inside the mountain," said Medusa after a while.

"You're right," said Sus. "They are changing the energy on the whole island. It won't be activated until the first circle of light reaches the island, then the three circles will merge together."

"Where is the first circle?" asked Medusa.

"A Norwegian Viking king took the third circle back to Norway. It was Dian's grandma Ailsa who was so foresighted that she let the last remaining druids show the king how to make it."

"How come it's a secret how to make a circle of light, after all it cleanses the landscape?"

"It cleanses the landscape from evil, but there can only be three of them."

"Explain," said Medusa.

"Imagine that there are more than three circles."

Medusa closed her eyes and imagined hundreds. It was a complete chaos; the balance had disappeared from earth.

"I understand what you mean," she said, "but explain it anyway."

"Three circles balance each other, it's like a slingshot."

"And the point where it's pulled back is in Norway?"

"Right," Sus said and smiled.

"What happened when Dian started the first circle of light?"

"Dian went to a field with a view to the mountain with a small fort on top. It was Friday the thirteenth of June in 2014."

"It was Heimdal who stood on the other side of the moonbeam, that's what I don't understand."

"You have to remember it was all new to Dian at that point. The ghosts she got rid of in Glasgow and the heart she sent a beam of light into was her only experience. It was a month without a new moon in February that year, it only happens every twenty years. The full moon was at 06.11 that morning, but what Dian was going to do, had to happen exactly at twelve o'clock.

If Dian wasn't standing on a small point that was 4x4 inches on that day, there would be no point trying to get the next two circles started. The first one needed to be activated first, in order for the next two to be activated."

"I still don't understand why Heimdal had to be on the other side of the beam."

"As I said, Dian had not understood much of what was going on at that time. How do you say to a human: Today you are going to start a circle of light?"

They both burst out laughing.

"What was Heimdal doing there?" Medusa asked once more when they had finished laughing.

"Heimdal is the one who has the greatest powers of the gods. He is master of the rainbow; it can be formed in fog as well as in rain and sun. Heimdal made a nebula that Dian didn't see, but it was there. He showed Dian where she was going to stand, then he opened the small leather bag he had been given by Håkon Håkonsson exactly at twelve o'clock. The moonbeam hit Dian in the chest, and she sent it back right away, and the circle began to move slowly around the small mountain."

"How did it look?"

"It's still going around the mountain with the small fort on top. It has a strong beam of light that travels in a radius of 3.4 miles, the width of the beam is 4 inches."

"Then I reckon it was 3.4 miles between Dian and Heimdal?"

"Correct!"

There was something Dian didn't understand, she went to the top of Goat Fell where she knew Raven and Lusifer would be.

"You wonder how the circle of light could be made in darkness. In 2014 when you started the first one, there were two new moons in January, and two new moons in March," said Raven.

"Why was it so important that there wasn't a new moon in February that year?"

"You got an extra new moon."

Dian laughed and said, "I needed an extra black moon to hide the moonbeam."

"Exactly, the same thing happened when you started Arran's heart on Machrie Moor. It was pitch black and there was a new moon, but the heart lit up everywhere. The moonbeams are just as bright even though you can't see them. They are just as invisible as we are. Had the moon made the circles of light under the full moon, it wouldn't have been possible to preserve them."

"The circles of light had been discovered immediately," Dian said thoughtfully, "everything is there whether it's light or dark."

"It's the same as with faith," said Lusifer. "It's there even though you can't see it."

"Is what you can see stronger or weaker?" asked Dian.

"What is hidden is much stronger," said Raven.

"That's where the miracles are," said Dian and looked at them. She knew she wouldn't get an answer.

29

Volven dreamed of a new man, she was tired of being with Evil. Dian asked her if there was somebody she was secretly in love with.

"Gilde!" Volven replied without hesitation.

"Who is Gilde?"

"He lives on top of Dovre Mountain."

"He's the Mountain King?"

"Correct!"

"Nice piece of music that has been composed in his honour," said Dian.

"I like it too," said Volven.

"So, he's a troll?" asked Dian.

"Usually, he's an ordinary strong man who likes to build things in stone. His hair is brown, and his eyes are green, he looks like he comes from nature."

Just the way you look, Dian thought.

"Gilde and I are expecting trolls."

"Is it you who has made the song: When the troll mother put her eleven tiny cubs to bed?"

Volven nodded and smiled.

"Then you have known about the eleven tiny cubs for a while."

"I have."

"Are you going to stay at Gildevangen or in the Mountain King's Hall?"

"We shall live on Iceland," replied Volven.

30

Dian was sitting on the coach relaxing, she suddenly farted like thunder. Blackbird came over to her and looked wide-eyed at her. It looked like he had fallen off the moon.

In the background Dian heard Snowflake talking to Sus. Blackbird was still staring at her with big wondering eyes.

"What was that sound?" Snowflake asked Sus.

"It was Dian who farted. It's gas coming from her ass."

Snowflake thought for a long time before she asked, "What about the awful smell? It never smells that way neither from me nor Blackbird."

"It's something she's eaten," said Sus.

"She should try to eat grass," said Snowflake.

Blackbird tripped across the concrete floor; he was at Purple's work. As usual, Sus hadn't been able to stop him, but this time he was with him. Snowflake was with Dian.

Purple turned around, he felt someone behind him.

The sun shone through the windows high up on the wall in the workshop and hit Sus on one wing and his turquoise eyes. Soon after the sun rays hit Blackbird's shiny and glossy black mane. *What a sight,* thought Purple.

"Do you have a moment?" asked Sus. Purple nodded.

"Do you remember when you became so furious that you became red-hot?"

Purple nodded again.

"Dian was just as furious as you, she didn't become red-hot, she blew up all the continents instead. None of us have thought of blasting the continents, so it made us think. Since water needs to be moved in order to get oxygen, what if we made her blow up the oceans as well. Some of the water in the depths hasn't moved for millions of years."

"I got to join in," said Purple and smiled.

"She wasn't mad at you anymore?" asked Sus.

"I think she got rid of all the aggression when she blew up all the continents. She asked if I would like to get rid of some steam, we blew up the oceans together."

Now it was Sus who smiled. "Is that how you got the pink energy that suits you so well?"

Purple looked perplexed at him.

"Relax, light pink is the most powerful of all colours. No worries, you still look like a man and not a baby," Sus said with a crooked smile. "That's not why I came by. Do you still think I live in the other world, and you in the real?"

Purple just looked at him. That was good enough for Sus, he saw the answer.

"What in Helheim is it Dian and Purple are doing?" Volven asked Gilde. "The geysers soon erupt into the sky."

"Dian shook up all the continents yesterday, but fortunately she did the same thing today without the same raging energy."

"If she hadn't neutralised the energy, I don't know where we would have sailed off to."

"Maybe no one has told her what she's capable of."

"What was it that made Dian so angry?"

"She called Purple a baby."

"Why did Dian get angry because she called Purple a baby?" asked Volven surprised.

"Purple became red-hot with rage, he was about to explode, Dian got angry because he got angry. She is right you know; Purple is a big baby."

"If I said you were a baby, would you have crushed all the mountains in the world then?"

"Try me!" Gilde said and grinned.

31

The squirrel looked at Purple.

"I want a name too," it said.

"Why?"

"Because Blackbird has a name."

"What about Robin?"

"Why should I have a bird's name?"

"Because Blackbird has."

The squirrel sat down on its hind legs, while itching his stomach, thinking.

The white deer had heard that the squirrel had been given a name, it went to Angus and said it also wanted a name.

"Do you like John?" asked Angus.

"Why?" asked the deer.

"Heard about John Deer?"

"You mean the tractor?"

"Exactly! I'm named after an ox, and you after a tractor."

"That's not quite how it was," said the deer, "the ox was named after you."

That's how it was, thought Angus smiling to himself.

32

The eagles had found the right girlfriend for Angus. They found her in a pub, deep inside her own thoughts and beer glass, she drowned her sorrows, she was done with men. The eagles knew the right time had come.

Angus walked past the pub The White Deer. *The pub must have emerged lately,* thought Angus, he had never seen it before. He opened the door and went to the bar and bought a beer. At the other side of the bar sat someone that caught his eye, she speared everyone with her gaze. Angus went over to her.

"Do you like dandelions?" he asked.

She was so surprised that she laughed out loud. Angus looked at her and smiled his secretive smile.

"It happens," she said.

"Happens?" asked Angus.

"Sometimes I see how nice they are and other times I don't see them, it depends on what I'm thinking."

"What are you thinking when you like them then?" asked Angus.

"Then I think it's a strange plant."

"What's your name?"

"Angina."

"Is it possible to be called Angina?"

"It is, if your father has angina when you are born."

"Strange name."

"I thought you liked strange?"

"I think you're right," Angus said smiling. *I'll never distrust the eagles again*, he thought.

Angus asked Angina a month later if she would marry him, and she said yes. Angus said it was one thing he wanted to decide, and that was the bridal bouquet.

Angus asked Purple if he would be his best man. Purple was moved and could hardly answer. What Purple didn't know was that Angus had asked Dian too.

Angus wondered if a yellow suit would be accepted by Angina, she was traditional and wanted a white wedding dress. *The dress suits my hair,* thought Angus. Angina had brown short hair and brown eyes.

"I have never fallen for anyone with short, dark brown hair and brown eyes before," said Angus to the eagles.

"She looks like us," said the eagles.

Angus' wedding day was finally here. He stood in front of the mirror in his yellow suit, he looked radiant.

Purple appeared in a light blue suit.

"You look like the sun," said Purple.

"And you look like the moon," said Angus.

Angus asked Purple regarding the second flower in the bouquet.

"Take a couple of red poppies, you need some drama."

Dian saw the backs of Angus and Purple as they stood looking into the huge, gilded mirror. It stood in the hall in the old hotel they had rented for the venue. She wanted to back out again but it was too late, Angus had seen her.

"You came," he said, turning around.

"Of course, I'll come when you call."

Angus asked Dian what kind of flower she would put in the

bouquet. She said blue cornflowers without hesitation. Angus hugged her and said, "I just have to get something; I'll be right back."

"You look nice," said Purple.

Dian was wearing a light pink dress.

"We look like we're from the '80s," she said, laughing.

"Especially with Angus in a yellow suit," said Purple smiling. Purple took a dandelion out of the bouquet and attached it to Dian's dress.

"Now we look just as nice as Angus," he said.

"As long as we do not surpass the bride," said Dian.

"I never thought Angus would get a nice girlfriend."

"Why not?"

"I don't know, for some it's just difficult."

"How is it for you?" Dian asked hesitantly.

"You know."

"No, I don't."

Angus came back. "How are the turtle doves?" he said smiling. They just looked blankly at him.

"You must be kidding," Angus said furiously. Purple looked at the floor and Dian at the wall.

"What's the problem?" asked Angus.

None of them responded. The church bells began to toll.

"Are you ready?" Purple asked Angus.

"No, I'm not."

"What's the problem?" asked Purple.

"You are," Angus replied.

Purple looked down at the floor again.

"When will you realise that you either have to say something or do something," shouted Angus.

Purple knew very well how the floor looked by now.

"We're going," Angus said to Dian. "And you stay here," he said, pointing at Purple with a trembling finger.

Angus was so furious that he turned the key and locked Purple inside the room.

"Won't you need him as your best man?" asked Dian.

"Not any more, I have you."

Purple couldn't remember ever feeling so stupid, Angus was not going to let him out again. After a while he heard the door unlock, Dian stood in the doorway.

"I can't get out," said Purple, "Angus doesn't want me there."

"I brought you some food," said Dian and sat down on the edge of the bed.

Purple kissed her, why hadn't he understood that he should have done this a long time ago? Purple couldn't stop, he kissed Dian until she said they had to go. He took off his light blue jacket, below he had his favourite shirt, the deep red colour made him feel good.

The eagles sat in the trees and watched all the guests on the lawn, the dance floor was in front of the stage, a band played Angus and Angina's favourite songs.

Purple watched Dian and Angus dancing.

"How are you?" he heard someone say behind him.

Purple turned and saw Angina standing there. He understood why Angus had fallen for her, there was something real about Angina.

"I'm fine."

"That's not entirely true, is it?"

"How do you do something you know is right, which is the best thing that's ever happened to you, and yet you are unable to do anything about it?"

"That was enlightening," said Angina dryly.

"Wasn't it," said Purple, and smiled at her.

"Let's dance instead."

They had just gotten out on the dance floor when Angus released Dian and grabbed Angina instead. Dian and Purple stood looking at each other.

"Stop behaving like mongrels," said Angus angrily.

He pushed them against each other. They had no choice but to continue the dance to "Back to Black." *My God,* Angus thought, *I'll soon hit them both.* Angus was so bored, he decided not to talk to them anymore, he wondered if they danced one step forward and two backwards.

33

"Oh my God! What is going on?" Purple asked Dian. The whole mountain range shook.

"Sounds like Gilde is singing and playing the violin," said Dian.

"He's singing Fairytale," said Purple and laughed.

"He sounds cursed," said Dian.

They were invited to a party at the Mountain King's Hall. Purple and Dian lay on their backs in the heather, while listening to Gilde, his love for Volven was obviously hurting like hell.

"It can't hurt that much," said Purple and laughed even more.

Sus and Medusa stood and watched Purple and Dian writhing with laughter in the heather.

When Gilde finished singing, Dian and Purple caught sight of Sus and Medusa.

"Stood there long?" asked Purple.

"For a while," Sus said laughing, "looks like you're ready for a party."

"I think all folks are," said Purple.

"And trolls," added Sus.

"Hopefully trolls who can sing better than Gilde," said Dian.

"Angus is on his way. He is a troll sometimes, but he knows how to sing," said Purple.

"Storm can't sing," said Dian, "but don't tell him."

"If butter could sing, that's Storm for you," said Sus.

"Maybe he dances sensually as well," said Medusa.

Fortunately, Purple wasn't one of the sensual dancers, thought Dian.

They began to walk towards the mountain range and the Mountain King's Hall, Gilde was about to light all the torches on the path leading to the Hall.

"Started the last circle of light yet?" Sus asked Dian.

"Not yet, I'm waiting for the final sign from the gannedruids."

"How are things between you and Dian?" Medusa asked Purple.

"It's okay," Purple said quietly, then he shut down.

Dian wasn't wearing pink tonight; she wore a long brown dress. Purple had stopped wearing red as well, he wore a blue-black metallic silk shirt and matching trousers. Both Dian and Purple disappeared into the natural colours of the surrounding scenery. Sus and Medusa did the same. Sus was as usual in black, and Medusa wore a grey-green long dress. She had no snakes hanging from her hair any more, she looked normal.

Tue's owl followed them. Tue should have been there, but he was busy overturning loads.

Volven came out of the Mountain King's Hall when they arrived, she had a large silver platter in her hands, with blue sparkling drinks in tall glasses. The tray was garnished with blueberries and sage. Volven was dressed in metallic colours, and of course Gilde wore the same colours.

Purple took Dian's hand and squeezed it hard.

"We'll start the party when the glasses are empty. I mean the first glass of course," said Volven laughing. Her body shook so much when she laughed, that the glasses on the tray splashed everywhere.

"As usual Volven has ordered the northern lights," said Gilde while Volven finished laughing.

The northern lights were fortunately green and not red, they didn't have to be on heightened alert tonight.

There were no tables or chairs inside the Mountain King's Hall, just a stage and a bar. A disco ball hung from the ceiling, and lit torches hung on the walls. The bar was full of drinks in the colours of the rainbow. There were large colourful bottles with a grey stone on top, shaped like a drop.

"Where do you think she's hidden the whisky?" Dian asked Angus.

"Try the yellow bottle."

Angus was right. Dian poured herself a glass and went outside and sat down at one of the tables. The mountains were dark blue, and the torches along the path lit up the purple heather.

Inside the party had started. "Eloise" with The Damned was the beginning of a party that would probably last till early morning. Dian looked through the open double stone doors, Purple asked Storm for a dance. Shortly afterwards "I Will Survive" filled the air. There was nothing sensual about Storm's dancing, he was a disco lion.

Dian could see a light aurora borealis approaching slowly, the light blue and white colours were subtle. Dian imagined the solar storm that had to happen before the aurora showed itself. Not many people knew that the aurora happened during the day as well, it was invisible on the daylight side of the pole.

The magnetic field and the particles from the solar storm formed a funnel, then the magnetic field stretched rearwards and the funnel of particles followed to the nightside, and there it was possible to see the aurora.

The particles from the solar storm collided with the atoms in the atmosphere, but the strange thing wasn't the lights it created, it was the shape. The aurora Oval looked like a halo on top of the earth.

Dian thought about the funnel that was hidden in daylight, but it was still there. It was the perfect place to send all the evildoers, she only had to figure out how to close the entrance so they couldn't leave the funnel again.

Sus was heading across the floor towards Medusa. His wings were half folded. Gilde played his favourite song, "Something's Got a Hold of My Heart."

Suddenly Volven stood in front of him smiling. Sus didn't want to annoy Volven, but he had been looking forward all evening to dance with Medusa to that particular song. Purple saw what happened, he came running and smiled at Volven as he held out his hand.

I owe him one, thought Sus.

A stage with a microphone was rigged next to the bar. When Marc Almond and Gene Pitney stopped singing, Gilde waved at Volven and handed her the microphone. Volven smiled broadly and began to sing.

Wow! She really knows how to sing, thought Purple.

"Is it California Volven dreams of?" said Medusa to Dian.

"Who would have thought," said Dian.

Sus and Storm were chorusing the song. Everyone suddenly left the Hall. They had cheered and clapped when Volven began to sing, it lasted until Storm opened his mouth. His singing went through marrow and bones, it was the worst they had ever heard.

Sus and Volven exchanged glances while they sang, Storm didn't notice anything.

"I have a song for you," Volven said to Purple when everyone had entered the Hall again.

What has she figured out now? thought Purple.

Volven dragged him up on stage and gave him the microphone. Gilde started the music and Purple had no choice, Volven stood in front of the stage staring at him.

Purple began to sing "The Long and Winding Road." They

all wiped a tear when he had finished singing. Purple couldn't stay any longer, he went outside into the darkened night.

Volven wondered if she had done the right thing. Why it was so difficult, she couldn't comprehend. Everyone knew that Purple and Dian belonged together, including themselves.

Sus got an idea; he knew Dian didn't have much chance of surviving Edinburgh.

The gannedruids could develop a deadly weapon she could use. Sus had seen how everyone escaped when Storm sang. If they turned up the volume on the worst tones, evil would be destroyed. The sound waves would crush their bones, and the evildoers would turn into dust. Sus smiled to himself; he knew it was going to work.

Gilde wanted to swim in one of the hot springs. Volven stood and watched the garments fall, until Gilde stood in all his splendour, before he plunged into the water.

Volven couldn't help herself, she made the geyser spew up to the sky with Gilde on top.

Gilde shouted at her to stop. Volven did as he said, and he got himself a solid belly splash.

"Not so fast," he groaned.

It was the day after the party, they had gone to Iceland for a swim, Volven saw that Storm and Purple looked at her.

"You can go ahead," she said, "it's only fun doing it with Gilde."

The water was warm and turquoise, Medusa and Dian sat on a rock and watched. Angus jumped in too, Angina had to be with her father, he had heart trouble again.

Tue stood and watched them swim with his owl on his shoulder. He was angry that he hadn't been invited to the party.

Volven thought he should watch the earth while they were partying. His job was to avoid the little strokes to fell great oaks.

"It's good that someone holds the world into place while you party," said Tue angrily to Volven.

Volven gave him a look that was cold as ice. Tue got scared, he had never seen Volven angry before.

"What do you think we have done for hundreds of years?" she yelled at him.

Tue said sorry apologetically as he threw himself into the water. Volven gave him the same treatment she had given Gilde, only much longer this time, both in time and height. Finally, Dian said to Volven that she should get him down again. Tue wasn't used to being so high up, he stayed on the ground all the time, due to his work.

"How do you manage to control yourself?" Volven asked Dian. "You can make the geysers spew all the way up to the Milky Way."

"I have no choice," said Dian.

Tue landed in the water, and Purple and Storm dragged him up and lay him on the ground.

Tue's owl looked at them with its intense bright orange eyes.

"Don't look at us," said Purple, "look at Volven."

The owl didn't bother, Volven was too strong an opponent.

34

Satan had hidden in the huge rhododendron bush in Dian's garden, she sat on the bench that stood nearby. He turned into a large bright orange light almost as big as the bush, he wanted it to look like the bush was on fire.

Satan looked at Dian as he turned into the bright orange light, she looked interested at him, but not scared.

He disappeared and lit the light again with full force. *Now she must understand that it's not natural,* he thought.

Dian was stunned by the bright orange light, but she wasn't scared, Satan decided to get out of the bush. He walked towards her, it helped, Dian got up and left.

Just before she arrived at the house, she suddenly turned and looked straight at him.

"Forget it," she said, "you're not coming inside." Sus landed next to Dian and Satan had to give in.

Satan had been inside Dian's house many times. He had been standing in a small room at the end of a long hallway. Both his horns were visible through the small glass panes at the top of the door, but Dian didn't care.

Eventually Satan got tired of not getting a reaction, so he stayed outside instead. That was not entirely true, he couldn't get inside any more. Sus had created a protection that was too strong. The worst thing was that Dian didn't go outside alone any more either, Sus was always with her.

Satan had told all his friends that he was gonna introduce Dian to them in Edinburgh, he couldn't wait.

35

"I'm wondering what kind of connection you and Oak have with the phoenix," said Dian to Purple.

"What?" Purple didn't understand anything.

"The phoenix was originally purple, and the name comes from Phoenicia a region known for the colour purple, it's a royal colour. The phoenix is also associated with the sun. Arizona was a part of New Mexico in the old days, and the capitol is Phoenix. The name Arizona comes from the Basques who settled there, it means the Good Oak. The Basques believed in a good and a bad force. The Secretary of Arizona was Richard Cunningham McCormack. The Cunningham clan comes from Ayrshire where Arran is located.

In the Cunninghams' coat of arms there is a unicorn, and in the McCormacks' coat of arms, there are three red phoenixes." Purple still didn't understand the connection between the phoenix and himself.

Dian started telling him about a book called *Phœnician Origin of Britons Scots and Anglo-Saxon* by L A Waddell. "Listen to this," she said. "In the old historical books the Britons were said to be savages roaming wild in the woods."

"That was obviously not true," said Purple.

"It looks like the Phoenicians beat them to it," said Dian.

"And that was supposed to have happened over a millennium and a half before Christ?" asked Purple.

"It says so," said Dian. "The Phoenicians were Aryans in

race, and they were from the fair Northern race. They were the lineal blood-ancestors of the Britons and Scots.

The early settlements of the Phoenician Catti, meant: the first settlers.

Arran is anciently spelt Arran as well as Arran-see. Land of the Arri or Arya-ns, they lived on the flanks of Goat Fell and in the ancient Kil-Michael and Catacol."

"So, it wasn't named after Frøya's cats after all," said Purple and laughed.

"Arri or Arya English into Arya-n derived from Sumerian Ar, a Plough. They made ploughing and sowing secret rites under the Sun Cross in 1350 BC.

It also says that London was called New Troy, and Lusifer was the Gothic name of Loki."

"It's all connected. Tor and his hammer is found in the old cultures as well. He was a sun god."

"Tyr is on the oldest stone carvings in the north of Norway. He is easy to recognise, since he's missing half of his arm, maybe he was the moon god.

The Sun Cross also appears on some of the rock carvings alongside Tor and Tyr, they must be at least three thousand years old."

"The ships on the rock carvings look a bit like the galleys the Phoenicians used," said Purple.

36

Purple stood on deck on the CalMac ferry and saw the Isle of Arran drew closer.

He saw himself riding on the beach wearing a red sweater and red pants. Purple thought he looked like he was about ten years old. Two riders came and joined him. He recognised Angus in his yellow clothes, and Dian in her pink clothes.

All three of them had the same hairstyle, half-length and cut straight off, none of them had fringes. *Maybe they didn't have fringes back then*, thought Purple.

The ferry was almost at the pier. When it docked, Purple strolled slowly down the gangway with his jacket over his shoulder. It was the freshest air he had ever felt. Purple asked one of the men at the ferry terminal, if there was a taxi on the island. The man said he was off work soon; he could give him a ride. Purple accepted and sat down to wait.

There was a Christmas tree in the waiting room with a toy doll on top that looked like Mickey Mouse, it looked completely natural. The man finished work and they went to his car, which was parked near the well of happiness. Purple threw a coin into the well and mumbled something.

"Love trouble?" asked the Scotsman.

"Hope not," replied Purple.

The Scotsman pointed at Goat Fell, it was an impressive sight. The shadows were extra strong when the sun was going down. Purple asked if the Scotsman knew Dian.

"Ay!" he replied.

Jeez! Purple thought, *he speaks less than I do.*

They drove towards Goat Fell and the car stopped in the middle of nowhere.

The Scotsman pointed to a path and drove on. Purple looked up at Goat Fell, the shadows ran along the mountainside, the weather was about to change.

Suddenly there was a violent hailstorm. It flashed now and then inside all the hail, it looked completely insane. Purple began to trudge along the path, it twisted inward into the forest. He saw the same horses he had seen on the beach in Brodick.

Purple and Dian tethered the horses to a tree while they shouted, "Come on, Angus!"

Angus stood on the back of an ox while galloping away. Every time he was about to fall off, he bent down and held on to the ox's horns. Dian and Purple sat on a large rock and watched him, none of them had the same fascination as he had to tame oxen, Angus could keep at it for hours.

"Look, there is Flora," said Purple to Dian.

"Come here immediately, Angus Moon!" she yelled. "That includes you too, Dian Rowan and Purple Black."

Angus fell off the ox, and Dian and Purple walked slowly towards Flora, she stood with her hands on her hips.

"How many times have I told you not to mess with the Hamilton clan? They are not like us."

"We know, "Angus said, "but it's too difficult not to."

"I know, Oak and I used to do the same, but those times were different."

The image disappeared, and Purple trudged on, he thought he had walked for miles when he finally spotted a whitewashed house with smoke rising from the chimney. Purple knocked on the door and waited. It lasted and lasted; he began to wonder what was happening inside.

Dian froze to ice when it knocked on the door, she hoped, but dared not to hope at the same time. It took a long time before she opened the door. When she saw Purple standing there, she could neither speak nor move.

The wind had increased in strength, it was a hailstorm out there now. Dian didn't know how long she stood in the doorway; time had disappeared as soon as she met Purple's eyes. Finally, he said, "Can I come in?"

Dian laughed and let him in. Purple didn't need to convince Dian that they belonged together; he had come home. They both knew it was just a dream, but it felt real.

37

It was time to go to Edinburgh. Dian was going to spend a night near Falkland, she had to find the two unicorns that were trapped there, and free them before she could go to Edinburgh. Dian knew the unicorns were in Falkland, because it was the only place, she had seen a unicorn, without a chain around its neck.

The great battle in Edinburgh was approaching at a hasty speed.

Lusifer, Sus and Raven kept a close eye on Dian, they couldn't tell her anything important, the Devil watched every step they made.

The information about the unicorns' whereabouts would be given to her at the last minute, so evil didn't pick up how much Dian knew, they could enter people's minds. The unicorns stood for faith hope and love, without the unicorns the battle was stillborn.

Dian took the earliest ferry that went from Brodick to Ardrossan the next day at 08.20 a.m.

She only drank coffee; it was too early in the morning to think about food. Dian was still sleepy, but excited about what the day would bring. She was on her way and that was the most important.

When she got off the ferry, Raven, Lukas Evangelium and Midas Valiant waited for her. Storm came while the train was standing on the platform. Dian looked angrily at him; she had heard Storm's miserable singing the night before.

"Use butter," said Sus," it's the only thing that helps."

As soon as Sus said butter, Dian jumped into a huge packet of butter from Tine, it was the only butter that had high enough density to repair her cells, she kept the golden paper on. It was only her head, and some of her arms and legs, that protruded. The cells began to repair themselves immediately.

I will stay inside the butter packet for a long time, thought Dian happily.

Storm had disappeared into another train carriage. Dian looked at Midas, Lukas and Raven who sat on the other side of the aisle, she thought their behaviour became more and more strange. Midas and Lukas looked straight ahead, while Raven constantly stared out the window.

Raven saw that Dian suddenly sat in a large packet of butter, he couldn't believe his own eyes, she was so happy and didn't care at all how she looked.

Raven exchanged glances with Lukas and Midas, they struggled just as much as him not to laugh. If they laughed, Dian would probably take off the butter. They couldn't risk it; it was important that her cells were repaired again. None of them knew how much damage Storm's singing would do, they had never tried his voice before, Dian received an overdose.

Raven said quietly to Lukas and Midas that they shouldn't look at each other or Dian. He forced himself to look out the window for the hour the train ride lasted. When the train finally arrived in Glasgow, he said to Midas and Lukas that they had to watch Dian, so she didn't take off the butter.

Raven barely managed to get off the train before he lay down on the platform and bounced with his legs and arms, howling with laughter. Dian saw Raven laying on the platform bouncing, but she didn't understand what was so funny, she was talking to a woman. The woman told her to write down everything she saw. *A strange thing to say*, thought Dian, but she had a small notepad and a pen in the bag.

The train to Falkland left from the other train station in Glasgow. She arrived at the station five minutes before the train was leaving. *Perfect timing*, thought Dian, I'm surrounded by three black angels who know when the train leaves and where to go. She felt confident that she would find the place where the unicorns were trapped.

The train went through rolling hills and small villages. A tower suddenly appeared; it had a silver construction on top of a church tower.

"That's a strange construction on top of an old church, isn't it?" Dian asked Sus.

"Lilith and her hundred nutcrackers stay in the tower. They have a counter-formula ready for every formula you find. The strange church is a part of Linlithgow Palace."

Dian had never taken off the packet of butter, it felt like she was inside a duvet. Had she taken off the butter, the nutcrackers would have discovered her the minute she entered the train.

The train crossed the firth of Forth which lay in the kingdom of Fife. On the other side of the bridge, boxes of various grey colours and sizes began to appear. Dian remembered what the lady on the platform had said, that she should write down everything she saw. She started writing down the boxes. Eventually there were some dark blue and black boxes as well. Dian wrote down the colour and size of all of them, there were several hundred of them, she ended up with an endless line of boxes. There was a pattern within the long line, it was an abbreviation of the formula that consisted of five boxes.

The nutcrackers were so sure that Dian would never write

down hundreds of random boxes. They didn't notice the woman on the train station, they had been too busy watching Raven bouncing on the platform.

The nutcrackers could see Dian, but they couldn't harm her as long as she used the protection formulas, or the butter package she had used, while the train passed their headquarters in the silver tower in Linlithgow.

The train finally stopped at the small square where she had booked a room at an inn half an hour from Falkland. Dian walked through a park on her way to the inn. It had been a tiring train ride with endless formulas, all she wanted was to lay down for a while. Dian went up to the room and decided to make herself a cup of tea. She took off her shoes and put them nicely together on the floor, then she hung her jacket in the cupboard, while she waited for the water to boil. All Dian wanted was to lie down on the bed, but something stopped her.

Finally, the water boiled, and she drank the tea standing, looking longingly at the bed.

Sus had a quick encounter with Raven and Lusifer in the park.

"Dian actually wrote down the formula with all the boxes," said Raven and bowed his eyebrows.

"Thanks to Flora," said Lusifer.

"So that's who the woman was," said Raven.

"Remember, you can't tell Dian to write down the lion formula," said Lusifer to Sus.

"In order for the formula to work, she has to find out for herself," said Sus, "I remember."

"You have just enough time to get Dian and catch the bus to Falkland," said Raven.

"Good luck," said Lusifer, "you're gonna need it."

Sus rushed back to the inn, up the stairs and opened the door to the room. He didn't go inside, he just said holding on to the door handle, "We have to go now."

"I just want to lie down on the bed for two minutes first."

"If you lie down now, you'll never get up again."

Dian sighed heavily and followed Sus down the stairs. When she came outside on the street, her strength returned.

"Do you remember when we passed the Forth Bridge?"

"There was a message on one of the outbuildings," said Sus.

"It said: Fine Furniture Stop Forth of Fife. It was a message for me: Do not touch the furniture."

"The druids have left messages everywhere for you," said Sus and smiled.

He knew the druids had planned the trip for a long time, still he was impressed by all the boxes the druids had managed to put by the railway tracks, hidden as a formula.

They caught the bus to Falkland. The formulas were approaching at an ungodly speed. Sus had to help Dian sometimes to write all of them down, they appeared on street signs, cars, people and in shop windows. Dian sent them all off at the right time. They drew closer to the unicorns every second, and that was something Lilith's nutcrackers didn't appreciate.

They got off the bus and walked a narrow paved road that led to the square. It was impossible to pass Falkland Palace without going inside. They entered the Palace through the garden at the back.

Dian knew she had to find the unicorns, but the only information she had so far, was that they were kept close to water.

In one of the rooms, a huge rug covered an entire wall, it showed two white unicorn stallions with a heavy chain around their necks, their red tongues hung out of their mouths.

Dian couldn't hide her disgust.

The woman, who sat and watched the room, smiled at Dian and said, "You know that unicorns don't exist don't you, they're just a mythical figure."

"Do you think any animal likes to have a chain around its neck?" Dian said harshly to her.

"You know it's only a symbol of the union between Scotland and England?" asked the woman sweetly.

Dian didn't bother to answer her, she asked if there was any water nearby instead.

"You have the sea which is a few miles from here."

"Do you have a small puddle then?" asked Dian.

"We do," said the woman still very friendly, "we have a small burn." Dian felt in her bones that it was the right place, she asked how to get there.

"Past the square, then you follow the road to the left and continue until you see the burn, it's not far."

The woman looked indulgently after Dian as she left the room. She couldn't comprehend that anyone could react to such a beautiful rug, it symbolised the history of Scotland, they liked being chained to England.

Soon after she thought that it couldn't be the symbol of the picture. She had watched the rug for hours every day for years. Then it dawned on her, it wasn't the symbol of Scotland and England, it was two unicorns fighting for their lives with their tongues hanging out of their mouths.

She knew her bible very well, and she knew it said: The tongue is the instrument either of a great deal of good, or of a great deal of evil. The woman left her post for the first time during all these years and went to find the two lions with their tongues hanging out of their mouths.

It dawned on her for the second time that day. The Palace held a secret, the two lions' tongues and the two unicorns' tongues were connected. The lions could help the unicorns, she was sure of it. She started to laugh and reminded herself that she didn't believe in unicorns.

The Palace had a lot of lions on the stained glasses, they were everywhere. Dian took her notepad and pen from her purse and wrote down the colours of all the lions she saw. After she had been through all the rooms in the Palace, she had managed to write them all down.

Two orange, two blue, three golden, four orange, five red, two red, six red, one red, one red, one golden, one red, one golden, one blue, one red, two silver, one red, one black, one black, one silver lion with its tongue out, and a blue lion with its tongue out.

She wrote down six orange, four blue, five golden, eighteen red, three silver, and two black. She put the numbers in a row and got 1234568. "I wonder if she knows that she represents number seven," said Sus.

"It doesn't matter," said Raven. "The formula will work, because all the first eight numbers are present."

"And it helps that number eight is the eternal number," said Lusifer.

Sus said it was time to leave, the Palace wasn't safe anymore. He asked Dian if she wanted a cup of coffee, he knew a nice cafe by the square.

Dian just looked at him.

"Of course, you want coffee," said Sus and laughed.

When they came out on the street, Sus stopped and looked at a statue on the house on the other side of the street. It had a rope around its neck. Dian saw it too.

"A statue of you, outside a house with a rope around your neck, do you by any chance own the house?"

"I do, it's my old house. We have to be more careful from now on, the nutcrackers have discovered that we have been inside the Palace, the rope wasn't there when we entered."

They went to find a cafe and passed four pink lions sitting around a spire in the middle of the square.

"I have a feeling I will experience a lot of hardships before all of this ends," said Dian.

"The hardest time will be when this book is almost done. You don't know how long you will manage to stay afloat to finish it. The date you have to be ready won't be revealed to you, but it's close to this date. You must be willing to sacrifice a lot."

"I know what you mean," said Dian.

"You do?" said Sus surprised.

"It gets worse every day, especially the last week, I'm so close, and I'm about to give up every day."

"So how do you think you will survive?"

"I give up, but I keep on writing because I give up. I have nothing else to do."

Sus laughed and said that it actually was a good plan, nobody expected her to give up and at the same time continue. They went inside the quiet cafe by the square.

"No wonder it is quiet," said Sus," it's out of season."

The coffee was delicious, and Dian felt calm, it was time to go and find out if the unicorns were captured somewhere close to the burn.

"It's a lovely street," said Sus, "so idyllic. It's almost strange that there is so much evil here."

A small house lay on the right side of the road. It said: Out sailing on a sign in the window. In the garden stood a miniature of the four pink lions from the square, except they were red. A miniature house with purple windows stood behind.

Dian saw three numbers as she approached the gate, it was 659. The gate lay at the entrance of the Hidden Place. An old stone house on the left side of the road was decorated with a string made of clay that hung in arches under the ridge.

Both Dian and Sus felt a shift in the atmosphere when they passed the gate.

The burn came floating quietly down into a small pond on the left side of the road. A small stone bridge, with two stone pillars, went across the burn by the pond.

Dian walked onto the bridge and looked down into the pond. She saw two black unicorns, chained to the stone pillars on each side of the bridge. Dian sent a rainbow on the chains around the unicorns' necks and said 659 at the same time. The two black stallions were free of their chains and galloped at maximum speed down the plains towards the hills.

Afterwards Dian used the lion formula as a protection so the unicorns wouldn't get caught again. Without the lion formula the unicorns would have been dragged back by their chains. The lion formula was so strong that it broke Lilith's curse.

Dian saw the two huge eggs containing Snowflake and Blackbird. She sent Snowflake into the nearest tree. Snowflake was restless and kicked the egg until it cracked.

Dian repaired the egg with milk and honey, and made a new membrane around the egg, she did the same with Blackbird's egg. Then she sent Blackbird into a tree nearby which had a solid bird's nest. On the other side of the river stood a tree with a similar nest. Dian understood that she had sent Snowflake into the wrong tree, so she sent her into the right tree. Snowflake lay down calmly and fell asleep.

Dian saw that Sus and Medusa stood on the plain between the large deciduous trees. Medusa was pregnant, their bairns would be born the same evening, same as Blackbird and Snowflake.

Dian laid stones in different colours around Medusa and Sus. It was pink, turquoise, purple, blue and red with a red lion on top, she had found the coloured stones on two crowns in Falkland Palace. Finally, she made a huge transparent bubble around Sus and Medusa.

Dian decided to go back to the inn and get some sleep before the big battle in Edinburgh the day after. There wasn't anything else she could do for the moment, at least that's what she thought before she saw the hundreds of evildoers that had gathered outside the wrought iron gate.

Dian bent down and picked a snowbell which stood by the fence, it was white with a green zig-zag pattern on the innermost petals. Dian smelled and studied the snowdrop carefully.

The evildoers' faces touched the fence, while they were holding both hands firmly on to it. They didn't understand why Dian didn't walk through the gate right away, the black angels didn't understand it either.

Dian finally went through the gate; she picked up a wrought iron flower stand and used it as a wand. She swung the wand against the evildoers and turned them into dust. Each time there was an attack from above, she turned the wrought iron flower stand against them, and they turned into dust.

The black angels walked calmly behind Dian; they didn't have to do anything.

Raven jumped off at the Puppet master's house. It said Out sailing on a sign in the window. The only boat Raven had, was a boat made of paper which looked like a sailor's hat. In the boat stood a tin soldier. Raven saw that the windows of the miniature house shone brightly in purple, he knew who was hiding in the house.

"You can come out now," he said.

Purple crawled out of the little house and disappeared down the road. Raven looked at the little tower with the four red lions sitting around it. *One day I will paint them blue*, he thought, *when the earth becomes the blue planet again.*

He went inside and sat down to make another toy, what it was going to be, he didn't know.

Lukas Evangelium lived a little further down the street, he was God's rat shepherd. Much had changed after his rats had been valued for the job they had done, and still did. His house lay in the second row from the road. Lukas enjoyed his backyard hidden away from curious eyes, he had only visits from those who knew where he lived.

Lukas sat in his backyard and smoked a pipe while watching the sunset. He and Raven used to walk along the burn and look at the stupid paper boat Raven had made. They bet on how long the tin soldier managed to stand before falling into the burn.

If the tin soldier stands until the boat reaches the tree, you have to clean my house, Raven always said.

Now everything was turned upside down. *Maybe I will have to clean Raven's house one day,* Lukas thought and bowed his eyebrows.

Friday the thirteenth of March 2015 was drawing to an end. Dian was on her way back to the inn. On the way she passed a window which had squares of a pink and green film.

Volven had once told her that she had to look for that particular colour combination. It was the colours and the pattern of Volven's invisibility rug she stood and looked at. Dian recollected it and walked slowly back to the inn; she was so tired that it was hard to remember the way back.

At the Hidden Place the black angels and the druids had gathered to celebrate that the unicorns got rid of their chains, but it was too early. Evil had a surprise that none of them expected. Arnold Clark came flying out of the blue and killed thirty black angels at once, twenty died shortly after. The druids didn't know how to fight, so they just disappeared.

Dian saw that Sus needed help, he couldn't get out of the bubble she had made around him and Medusa. It was a good thing Sus didn't get out when Arnold came flying, then he would have been killed.

Arnold had a tight-fitting suit in red and white with the Sun Cross in red on his white chest. The red cloak fluttered around him as he flew. Dian stood in the sky above the pond, she was wearing her finest druid dress, it was turquoise with small stones in all the colours of the rainbow.

She used blue around the Hidden Place, while the seven star and number seven moved through the air like a boomerang heading against Arnold. Dian got him off course time and time again, Arnold was zigzagging in the sky. She sent a long DNA-row made of silver triangles and got Arnold down on the ground, but it wasn't enough.

Dian had to use the ganne formula she had found on the train ride, fortunately she was able to use the abbreviated version which consisted of five boxes.

She used the formula around Arnold, and he disappeared like the air released from a balloon.

The formula also exterminated the rest of the wicked who had gathered around the Hidden Place.

Dian now understood that she had to be prepared for everything, nothing was certain. She also understood that she needed to get some sleep every time it was possible. The war was upon them, it was happening in both the worlds at the same time, but it was hidden in the real world.

She woke up at 04.58 a.m. on the fourteenth of March, the unicorns were captured again. Dian didn't have to go back to Falkland, she could do it mentally. She saw that the unicorns were trapped on their respective stone pillars again. It was pitch black by the pond; Dian could hardly see them. Both hung with their heads down in the dark water, the chains weighed them down.

It was God who had captured the unicorns again, he needed to see if any of the black angels would betray him by telling Lilith, but none of them did. God was relieved, he needed to trust all of them before the big battle in Edinburgh the day after.

All the black angels cried because the two black unicorns were captured, they thought Dian had failed. When God saw that the black angels' grief was sincere, he asked Dian to use the reverse formula.

To get the formula to reverse that they were caught again, Dian had to use the numbers in reverse. She said 956 towards the left unicorn first, then 956 to the unicorn to the right, but nothing happened.

Dian tried to figure out what she did wrong, it was the first time she had used the reverse formula. Then she did the opposite, she said 956 to the right and then to the left. It worked; the unicorns were free again.

Dian went back to sleep. She woke up a few hours later, it was time to go Edinburgh.

She walked through the park on her way to the bus, a white banner with black writing hung on an old stone building in the park, it said: Dian Airbus.

Dian read Airbus and understood that it wasn't the bus she was going to take to Edinburgh, but the train. There were 880,000 evildoers in the area around the train station and the bus station this morning. Raven was the only one who was sent out to help her to get onto the train.

The train thundered into the station soon after, and Dian was the only one standing on the platform. She set one foot on the train and the other foot on the platform. Raven had to make sure it was safe before she entered.

The conductor came over to her and said the train had to leave. Dian looked at him and said she was waiting for a friend, the conductor became more and more furious, at last he hissed. Dian could literally see the smoke rising from his head. "We have to leave the station now," he said over and over again. Dian just smiled at him and refused to move.

Soon after Raven told Dian it was safe to enter the train. The conductor snorted and began to weigh the flag and the train slowly set in motion. Raven jumped on the train as it started to move. He said she had to find the Needle.

Just before Edinburgh they passed the Haymarket, Dian thought of the needle in the haystack, but she saw nothing reminiscent of a needle.

Shortly afterwards the train stopped at the Waverley train station, it was located in the middle of Edinburgh.

"You can't use the main entrance," said Raven, he pointed to a small exit that lay on the right side of the building.

Dian stopped and looked around when she came out on the street. KGB was written on one of the walls, on another hung a poster with bubbles in full spectrum. KGB made her shut her mouth until it was safe to talk.

They walked up the street until they came to St Andrews

Square. It contained an exhibition called Full Spectrum. There were two pictures, one had an oval form with different colours, the other had colours that stood straight up like pillars.

Dian could feel that it was urgent to write down the formulas. When she was done, Raven waved at her to come to a stone staircase. Dian saw a black monument when she looked down the street, it looked like a needle.

"You have to say the formulas now," said Raven. "The black angels are dying like flies; you have to get them into the Needle."

Dian said the formula that was in the oval shape first. It was so strong that it sent the black angels and the evildoers in spirals through the air. The black angels had to use a special flying technique to get into the Needle. They plunged in with their wings closed around them.

They were completely exhausted; the fight had lasted ever since Dian had left Arran. Once inside the Needle, Dian used the latter formula around them which was a formula of protection. It was the colour poles in green, red, orange, yellow and purple. The black angels finally got a respite.

Dian found a cafe nearby, she bought a Jura 16 and sat outside the cafe, she needed some fresh air. A nice lady passed by on the sidewalk. Suddenly, she said out loud, "Freezing!"

"Something is frozen," said Dian.

"It's the sea around Edinburgh," said Raven.

Dian let flames thaw the sea, then she filled the sea with full spectrum bubbles.

It was time to move on, Dian could forget finding a place to stay, evil struck all the time, she changed the formula of protection faster and faster. She went to the pub The World's End and bought an Innis & Gunn.

Dian had found the formula for cracking Hell and Helvetia,

they were the most dangerous evil couple, they could divide into several parts and go into many people. She just had to find the biggest part of Hell and Helvetia before she used the formula. Dian finished her beer and went outside to wait for Hell and Helvetia to show up.

Two cute girls came walking towards her.

"There they are," said Raven.

Dian put them in a black cauldron and said the formula: Brown one red, green one white. Hell and Helvetia disappeared into the black cauldron and it was quiet for a wee while.

Volven kept an eye on Dian, she saw that Dian and Raven went up the Royal Mile, Volven also saw the hundreds of thousands of evildoers who followed her.

"The hotel we are staying in, is on the next street on the left," said Dian to Raven.

It wasn't, but the evildoers thought so. They went down the next side street to wait for them.

At the bottom of the street stood Volven, she didn't have to do or say anything, she just looked at them, and they died of fright and turned into dust.

"The hotel is on the next street on the left," Dian told Raven again. Volven killed all the evildoers who were stupid enough to believe that the hotel actually lay there.

When Dian said for the third time that the hotel was on the next street to the left, Raven thought she had lost it. He didn't see Volven, but Dian did. She understood that it was Volven who had made her say that the hotel was located on the next street to the left, three times.

It was too dangerous to approach the hotel yet, Dian had to wait for the right time. She had to change the protection formulas faster and faster.

She sat outside a cafe on the Royal Mile and wrote down all the moving formulas that passed by. The formulas were moving to fool Lilith's nutcrackers.

The first formula consisted of those with the strangest colours on their hair who passed by, then there were hats. It wasn't just hair or hats; the formulas were put together more ingeniously than that. It could sneak in a hat or a scarf occasionally, the pattern lay in how people stood in relation to each other.

The formulas Dian had written down had to be sent around at the right time. Sometimes to the right and sometimes to the left, or at the same time. Dian knew what to do half a second before, she had to trust herself and do it no matter how hopeless it seemed. As soon as one of Lilith's nutcrackers had solved one of the formulas, they had a counter-formula ready. If they managed to use it before Dian said another formula, all hope would be lost. The nutcrackers saw the same people as Dian did, she only needed to be half a second faster than they were.

It wasn't over yet, Dian made a protection formula for the black angels once more, it was a sunflower she saw on a sign across the street, inside a grey stone heart laying between the stones on the pavement. She had changed the protection formulas for the black angels almost as often as she had changed them for herself and Raven.

The hotel was on the next side street to the left. Dian had walked around the streets of Edinburgh for six hours, before she finally had fooled the evildoers long enough to be able to check in. It was a beautiful hotel with psychedelic wallpapers from Timorous Beasties.

It was expensive and luxurious, but it was tasteful and modern in a way that suited the surrounding buildings.

Dian sat down on the bed and looked out of the window. On the roof of the old sandstone building across the street, there was a black little door that led out to the roof terrace. The door opened slowly, and a black little witch came out, she looked at Dian with narrow eyes. Dian had no more strength left, she just looked at the witch with a blank stare.

A man came flying and landed on the roof, he had black hair and black clothes. The black wings disappeared as he landed. He impaled the witch with a pitchfork, afterwards he turned to Dian and smiled.

Dian didn't smile back; she was too exhausted. He left the witch on the roof and continued up the street towards Greyfriars Kirkyard. He was without any doubt the most attractive man Dian had ever seen, with his grey eyes and his straight black hair down to his shoulders.

Dian wasn't particularly hungry, but she had to eat something, the fight at Greyfriars Kirkyard was only hours away. She followed Cow Street down to the Grassmarket. All the cafes and restaurants were full due to St Patrick's day, it was celebrated on the closest weekend.

After a while she found a table outside a pub called the Beehive Inn. After the meal she followed Cow Street up to Greyfriars Kirkyard, Dian had been there before, but she managed to walk past the entrance without noticing.

Lusifer and God killed everyone in the kirkyard while Dian was walking around the block. There were millions of creatures crawling everywhere, some hid between the huge gravestones. God held his right hand over them and turned them into dust. Lusifer killed the ones who tried to escape through the gate. It was an easy match, they were so happy to see Lusifer, that they didn't realise he was with God.

Dian had only been a decoy, God and Lusifer had never meant for her to participate in the fight.

Dian finally found the entrance to the kirkyard. A group of people turned their heads and looked at her as she entered the gate, it was a guided tour that was about to begin. The fight was obviously over, and Dian decided to join the guided ghost tour instead. The guide boasted about all the tours she had guided without seeing a single ghost.

"My boss said there were twelve of you who paid for the tour, but when I count you, I count eighteen." The guide sounded surprised. They began to walk between the tombstones.

"We have decided to give the guide a bit of a scare," said a man walking alongside Dian.

They were sick of her saying that she had never seen a ghost, she mocked them almost daily.

"It's payback time. There are five of us on this tour," he said proudly looking at Dian wonderingly.

"I'm not. Have you noticed anything peculiar happening here just now?"

"It has been a big battle, but the hand of God made it extremely short lived. That's why the five of us decided to join the ghost tour, in order to celebrate."

The guide stood at the back of the church counting them again.

"You were eighteen, but now you are only twelve," she said trembling.

Dian just laughed and left the ghosts and the tour without paying. She had just reached the statue of Greyfriars Bobby when a homeless man approached her and asked if she had any money. Dian gave him a 20 pound note. The homeless man took her hand and pressed it hard.

"You don't have to thank me," said Dian.

"I will get myself a good bed tonight," he said, "I just want to cry."

"Promise me you will laugh afterwards," said Dian. He nodded and looked at her.

Dian stroked his cheek with her index finger. He looked at her with green transparent eyes, afterwards he gave her the best hug she had ever received. She looked at him while he disappeared down Cow Street towards the Grassmarket, he didn't look like a homeless.

God had promised Dian to laugh, and he kept his promise. He thought of the meal that she had eaten at the Grassmarket, he thought it was hysterically funny.

Dian was sitting outside the Beehive Inn; it was a message to Dian to behave. They had to hypnotise her so she didn't start to laugh at a terrible meal, it was important that she behaved differently than usual, so evil wouldn't recognise her, they had to believe that she was on her way to the kirkyard, where they were waiting for her.

Dian had ordered fish and chips; it was less than one hour until she had to face all the evildoers on Greyfriars Kirkyard. Dian ate and ate, but the fish didn't get smaller, it got bigger. They had to keep her there, until the fight was over.

God made the fish taste of glue and the chips of cardboard. He saw that Dian sat and stuffed herself, while evil accumulated in millions on Greyfriar, they were alive and dead on top of one another. Dian ate and ate, it was the worst meal she had ever tasted, but she couldn't stop.

She thinks it's the last meal, thought God and began to laugh so hard that the whole sky shook. *I have to keep my promise*, thought God and laughed even more.

Later in the evening he planned the funeral for the hundred and thirty-three black angels who died during the battle of Edinburgh.

The next day the hundred black angels who survived were present alongside God inside the Greyfriars Kirk. Dian opened the door and tried to sneak unseen inside the Kirk. There was a little grey choir singing, they looked bloodless, like they were soaked dry. The people who sat listening looked equally bloodless and grey. At the second service, that only Dian and the ghosts could see, sat the remaining black angels. Fifty died in Falkland and eighty-three in Edinburgh the day after.

Raven sang "To Be by Your Side" by Nick Cave. The black angels sitting on the hard benches longed for another world, where they could lie in the grass, and chew on a straw, and look at Blackbird and Snowflake while they grazed peacefully.

When the ceremony was over, the black angels and God went outside and discussed where the Mercy Seat should be.

"It can't be in heaven," said Dian, "they will be bored to death. Send them on to the top of Vatnajökull on Iceland so they can get some action, Volven will entertain them."

The black angels and God agreed that Vatnajökull was a good idea.

The golden bell on a tower nearby struck twelve, it was time for the dead black angels to leave, the Mercy Seat was waiting for them. It was a completely different death awaiting them this time, they could relax on top of Vatnajökull and choose where and when they wanted to be born again.

38

Dian thought the living formulas passed by too slow when she sat outside the cafe on the Royal Mile. She noticed that the formulas began to change at the last minute. Originally it was thought differently, but now it had to sneak in a small element in each formula in order for Dian to get the half second, she needed, it became more and more precarious.

Markus saw that Dian struggled at the end on the Royal Mile, she had only seconds left before they broke her. Markus had infiltrated Lilith's nutcrackers, he looked exactly like them. Brown corduroy trousers, middle-aged and half fat, a knitted vest with stripes in brown and dark red colours with a beige shirt underneath. Everyone was almost bald and wore glasses. None of them realised that it was wise to count how many nutcrackers they were. Markus was number one hundred and one.

Markus shouted out if he could get everybody's attention. He had found the formula that would send Dian to eternity. Everyone corrected their glasses at the same time and turned interested towards Markus.

He showed them a formula which went back a bit in time, but at the same time accelerated forward into eternity and destroyed everything on its way. Everyone got up and clapped and cheered. They were tired of solving all the formulas Dian had sent them. None of the nutcrackers had been outside the tower for at least a thousand years, they had been busy trying to nurture their small and grey braincells.

Markus snuck out of the side door of the church tower that

lay in the grounds of Linlithgow Palace. He heard everyone saying the formula at the same time, he had told them that they had to do so, if they wanted to destroy Dian. The nutcrackers didn't realise that they were the ones who were destroyed.

Markus transformed back to himself and strolled down the green hillside to the train station, he had a train to catch. Raven was right, in the midst of evil was the place to be, if one wanted to succeed the hundred and first time. God and the black angels had tried to succeed a hundred times before.

There was a time setting on the formula, it worked at 20.17 the same evening. Before that time Lilith's nutcrackers worked very hard, both they and Lilith thought. None of them felt that they had lost the ability to solve a single formula, it had to look like they had the upper hand.

Dian had long wondered why it suddenly was so easy to get into the hotel in Edinburgh. She understood why, when Markus told her what he had done.

39

Dian stayed only a couple of days on Arran after the arduous trip to Edinburgh. Raven said she should indulge herself with two days on the Isle of Bute.

She took the earliest ferry the next morning, she was looking forward to some peace and quiet, but it didn't last long. Lilith had hidden the best nutcracker till last, he was on the ferry, and he was good.

Dian wrote down formulas constantly for forty-five minutes, then she realised it was hopeless. This nutcracker couldn't be fed with too many formulas, he swallowed them and turned them into dust as soon as she wrote them down. Dian tried to write down the most unlikely things she saw, but nothing helped.

"He's too good for me," she said to Raven.

"This guy has been training for three thousand years, that's all he's been doing."

"I can tell," said Dian.

They went up on deck, Dian had decided to find a formula just before they got off the ferry, but the formula lay floating on the sea. It was five birds floating in a V form, the sixth bird floated just below the one in front. Dian saw a flag with St Andrew's Cross on the ferry. She put the cross on top of the V shape the birds made, and saw that the sixth bird indicated a line, she drew the line mentally in her head and saw that it formed a five star.

Dian didn't write down anything, she told Raven that they

were going to die, she didn't know what the nutcracker picked up.

When they were about to get off the ferry, Raven whispered to Dian, "Do you remember the two who got angry?"

"I remember the two," whispered Dian back.

"Say the formula you found when we get off the ferry."

A fat guy in a light blue duvet jacket suddenly pushed himself between them.

It's him, signalled Raven to Dian. Dian said Suslus and Lussus before she said the formula with the birds and the St Andrew's Cross. Lilith's nutcracker hadn't cracked the code that was in the names of Jesus and Lusifer. Raven used the Phoenix to destroy him, and they could catch the bus to Bute.

They passed Croft Town where evil had its core of power. Dian used all the symbols of evil just as the bus drove through the city. She sent 666 around and turned it upside down to reverse evil. Then she put two five stars on top of each other and sent them in their respective directions around the city. Afterwards she put two hay forks against each other with a white ball in the middle. It spun around, while the hay forks went high and low. She did the same with the St Andrew's Cross.

The bus arrived at Largs which symbolised all the battles that had taken place. Dian sent the number 1066 around the city and to Wychwood in England. Why Wychwood she didn't know, but it represented a place where a battle had taken place. She asked Raven why Wychwood was present all of a sudden.

"Just the taste of the name," said Raven and laughed. "Seriously it's a wood full of little people, fairies and nice goblins. They insisted upon being present somehow, and it was the only way I could think of letting them."

"There were two significant battles in 1066."

"Stamford Bridge and Hastings," said Raven.

"You have two Harald, one on each side, and you have two Godwinson, one on each side, and the numbers of men fighting the battles are seven thousand and something on each side, and the coat of arms in Hastings and Stamford contains three lions."

"So?" asked Raven.

"It's just strange," said Dian.

The ferry ride over to Bute was blessedly calm, nothing happened. Raven wanted Dian to check in at the hotel on the corner. Dian understood why, the hotel was magnificent. It had a strange dark pink colour on the walls in the bar and dining area, the curtains were faded in weird beige and pink stripes. There were various links of light hanging around in bright colours.

Everything was dilapidated, it looked like time had stopped there during the '50s. The landlady said they didn't have any rooms available, but she owned a hotel down the street, it was newly renovated.

Dian thought it was probably a charmless and soulless hotel, but she didn't bother to look for another, she desperately longed for two days off, she was still exhausted after Edinburgh.

It was so boring at the hotel that Dian decided she wanted to see the island. While waiting for the bus, she entered the pavilion by the fjord, she found so many formulas inside, that she barely had time to write them down before the bus arrived. She said one formula after another while sitting on the bus, the island was full of wicked creatures.

Storm asked Lusifer what all the fuss about free time on Bute was about.

"We told Dian that it was a good thing that she and Raven went to Bute, she needed a rest, but that was just something we said. It was too important what we wanted her to do on Bute."

"You thought she would say no if you told her that Bute wasn't a place to relax, it would be ten times worse than Edinburgh?"

"Something like that. It started on the ferry from Arran, Dian had to fight Lilith's best nutcracker. Then she passed Croft Town where you know what lingers, before she arrived on Bute. I think Dian had two minutes free without anything happening at the most, except during the night, then it was free on Bute."

"What happened?"

"On the first bus drive Dian had to say formulas all the time, evil was everywhere. When the bus stopped, the bus driver said she had to go up the hill, and to the left. It was important that she did so, we wanted her to activate the energy in that particular area, it's the core of evil on Bute.

We wondered if she would listen to the bus driver, but she did. When she was going back, we got the bus driver to drive right past her, she didn't realise it, but she needed time to write down dozens of new formulas that could keep her and Raven alive on the way back. She blew up cars, people and houses and counted hundreds of pipes, flowerpots and I don't know what, and found the right number combinations for the formulas.

After that she went to the Serpentine Road where she knocked her head hard on the walls of the houses along the street to release enough energy to set free the black angels that were burned there in the seventeenth century, she used the reverse formula. Dian made ten different formulas on Serpentine Road. Every time she ate, there were some people sitting next to her who had to be sent to the funnel."

"Funnel?" asked Storm. "What's that?"

"It's a funnel which sends people to the other side where no one has been before, they can't come back again.

The next day we needed a formula to keep the evildoers down, but we struggled to find something that evil hadn't seen before, they were prepared for everything after Edinburgh. Dian said we should sit on it, it's an expression that only exists in Norway. The gannedruids constructed a large butt, it helped to keep evil down for a while.

Is this what you call free time on Bute? asked Dian every time she had two minutes without anything happening, she thought it was hysterically funny.

She had to send plenty of people into the funnel and blow up boats and all sorts of other stuff all the time. When she went to the ferry the next day, Dian started to get sick of it all."

"Then she had solved the most difficult formula on the southern end of the island?" asked Storm.

"She had, that formula was so impossible to solve that I didn't think she stood a chance."

"Dian counted on her fingers, didn't she?"

"She did, but it's a weird finger system she has. I understand that five goes up in one hand, but when the number is seven, she counts three on her middle finger, so the formula became five and two."

"I don't understand anything," said Storm.

"No one does, that's why she is still alive, she's the best nutcracker the world has ever seen, "said Lusifer.

"There are several who would have been dead if she hadn't been."

"Dian continued with a boat that was right next to the ferry, she counted the poles around the boat and moored the boat to the ground, while God's hand pulled out the evil with the help of Ailsa Craig, it was a complicated formula."

"Pulled the evil out of what?" asked Storm.

"I don't remember any more, Bute was the worst nightmare, but it was fun because Dian laughed so much that we called it free on Bute. What we really meant by free time on Bute, was the formula we hoped Dian would solve.

As I said, Dian started to get bored of all the formulas. She was waiting for the ferry back to the mainland, when she decided that she had to find a formula, so there was an end to the protective formulas we all needed endlessly. That was the test, she had to find it without thinking about herself. If she had, it wouldn't have worked. When Dian said the formula she had found, we were all free, none of us needed a formula again for protection, that was what we meant when we said free on Bute."

"Where did she find the formula?"

"She found the numbers on the digital clock in the waiting room. The only thing I remember is that she sent a lying eight around at the end to make it eternal."

Dian took the bus to the South end of Bute. Raven said it was a formula she had to solve; it lay in the landscape at the southern end of the island. There was no hurry, she had the rest of the day to solve it. Dian was about to get off the bus when the bus driver stopped her and looked straight at her, he said the next bus would leave at twenty minutes past four. It was the way he said it that made Dian write it down.

She had seen five black horses, five large water tanks and five couplings attached to a fence on the bus ride, she understood that number five was important in order to find the formula.

Dian sat down at a table and began to study the landscape. She wrote down some poles and windmills, but shortly afterwards she knew it was wrong. She looked behind her, there were five fence posts.

This is where the formula begins, thought Dian turning around on the bench. She started counting the posts on her fingers, the next row of posts was five forward and four back. Some people sitting at the next table were singing, it was a song she needed to add. Dian wrote: "My Bonnie Lies over the Ocean". She continued to write down things she saw in the landscape: 4-1-1-2-1-2-1-3. The formula ended with twenty past four.

Dian read the formula, then she said to Raven: "Now I'm going to read it," and then she read the whole formula again. When she was done, she asked Raven why they had collapsed in the seventh heaven.

"You did it," said Raven, "they held their breath for so long that they collapsed when they started breathing again."

"Why?" asked Dian, "I had the rest of the day to find the formula."

"You had five minutes to solve the formula, I lied so you wouldn't give up, you managed it within two and a half minutes. The last word had to be read at the right time, that's why you said I'm reading it again now."

Dian felt nervous.

"Now she's nervous," Dian heard them say in the seventh heaven as they began to laugh. Shortly afterwards it became completely quiet, they had collapsed again. They had only woken up for a moment when they felt Dian was nervous, she had never been nervous before.

The bus came long after the bus driver said it should. Dian looked at the bus route that hung at the stop. There was no bus at twenty minutes past four.

"You have probably started to get used to the fact that the bus drivers are reborn druids," said Raven laughing.

They decided to go to a pub when they got back. They ended up at a pub on Serpentine Road. Raven ordered a Captain Morgan, Dian did so too, the whisky selection was lousy.

"The Land of the Silvermoon," said Raven out of the blue, "that's what Finland was called in the old days."

"What happened?"

"A thousand years ago, Volven fell in love with Nøkken who lived in Finland. Nøkken wasn't interested in Volven, she became furious, and cast a spell over Finland. They should freeze and live in darkness and get lost in the landscape that consisted of spruces and lochs. Everything should look the same, and all the adventures should be completely gone. Even Karelia, where the soul and heart of the Finns lies should be lost."

"They manage to keep half of Karelia," said Dian. "I think it's time Finland got its magic back."

"Use the three Phoenix plates you inherited from your grandmother," said Raven.

Dian put the three Phoenix plates in a triangle around her and went back in time before Volven cast a spell on Finland. She used the reverse formula and reversed all evil Volven had caused.

They left the pub and continued further up the Serpentine Road which twisted like a serpent upwards. They came to a small park; Dian went to the top of the grassy slope and lay down on the grass and rolled down while Raven sat calmly on the bench.

The bells on an ice cream truck nearby started to chime endlessly, it was church bells instead of the usual bells. Dian's hands were icy cold.

"Something is frozen," she said.

"You're right," said Raven. "It's God's right hand."

"The answer lies in the pub where we just were, did you see the big empty whisky bottle? It was chained to the countertop."

"We have to use the big sledgehammer on the chain," said Raven. They did, and God's hand was free again. There had been a time setting on hand.

"What would have happened if we hadn't got his hand loose before time ran out?" asked Dian.

"Then God's right hand would have been frozen for at least two thousand years."

"What happened?"

"God has four nutcrackers now; they got a little too eager after you said the reverse formula could probably be used as a future formula if you turned the numbers around. The reverse formula was too advanced for them, only you are allowed to use it from now on."

"There's something else I've been wondering about?"

"What?"

"You said the black angels were on Machrie Moor for the first time when I was there."

"That's correct. Our rage was so great that the earth shook in its foundations. We still had hope, but it was a tiny hope, it was three thousand years of frustration that was released between the mountains.

We sang the chorus of the Mercy Seat over and over again, while the drums echoed all over the place. We were sick of the truth being measured all the time."

The rage of the black angels made the stars go crazy, they changed places and suddenly disappeared, only to reappear. There were strong inexplicable lights that could be seen from the moor that night.

"I remember the insane lights," said Dian. "What I don't understand, is how the druids and the black angels started to collaborate."

"Close your eyes and I'll take you back a thousand years in time." Dian closed her eyes and could see the black angels gathering, God had summoned them to give them courage to continue fighting. None of the black angels thought it was possible to win the battle any more, evil was too strong.

Raven took a step forward and said, "The druids."

"What do the druids know that we don't?" asked one of the black angels.

"I don't have a clue, but something happens when they are doing their rituals," Raven replied.

"Raven is right," said God. "The druids are the ones you should collaborate with."

"The druids have thought we were demons before, but they don't any more. The black angels will go to war one last time," said Raven.

"What do you have in mind?" God asked Raven.

"The best of the druids will help us."

"I know who you mean," said God. "I've had a plan together with the holy ghost for more than three thousand years, now the time has finally come. I hate to be the one who doesn't give you any hope, but there isn't much hope, not more than a grain of sand."

"Impossible then," Lusifer stated.

"As I said," God said, "we have a grain of sand."

"Does anyone think it's gonna work?" asked Lusifer.

There was one who raised his hand, and that was Raven. The hope was so microscopic that they wondered if it even existed. They were to go the first step on Friday the thirteenth of March in 2015.

40

The rats went to Lukas and cried.
"They are trying to kill us all the time."
"I know," said Lukas.
"Wish I was a black angel," said one of them.
"I'm making a statue, it will stand on the best place in the square, next to the pink lions."
The rats gazed at the statue; it was the nicest rat they had ever seen. The crown had precious stones all around in blue, red, pink, turquoise, yellow, light green and scarlet. They sat completely still and looked at the statue, their sorrows vanished like dew from the sun.
"Every time you're sad, you can go to the square and look at the statue," said Lukas.
"We will!" said the rats excited.
Lukas smiled and went outside and lit his pipe, the sun shone through the cloud layer. Lukas was in love, but he had no idea how to get Dine to be as fond of the rats as he was.
Finally, he got an idea, he would teach Lady how to curtsy and the rest of them how to bow. He went inside and asked if they would help him.
The rats nodded, but they still didn't take their eyes off the statue. Lady tried first, it was very difficult, she had such short legs and stiff tail. She practiced and practiced, and in the end she did it. Lady held her hands straight out as she curtsied. The rest of the rats stood on two, while holding one hand on their chest, and the other straight out, while bending their heads.

"Now we go and meet Dine by chance," said Lukas.

They nodded and followed him. They met Dine while she was out walking.

Lady lined up in front and curtsied while the others bowed.

"Why do they curtsy and bow to me?" asked Dine.

"I have absolutely no idea," said Lukas and smiled.

"What's their names?" asked Dine.

"It's Tim, Pling, Plong, Heaven, Lady and Mantle. Lady is the one who curtsied."

"I understood that," said Dine.

Lady curtsied once more and fell over. All the rats began to laugh and rolled around on the ground.

"Where are you headed?" asked Lukas.

"Nowhere."

Dine was wearing a long grey dress with many small pink stones. *She is dressed in the rat colours*, thought Lukas. "Maybe we should stroll together?"

"We can," Dine replied and smiled at him.

They strolled into the sunset with a long tail of rats behind them.

41

Blackbird asked Dian why the unicorn had no name.
"It has, but I don't like it, it's Edit."
"I think Edit has the same taste as your mother had."
"I think so too," said Dian.
Dian asked Blackbird if he wanted to hear her real name.
"I do!"
"Diandra."
"Help!" said Blackbird, "it was probably Edit who wanted you to be called Diandra since she wanted Snowflake to be named Crystal. What was your mother's name?"
"Sofia."
"But that is nice."
"She called herself Selina."
"See what you mean," said Blackbird.

42

Flora could see that Dian was scared; she was not like her when it came to men. Dian went the other way and Flora went straight on. *She encounters evil time and time again and doesn't care, but she is terrified of Purple*, Flora thought.

Flora had long brown hair and green eyes. She wore green clothes and decorated them with fresh flowers. Her favourite flower was roses.

Flora remembered the time Dian had come to live with her and Oak. She wasn't a child who sought adults, she sought to be with Angus and Purple. Oak and Flora were only two adults, who looked after them with clean clothes, food and a bed to sleep. Flora thought Dian was a little different now, it might be that she needed Flora's advice for once. She went to find Purple.

"You know how me, and your father became a couple?" Flora asked Purple.

"Oak told me you went straight to him and said you wanted him."

"That's right. Dian will never do that."

"Why?"

"Because she is like you and your father."

"Then we will never be together."

"No, you won't," said Flora sharply.

"You mean I should be you?" asked Purple astonished.

"Someone needs to be me," said Flora. "Dian is terrified that you don't want her, and you're waiting for her to do something she's never going to do."

"Do you mean I should say I want her?"

Flora rolled her eyes and answered him one last time. "Yes," she said and left.

Purple thought for a long time. Robin came over to him and asked, "What is it?"

"I have to be a different person for a while."

"Who?"

"Flora."

Robin didn't understand anything, but he didn't bother to ask.

43

"The Devils present are growing stronger every day," said Sus. "I can feel it and I know you can feel it too."

"We both know that he must be someone we trust and care about," said Flora.

"How is it possible for a person to hide in plain sight?"

"The person has to say the right things and do the right things, I wish there was a test that could reveal who it is."

"Nobody knows who it is."

"I'm not so sure," said Flora, "I think there is one other person who knows who the Devil is."

"Who are you talking about?"

"I think Jesus knows who it is."

"I think you're right," said Sus. "Jesus feels that it's important to keep his path clean, but it's not him who's doing all the work, that's for someone else to do for him."

"He has a lot of people who give him an alibi, they are all fed up, but Jesus thinks they like him and care about him."

"It's easier," said Sus, "you don't have to do anything or say anything, you just let him keep on doing the things he has always done."

"Exhausting people close to him," said Flora.

"Gyda doesn't help him either, she is protecting him when she should have told him the truth instead. It's probably too late now."

"It is too late," said Flora. "Jesus feels he is the most important person in the world, and nothing can stop him."

"So why would he want to be close to the Devil?"

"The Devil probably tells him how important and fantastic he is, and that he deserves the best that life has to offer."

"He has never fought a day in his life," said Sus, "and still he deserves everything."

"The world wants to be deceived," said Flora.

44

God slid for the first time in his life. The black angels followed him closely. God howled like a stung pig all the way down, he had started on top of Vatnajökull.

It went downwards insanely fast. Some of the bravest black angels put their wings in front of them and slid down on their stomachs with their heads first. When they got to the bottom of the hill, they fell in the snow with their faces first.

Afterwards they had a snowball fight, everyone thought it was fun to throw snowballs at God. Finally, they lay down on their backs and looked at an icy blue sky while moving their arms and feet back and forth.

The black angels who were sitting on the Mercy Seat at the top of Vatnajökull didn't believe their own ears and eyes when they saw God slide at a wild speed down the mountainside. They couldn't find any words; they just opened their eyes widely and looked at each other.

The black angels stood at the top of the Lyngen Alps. Their wingspans were enormous, and they felt completely free and calm.

It lasted until they went downhill on a snowboard they couldn't control. The snowboards picked up speed, and the black angels folded their wings behind them, as they leaned backwards and howled in terror.

Sus and Storm saw that Lusifer bent forward and crouched a

little as he unfolded his wings. They did the same and began to gain control, until they got scared and leaned backwards again, howling while the snowboard went too fast.

Sus was the first to reach the fjord, he lay with both hands and his face deep down into the snow. It took a long time before he dared to feel if he was in one piece. In the end he found out that he was absolutely fine and shook off all the snow.

Lusifer whizzed past him and swung gallantly in between Sus and the fjord. At the same moment, Storm came at a wild speed and drove straight into the fjord, he hadn't figured out how to stop. He snuck up from the fjord and sat down on the snowboard.

Dian stood on top of the Lyngen Alps, looking at Blåisvatnet, the Blue Ice Water, it was the most incredible icy, turquoise mellow transparent blue she had ever seen. She decided to show Blåisvatnet to Lusifer, Storm and Sus. The blue hour had arrived, together with the northern light that went across the sky at full speed.

Dian did the same, she rode all the way around the Lyngen Alps at full speed, on her way down to the fjord. Storm was sitting on the snowboard shivering. Lusifer put a finger on the back of his neck and sent the heat back into his body.

Dian told them about Blåisvatnet, they flew up and looked at the colour of the water.

"Were you on Machrie Moor with the black angels?" Dian asked Lusifer.

"The black angels had never been so tired of being mistaken for demons before. We sang the same verse over and over again facing the fjord, while the rain was trickling down our faces. It was the first time the black angels and druids were gathered on Machrie Moor."

"I made sure there was enough shine in the puddles so you could see where the road went," said Sus.

"I could barely see you, all I could see were a few of you standing on both sides of the narrow road. You all had black smooth hair down to your shoulders, no beards or moustaches, black wings and black clothes. The drums sounded far away beyond the mountains. Why were you there?"

"There was a lot going on that you couldn't see," said Sus. "The light you sent into the heart went straight up to the Milky Way, and the light waves made rings on the water that went beyond the seven seas."

"Where did you go after?" asked Dian.

"We went to England," Lusifer replied.

"It doesn't matter where we are, but nothing beats the feeling of being home," said Sus.

"Are you are going back to the Grassmarket in Edinburgh?" asked Dian.

"We will, but first we will have a good night's sleep," Lusifer said and smiled.

45

Dian read about Lusifer that he was closest to God, and the most beautiful thing God had ever created. She thought of Satan who no longer stood at the end of her hallway. She realised that he had the same energy as Lusifer. Satan looked ridiculous but had a devilish charm and charisma.

"So, Dian has found out that you were Satan?" God asked Lusifer.

"She realised it after reading that I was the one closest to you," Lusifer replied.

"She spent a long time figuring it out."

"Dian was never afraid of me as Satan, she didn't care."

"It's so weird not to care about Satan," said God and stroked his chin.

"It's the first time I have experienced it."

"Did Dian understand why you were Satan?"

"She realised it when she read that I'm the finest you have ever created. She understood that I couldn't go straight into the midst of evil with my charisma and charm."

"I still think she spent a long time figuring it out," said God.

"We have fooled Dian about almost everything we have said to her."

"She's the only one we can't see straight through, we had to trick her to see what was inside of her. With the forces Dian has, there is so much mischief she could have done."

"But she didn't," said Lusifer.

"She didn't," said God, "and that's remarkable."

"We haven't figured out her DNA yet, have we?"

"I think she's a troll."

"You mean she is made of grey stone?" asked Lusifer surprised.

"Don't you?" asked God.

"I don't know," Lusifer replied, "but one day we will find out."

46

Dian was so pissed, she had almost no money left, it had always disappeared fast. Dian screamed how fed up she was, never having any money.

"You must have faith," said the black angels and God to her.

"How many of you have ever believed in me?" screamed Dian back at them.

They started sending heavy hailstones towards her window. Dian screamed at them once more, "How many of you believe in me, not even God believes in me. Soon I will ascend to the seventh heaven and pull your hair."

It was quiet for a moment, then Dian heard them saying, "Why don't you?"

"Seriously?" asked Dian.

"Seriously," they replied.

Dian went straight up to the seventh heaven and pulled Lusifer's hair as hard as she could.

It wasn't enough, the next in line was Storm. Dian was still mad at him for destroying her cells with his singing.

Sus just laughed when she pulled his hair. Still, it wasn't enough, Dian was still mad.

She didn't want to pull Raven's hair; he was the only one who had believed in her. God was next, he had a heavy tousled hair. *Does he never brush his hair*, Dian thought. She pulled his hair hard several times before she was satisfied.

Lusifer looked at God who grimaced and stroked his hair.

Dian looked at him too. Lusifer couldn't decipher her facial expression, he just knew she needed to get rid of all she had been experiencing lately. There were none who had fought so intensely towards so many in such a short time before.

Dian had not become angry, she had just laughed and continued to fight, what she had experienced had to come out, and most of it ended up in God's hair.

Lusifer saw that God shook his hair. Everything that fell out, turned into stardust. Lusifer did the same, afterwards he went over to Dian and held her, he knew how she felt.

"Did you line up first because you knew I was going to pull harder and harder?" asked Dian.

"I was so glad when I saw you didn't pull Raven's hair, then you would have understood that he was me, I thought it was too early, but you understood it anyway, didn't you?"

"I did," said Dian. "I didn't know at first that you could be two people at the same time, but of course you can. I do understand that you find your name a bit burdensome, it's easier to be named Raven. I fell in love with you at the Lyngen Alps, it was a nice backdrop."

"It was," said Lusifer. "Me on top of the Alps with my black hair and my black wings as a contrast to the white snow."

"Not to forget the Blue Lake and the northern lights."

"It's not a miracle that you fell in love. It was just impossible not to, especially since I have so much charisma too."

Dian just rolled her eyes and looked at him.

47

Dian and Lusifer were summoned to God and the black angels. They said evil had gathered in the outer bulwark and was ready to attack. Dian and Lusifer didn't need to hear any more, they went straight up to the outer bulwark.

A large ring of large grey trolls had gathered. Dian flew over them and turned them into dust. There were five little trolls who couldn't be killed, they had hidden inside a large troll.

A large creature came flying with a huge wingspan, the wings were beige and golden, and the face was hidden behind a golden mask, his eyes were deep behind the slanted black holes in the mask.

"Wait!" Lusifer shouted in the same second as Dian turned him into dust.

"I hope you're not gonna tell me he was good?"

"No!" Lusifer said baffled. "I just wanted to help you. It was the leader of the outer bulwark."

"It's too late now," said Dian.

They decided to bring the five star trolls to Gilde and Volven on Island. Gilde and Volven stood ready in the yard receiving them when they landed.

"We will take good care of them," said Gilde.

"I saw you were good when you came to visit, when I was still with Evil," said Volven to Lusifer.

"I never understood why you didn't tell Evil that you saw straight through me," said Lusifer. "Why didn't you kill me?"

"Kill the most attractive man I have ever seen?" asked Volven astonished.

"Thanks for last time by the way, we had a great time in Edinburgh, didn't we?"

"Never had a better time."

Volven turned and looked at Dian.

"Good to see that you got rid of Purple, he was a baby, now you are with a man."

Lusifer gave Volven a bag of stardust.

"Sprinkle it over the star trolls when they go to sleep," he said. Volven squeezed him hard against her chest. Shortly afterwards, she fell to the ground, some of the stardust had fluttered from the bag when she squeezed Lusifer.

48

God and Gyda didn't live in heaven, they only slept in the seventh heaven sometimes.

"Don't you wanna live in the seventh heaven?" Dian asked God.

"No, there are too many angels there."

"What about the Puppet master's house in Falkland? It's free now, Raven has found a new house across the street."

Both God and Gyda thought it was a good idea. Right up the street lay the Hidden Place, where Sus, Medusa, Blackbird and Snowflake, as well as Flora and Oak, lived.

Next door was Lukas' house, further down the street lay Falkland Palace belonging to Midas and Eloise. God and Gyda could go there if they wanted to dance in the big hall, a short while ago it had been strictly forbidden to dance there.

The miniature house with the purple windows was still available. God wanted to put up a House for Rent sign.

Flora stood and looked out of the window, she had heard that God and Gyda were moving into to the Puppet master's house. It wasn't coincidental that Lilith had chosen to keep the unicorns trapped in Falkland, it was the only place where both the druids and the black angels felt at home. Lilith wanted them to see daily, that there was nothing they could do to stop the unicorns suffering.

For the first time in a long time Flora felt a hint of

anticipation, that was before she remembered the dream she had. She put on her green coat and walked down the narrow road that led to the square.

She saw that Lusifer, Sus and Raven carried a large dark brown four poster bed between them, a long aubergine coloured fabric hung on the side. Flora went over and grabbed the fabric so it wouldn't drag along the ground.

Lusifer, Sus and Raven sat down on the bed and looked at her in astonishment.

"What is it, Flora?" asked Raven. "You are the first to always say hello, has anything happened?"

Flora sat down on the bed; they saw that she was in a long line of thoughts. At last, she came to herself. She embraced them in turn, before she said there was something she had to tell them, but not in the middle of the road. Flora was exceptionally quiet on the way home.

They approached the Hidden Place where the unicorns had been trapped to the two stone pillars in the pond. Lusifer could see that Flora still envisioned them, the phantom images were still there. Lusifer, Sus and Raven went up on the stone bridge while Flora disappeared into the kitchen to make coffee.

The pond was large and round. Between the stone pillars that stood on each side of the stone bridge, a crescent-shaped stone circle went into the water. Raven imagined the rainbow that had passed between the stone pillars, both above and below the water, when Dian set the two unicorns free.

"Do you see that the nests where Snowflake and Blackbird lay when they were born, are still in the trees?" he asked.

"Is there any reason why the nests shouldn't be there?" asked Sus.

"The only thing that separates unicorns from horses is the

horn on the forehead, and the fact that unicorns lie in a nest before they are born," said Lusifer.

The sun became visible for a moment and sent a fan of rays into the pond.

Sus wiped a tear and said, "I think we can remove the phantom image of the two unicorns now."

"I think so too," said Raven. "Flora needs to see that it's over."

"Coffee!" shouted Flora at the same time.

"Coming!" shouted Lusifer back. He took one last look at the solid nests in the two birch trees, where Snowflake and Blackbird had lain, before strolling down the grassy slope.

"It's a strange decoration on the house," said Lusifer to Flora. "It looks like someone has laid a pattern along the ridge with a twisted rope of stone."

"It's beautiful," Flora said slowly. She was far away again.

Lusifer and Sus exchanged glances, they had never been worried about Flora before, she was always the one who stayed afloat no matter what happened. Suddenly an icy wind came around the corner of the house.

"Let's go inside," said Lusifer and got up.

"Tell us what's worrying you," said Raven when they sat in the living room.

"I had a dream last night," said Flora, "it was from the future. The dream was about Dian, the first book is almost ready."

"What worries you?" asked Lusifer.

Flora told them the first sequence of the dream.

"Dian stops a ball that is coming towards her, it had unforeseen consequences," said Lusifer.

"The ball changed direction and got a tremendous force and put the woman who was so sure to win out of play," said Flora.

"You are afraid of revenge?" asked Raven.

Flora nodded and said, "All Dian did was to put her foot down, but the consequences were enormous because the woman lost face. Dian doesn't have much left before she can publish the first book, we must get control of the situation before it happens."

"I don't understand what can stop everything," said Sus.

"The last drop," said Lusifer. "Little strokes fell great oaks."

"We have always known that the most dangerous time would be just before the first book came out," said Flora.

"Domino effect," mumbled Raven, "the books are lined up."

"What are the books called?" asked Sus.

"*The Nutcrackers*, *The Sleeping Warrior*, *The Silver Thistle* and *The Bloodlines*," said Lusifer.

"Where should we start looking for the needle in the haystack?" asked Flora. "We all know a wee grain of sand can stop the whole machinery."

"Did you dream anything else?" asked Lusifer.

"The woman wants Dian to attach a piece of cloth with needles to her chest, but Dian refuses. She says they are done with each other."

"What about the last sequence?" asked Raven.

"A man yells to a man that he doesn't take care of the baby. Dian is heading down the stairs, when she turns and gives the baby to the man yelling.

There was another small detail."

"What?" asked Sus.

"A cupboard that originally had two doors, but now only a few rags hung in front of it. Dian thought she had to wash the closet and wallpaper it inside, so it looked nice again."

"We have to turn it around," Lusifer said firmly and put the cup on the table, so the coffee splashed. "Dian is on her way down and on her way up. We have to get her to move forward."

It sounds so simple, thought Raven, *but how the hell were they supposed to get her to move forward.*

"She continues down the stairs after she has delivered the baby," said Sus.

"It's no big deal," said Lusifer. "The most important thing is that she got rid of the baby."

"Then we are left with the cupboard," said Raven.

"It looks so nice here," said Sus, "maybe you can help me decorate my house?"

"What do you have in mind?" asked Flora.

"I want a large baking kitchen with a wooden table just as big as the one you have. I see you have chosen oak; I prefer elm."

Lusifer and Raven just rolled their eyes.

Oak came in from the garden. Flora told him about the sequence in the dream they couldn't figure out.

"Dian comes out of the closet," said Oak, "she is refurbishing herself, not the closet."

"You think Dian survives?" asked Lusifer and looked at Flora.

"I know she does."

"There's a sequence we have forgotten," said Raven. "The girl grows up and wants Dian to attach a piece of cloth with pins to the outside of her blouse, but Dian refuses."

"The woman is so ebullient in the dream," said Flora, "she forgets she gave Dian the blame for destroying her life."

"The main thing is that Dian hasn't forgotten," said Lusifer, "that is why she refuses to wear a piece of cloth attached with needles to her chest."

"I have understood one thing," said Flora, "none of us have made the dream."

Angus came into the room. "Smells good," he said, dumping himself into an armchair.

Raven gave him a cup of coffee. They knew it was no coincidence that Angus came, but they didn't know that he had begun making dreams.

Angus looked at them and asked, "Do you need any help?" They didn't bother to answer him, so Angus continued.

"You cover up the area that usually provides nourishment, the needles protrude at the same time."

"Give and take," said Raven.

"That's correct," said Angus. "You get a lot of milk, but at the same time you have to take the sticks. Dian intends to find out where she can get nourishment without being stung afterwards."

"You have solved the dream riddle," said Flora and smiled at him. Angus just smiled and scratched his hair.

"Who takes care of the baby?" Raven asked suddenly. Angus just looked at him in amazement.

"Who's the baby Dian delivers back to the man standing at the top of the stairs?"

Angus still looked at him in amazement.

"You didn't create the sequence," said Raven and gazed at him. They all knew what that meant. There were two who had made the dream.

"Do you think the same as me?" asked Lusifer.

They nodded and looked at the double porch doors. The handle was gently pressed down, but they couldn't see who it was because the sun shone brightly into the room. When they could see again, they began to laugh. It was Purple, he was wearing a red shirt and pants.

"Missed me?" he asked laughing.

Purple sat down on the sofa, and Flora gave him a cup of coffee. They all remembered what had happened when Dian called Purple a baby. Now it was Purple who knew who the baby was.

Purple took a sip, then he put the coffee cup gently down on the table.

"It's so nice here." Purple gently stroked his hand over the tweed from Isle of Harris that covered the sofa. It was sand coloured with thin purple stripes. The armchairs were light blue, with thin green stripes that made a grid pattern. At the end of the room lay the kitchen with apple green walls and aubergine coloured cupboards underneath. The house was built of the local sandstone and plastered grey on the outside, but inside the walls were preserved, one could see the beige sandstone, with black basalt in between. Old Windsor chairs stood around a solid kitchen table.

They were patiently waiting for him to tell them who the baby was.

"The baby is me," Purple said at last.

"Dian didn't want to look after you anymore," said Sus.

"No, she thinks I've grown up enough to take care of myself."

"Why did you make the sequence, do you feel ready?" asked Sus.

"As ready as I'll ever be."

"Dian delivered the baby and walked away. She doesn't want a baby," said Oak, smiling.

"Hear! Hear!" said Raven and clinked his coffee cup against Purple's.

Flora took the hint and got up and fetched a bottle of whisky. Lusifer, Sus and Raven only had one drink, it was time to finish helping God and Gyda to move.

"We forgot to ask why the unicorns are born in nests," said Raven. It was completely dark outside now. They heard snoring all the way up to the pond.

"I know who we can ask," said Sus.

"How long do you think he has slept in the middle of the road?" asked Lusifer.

"Impossible to say," said Sus, "but I think he has slept long enough." They sat at the foot of the bed, waiting for God to wake up. He suddenly sat up.

"Sweet dreams?" asked Raven.

God just tore his hair, and began to tell them the dream, with his hands explaining half of it. They heard the same dream as Flora had told them.

"We'd better head back," said Lusifer.

Flora looked astonished at them when she opened the door.

She was even more astonished when Lusifer told her that God had the same dream.

"The dark side of the moon," she said thoughtful. She put the whisky bottle in the middle of the table. "I think we need it; it's going to be a long night."

When Lusifer told Oak, Angus and Purple that God had dreamed the same as Flora, they just shook their heads, none of them had given God his dream.

"That's what I was afraid of," said Lusifer. "Someone is making a dream within the dream. If we don't figure it out, I'm sure of one thing, no books will be published. There are many who want the truth about the black angels, to continue being a hidden story."

"And the druids," said Flora.

"They have always been hidden," said Lusifer.

"Same goes for the black angels," said Flora.

Purple poured more whisky into everybody's glasses.

"We'll benefit from a little fire, earth, water and air."

Just as Purple said air, the Föhn wind opened the porch doors. They went outside and looked up at the sky. Saturn had made its arrival.

"Beautiful," said Sus.

"I don't think that's the point this time," said Raven.

"You think you have solved the riddle," said Saturn.

"The next time the sand grain will come, and it will stop the whole machinery."

"But it's not yet," said Lusifer and sighed heavily.

Saturn disappeared and the Föhn wind did the same, it got icy cold.

"Let's go inside," said Flora, "I don't think any of us will get any sleep tonight."

They must have fallen asleep at some point, for they awoke to a full storm outside.

"Someone who has dreamed something?" asked Flora.

"I have," said Raven. "It was the ebullient woman who lost face. She sat down in Dian's bed and told her that a friend had made a cosy corner in her living room, using bubble wrap. Dian said she wasn't interested, she didn't want a close relationship with the woman, and she didn't want her to sit in her bed. The fabric was, by the way, purple."

Everyone looked at Purple.

"We need coffee," said Lusifer and got up. Flora followed him into the kitchen.

"This must be the last little grain that Saturn warned us about," she said.

"Ebullient means it's a connection to the Devil."

"I've been thinking the same."

"It's one thing I've been wanting to ask you," said Lusifer.

"Go on," said Flora.

"Dian sent Snowflake and Blackbird into two trees with huge nests. Why did the druids think it was a good idea that the unicorns should hatch in a nest like a bird?"

"They look like horses, but they are birds. The unicorns can fly if they need to."

"Confusing," said Lusifer.

"Why?" asked Flora. "There's a lot that is confusing. We think it's more magical that the moonbeams light up the water, than it is when Saturn shows up for a visit, it's how you look at things."

"You are right," said Lusifer and gave her a kiss on the cheek.

You need to stop that, thought Flora, and shouted that the coffee was ready.

When everyone had coffee, they were ready to solve a dream none of them understood. God sighed heavily and scratched his hair.

"I have been left in the corner," said Purple and laughed.

"Bubble fabric keeps you warm, but it should be used outdoors," said Raven, "it went out of fashion in the '70s. Nowadays they use bubble jackets with thin stripes, the bubble fabric in the dream had large bubbles."

"The ebullient woman was so excited when she told Dian that the fabric was in the corner," said Lusifer. "Why?"

"Nobody puts baby in a corner," said Sus. "Who put Purple in the corner, did you do it yourself?"

Purple just shook his head.

"The fabric shouldn't be inside," said Sus, "it should be outside."

"Who made the dream?" asked Lusifer.

They looked at the porch doors, but nothing happened.

"Dian," said Lusifer, "she knows who made the dream." He sent her a thought.

"I made it," she replied. "When we go out into a storm, we need to be covered in a warm fabric. Bubble fabric is good outside, but hopeless inside. The woman who lost face is hiding in the corner, but what she is actually doing, is that she puts everybody else in the corner."

"She is hiding behind her kindness," said Lusifer, "so everyone feels sorry for her. How come she managed to put Purple in the corner?"

"She wants to make people I love disabled, so I would only care about her, she is sick."

"You can say that again," said Raven, "but how can she stop the book?"

"She can't," said Sus, "now we know what she is up to, we can make sure that she puts no one in the corner, except herself."

49

Dian and Lusifer decided to live in the small old house across the street from God and Gyda. New windows had been installed and the wooden floors had been sanded and oiled.

Lusifer painted the walls in different blues, light browns and mellow green colours. Dian hung up the curtains she had sewn, they all had patterns of acorns.

"Nuts everywhere," sighed Lusifer.

"Fits well since you are a nutcase," said Dian.

She had refused to let him paint the outside of the house. The house showed all the greyish green and greyish purple colours it had held during the centuries. The garden wasn't unnaturally prepared, it was natural with fox bells, straws and some large old deciduous trees that spread their long branches outwards, there was nothing that needed to be done neither in the garden nor in the house.

Lusifer wanted the same colours on bed linens he had always had. He flew up to the seventh heaven and picked up his old bed linens, silver on the cushion, light blue on the duvet, and light grey-purple sheets. The furniture they needed was already in the house, it was as if the house had been waiting for them.

50

Lusifer said to God that he didn't bother any more.

"I don't see the problem," said God. "Dian has you and Sus to take care of her, and you are the best. Dian is just a little girl, how much mischief can she do?"

"It's nine feet of snow, Dian has invented a new game."

"What?"

"She sees the snowplow coming at full speed, just before it hits her, she tries to climb the nine feet tall snowdrifts."

"Oh my God!" said God. "Did she manage?"

"With my help she did, but once isn't enough. Every time she sees the snowplow coming, she tries to climb the steep snowdrifts."

"She is only four years old," said God.

"The next thing she came up with was to put twelve kicksleds in a row. Then she sat on the last kicksled down the road completely without steering."

"It went well then?" asked God.

"It went well, until she decided to hold on to the bumper on the bus while it was driving down the street. She was slipping on the back of the bus as it drove at full speed on a layer of snow."

"Okay!" said God. "I'll take over."

God managed to endure one day. Dian had decided to ski, she set off at a wild speed down the hill and aimed at a rooftop which was half buried in snow. God groaned and stood on the other side to receive her.

Then she went jet skiing. The bottom of the hill was full of gravel. God had to grab Dian's waistband so she wouldn't scrape up everything on her body.

I don't bother any more either, thought God, *she must calm down soon.*

When spring arrived Sus and Lusifer had laid a battle plan.

They made her climb up a tall pine tree, when she reached the top, she sat down on a branch. Dian didn't dare to climb down again, so she sat there for hours.

Lusifer and Sus stood on top of a hill and watched Dian, she was six years old. She had planned to cycle down the steep hill over a small plank that lay across the burn.

"I don't bother to save her anymore," said Lusifer, "she will probably get both yellow and blue."

They watched Dian get on the bike at the top of the hill, then the small blue bicycle started to gain more and more speed down towards the burn. Dian ended up in the burn and got soaking wet. She dragged the bicycle up the steep hill and tried once more.

Sus and Lusifer lay writhing on the ground laughing, while Dian tried again and again.

"Are you sure that's the big nutcracker," said Sus, then they were about to die of laughter again.

Suddenly, Lusifer stopped laughing. "She did it," he said.

"What!" Sus said, shocked. "It was impossible to hit the little plank with the speed she had."

Dian was soaking wet, but she began to pull the bike up the other steep hill, which lay on the other side of the burn.

"She plans to try to hit the plank from that side of the burn as well," said Lusifer.

Sus just shook his head.

Dian fell once more into the burn. She took the little blue bike and pushed it up the steep grassy slope and began to walk home.

"Maybe she's done," said Sus.

"I don't think so," said Lusifer, "I think she's hungry."

Dian went home to eat, after she planned to go outside again. Sus and Lusifer felt they had had enough excitement for one day. They made her so tired after she had eaten, that she fell asleep on the coach.

Dian stood on Øysand in the grey weather and put on a wetsuit. She had received a short instruction in how to windsurf, but she had never tried it before.

"Where's the life jacket?" asked Sus.

"It doesn't exist," Lusifer replied. "At least not in Dian's head, it doesn't help that she's fourteen either."

The wind increased and the waves got bigger.

"Do you see Børsabergene far away on the other side?"

Sus looked at the steep black rock wall that rose from the fjord.

"That's where she's headed," said Lusifer.

"Should we go there in advance?"

"If she is stupid enough to hit the rock wall, then I stay here," Lusifer said gloomily.

Dian stood on the sailboard and got maximum speed right away because the wind was so strong.

"She's good," said Sus.

"She is but remember she doesn't know how to turn." Dian approached the rock wall with great speed.

"Now she has to turn," said Sus.

"She doesn't do it until the last second," said Lusifer.

At the last second, Dian turned, she barely managed to turn the sail before the board picked up speed again.

Lusifer was still angry. "I don't understand why she has to cross the line all the time."

"You don't think it sounds familiar," said Sus.

Lusifer looked at him astonished. "You mean I cross the line?"

"That's what you're known for," Sus replied.

Lusifer had not thought of it before, that he recognised himself.

51

Dian went over to Angus, his long white hair fluttered in the wind. They were invited to a big party; it was to be held at the Hidden Place in Falkland.

The druids and the black angels had tried once before to celebrate that the chains on the unicorns were gone, but they never managed to start the party until Arnold showed up.

"Do you want me to cut your hair?" asked Dian.

"Preferably not," said Angus laughing. "Good to see you're alive."

"Same," said Dian. "Do you want to meet a chatterbox?"

"Definitely not if it's a woman."

"It's not a woman," said Dian and took Angus to see Blackbird.

"A unicorn that is a chatterbox," said Angus astonished.

"It happens, but it's extremely rare."

"I heard that Blackbird isn't Purple's anymore, who does he belong to?"

Dian introduced Lusifer who showed up. Lusifer measured Angus up and down. At last, he said, "What saves you is that your yellow suit matches my yellow shoes."

Angus smiled at him, he liked Lusifer. *A man to be trusted*, he thought, *with a very good taste.*

Gilde had arrived with an enormous music system. He knew Midas had a good music system in Falkland Palace, but he didn't take the chance when it came to the Hidden Place. Gilde mounted the music system in the trees where Blackbird and Snowflake had been lying inside the huge nests.

Volven came along with sixteen little trolls, they walked behind her like ducklings. The star trolls had grown just as much as the other trolls, they just looked a bit different.

"Look at the sixteen little trolls," said Lusifer to Sus. "They had been easier to take care of than Dian was at their age."

"It is and will always be strange," said Sus.

"Let's forget the hardest job we've ever had," said Lusifer. Blackbird had loud opinions about the colours of the tablecloths. Angus stood by his side laughing.

When Dian said Blackbird was a chatterbox, she hadn't mentioned that he was like an old woman.

"Let's go to your house," said Sus. "We'll get Storm and sit in front of the fireplace, and drink brown rum or whisky while we wait for the party to start."

"Or both," said Lusifer.

They snuck away, hoping no one would notice them.

Dian went to see God; he was sitting on a stool in the room with all the toys Raven had made. Dian sat down on the work bench beside him.

"Don't you want to celebrate?" asked Dian.

"I like being in my new workshop, making things with my hands."

"What's wrong?" asked Dian.

"My heart has stopped inside of me; I have to remember to breathe."

"Tell me," said Dian. "What's on your heart?"

"It's the usual, Jesus is my everything in a bad way, he is everywhere."

"He is not at this party," said Dian, "so he can't be everywhere."

"He is inside my brain, demanding me to be a loving father, when all I see is a spoilt child."

"Forget about him and join us, it will do you the world of good."

"It probably would, it's no good staying here, this workshop was supposed to give me some peace, but it doesn't."

"It will," said Dian, "give it some time. I have to go and brush my feathers; they are full of dust."

"Wait a minute," said God and went to get a flat soft brush. "You have no idea how to do it, do you?"

"Not a clue."

"Spread your wings," said God and brushed them quickly free from dust. "Now they look good."

"Are you going to continue like Raven making toys?"

"No, I'll give away all the toys to Sus and Medusa's children, Blair and Andrew."

"What will you have here instead?"

"Wait and see," said God and grinned.

Blackbird had gotten his will; the long tablecloth was purple. The table went all the way from Sus and Medusa's house on top of the hill, and down to the pond close to Flora and Oak's house.

Flora hung in a tree trying to attach all the flowers she had picked. All the trees had different colours. A maple had yellow old roses attached to the branches, and an old oak was adorned with black tulips.

Most of the black angels and druids lived in Falkland. Those who didn't came from far and wide, everyone wanted to join, they finally had something to celebrate.

The druids filled the long table with food, drinks and large, five pointed candlesticks. The lights in the trees changed colours every time Gilde played a new song, as did the wooden dance floor shaped like a huge star, laying between the trees. Markus was the light master.

Elwin and Lennie came walking to see if there was anything they could do to help. Elwin thought life should be lived to its fullest, and it became full only when one had fun. Lennie was the one with the greatest singing voice of them all. Gilde had brought everything needed when Lennie entered the stage later. The stage was rigged up behind the dance floor.

Markus was hanging up lights behind the stage. He had made links of light shaped like DNA-links.

Lusifer looked at Snowflake in the garden at the back of the house. He went out to her and stroked her mane.

"Are you all right?" he asked.

"Not really," Snowflake replied, "I'm so tired."

"You can't stand so many people and chaos. You can stay in the garden if you want, until the party is over."

Lusifer had understood that she was a lone wolf. Snowflake lay down with her head on the grass and fell asleep.

"How is Snowflake?" asked Sus when Lusifer came back inside.

"She's asleep."

"Good, I saw she had enough when the little trolls started to crawl all over her."

"She's safe here. I have put up a sign by the road, with a picture of the big bad wolf, eating trolls."

Lusifer and Sus sat down by the fireplace in an armchair each. Storm came and sat down in the third. Storm and Lusifer chattered as they watched the flames, it was a huge fireplace compared to the size of the house.

Sus sat in deep thoughts for a long time.

"What's on your mind?" asked Lusifer.

"You remember when Dian was two years old, and we told her a story about the little bird that wouldn't sing?"

"I remember, every time the fairytale was finished, she smiled at us, before she closed her eyes and fell asleep."

"After, we were so sure she didn't see us anymore, but I think she just pretended."

"Dian was only two years old," said Lusifer.

"Never underestimate kids. You told me that every time you thought she couldn't do another dangerous thing, that's exactly what she did."

"Dian read my thoughts," said Lusifer thoughtfully.

"She did. Every time Dian did something that was life threatening, she was sure you were standing there to rescue her, but every time you didn't bother to save her, she did things that were dangerous, but not life threatening. Dian used us as test subjects."

"She did," said Lusifer shocked, "but why?"

"She trained herself in timing and combat. She used the two of us who are the best to give herself the best training. Do you remember how angry you were when she was going through the gate after the unicorns got rid of their chains?"

"She picked a snowdrop when she was supposed to fight."

"Dian knew exactly what she was doing. She calmly picked a snowdrop, then she smelled it. Afterwards she walked through the gate, where the evildoers stood so closely, that we couldn't fit. Dian killed half of them within a second, they were so shocked that she had picked a flower, that they just stood and gaped."

"It might not have been so stupid after all," said Lusifer.

"She hoodwinked both of you," said Storm and laughed.

They heard Heimdal blow Gjallarhorn.

"Hope it's not the start of Ragnarok," said Sus and rolled his eyes.

"Time to move," said Lusifer.

They got up and went out on the street.

"We are standing in the middle of the Hidden Place and Falkland Palace," said Sus, "where do we go first?"

Heimdal blew Gjallarhorn once more.

"There's your answer," Lusifer said and laughed.

The sound of the horn came from the Hidden Place. Heimdal stood on the small bridge and blew Gjallarhorn once more.

Dian came and stood beside Lusifer.

"You've brushed your wings?" Lusifer said impressed.

"God did," said Dian.

They walked slowly up to the Hidden Place, and saw that Mort and Myrt were standing beside Håkon Håkonsson, Haug and Erik the Red, he never missed a party. Tue had arrived together with his owl, Blanca and Beatrix stood and talked to Flora and Gyda.

"I wonder if Odin is here," said Lusifer and rolled his eyes.

"He's not," said Dian, "in this story he hasn't had a finger in the game, but his ravens are here."

Fog and Shadow were sitting in the trees. Flora and Oak had given the ravens new names. Angus' eagles flew over the long table covered with everything one could desire. Hundreds of druids and black angels had gathered. Gilde played "Gloria" by U2 while everyone sat down.

There was no talking while they ate, they just looked up from the food occasionally. The flavours were so quirkily put together that everyone lost their tongues. After they had eaten, they lay all the food that was left in a long row on the other side of the burn, for the rats and all the birds.

Lennie had entered the stage, she sang, "All flowers in time bend towards the sun." She wore a long silver dress that matched her silver hair. Lusifer came and joined her and sang the chorus. After they had left the stage, Gilde decided to lighten the mood, he played "This is the Sea" by the Waterboys.

The blue hour had begun. Markus' DNA-links began to glow in blue and silver. The lights in all the candlesticks changed colours into all the blues imaginable, as did the lanterns hanging from the long branches surrounding the Hidden Place. Everyone felt that all the grief disappeared from their cells, the blue colour made all the waves settle, but not for long.

When Lusifer entered the stage, all the lights changed to red and black, while "Paranoid" by Black Sabbath thundered over the Hidden Place. Lusifer made everyone lose control. Elwin was the next to enter the stage singing "Born to be Wicked" by the Phantom Chords.

Flora sang "Ghost Riders in the Sky" while Blackbird pranced and galloped around in the grey smoke that floated like a heavy fog over the area.

Heimdal made a solid rainbow that went from Midas' Palace and all the way up to the Hidden Place. Midas had finally started the party in Falkland Palace. The hall was decorated with light chains and flowers, but it was only an illusion. The floor was magical, sometimes you danced in water and occasionally in the clouds. Along the walls a full hailstorm could suddenly appear beyond the blue mountains.

Everyone could walk or fly up and down the street as they wanted, there was music everywhere. "Shadow of Love" by the Damned came floating from the Palace, down the street through the square, and almost up to the Hidden Place.

Dian went home and lay under the tree with Snowflake, she remembered what had happened when she was two years old.

Lusifer had read a fairytale to her, he said it was a gateway to all the darkness and evil that existed in the world. Every time Dian heard the fairytale, she would become acquainted with the evil in the world, she was a fly on the wall.

"A fly," Dian said.

"A fly," Lusifer replied. "You will meet Volven and Evil himself, Hell and Helvetia, Satan and Lilith. They don't know that you are a fly on the wall. It's crucial that you recognise them, so you don't get scared when you meet them in the future. You can't talk to anyone about what you are experiencing. You have no one to ask, and you have to do the right thing within a hundred millionth of a second."

"Millionth second," Dian said.

"Almost right," Lusifer replied. "I'm going to be there, and Sus, but you have to learn how to trust yourself."

Lusifer saw that something happened too Dian. She was already far away; she was a fly on Hell and Helvetia's wall.

Lusifer gave Dian the joy and laughter during the day so she could endure what happened at night. They didn't have time for Dian to get hundreds of years along with evil to get enough experience. A two-year-old was so open that they could go in and control what she saw.

Lusifer came and gave Dian a hand and pulled her up.

Dian petted Snowflake who was still lying under the tree, she was ready to return to the party again. They went down the street, through the gate to Falkland Palace and further into Midas' dance hall.

All the black angels and druids were gathered. The walls of the hall were full of moose standing in the sunset.

"You know we have been to a local party at the Public Hall in Verdal," Lusifer said to Dian. "What you didn't know, is that we learned how to speak trøndersk at the same time."

The music started, and Elwin, Raven, Sus, Midas, Lukas and Lusifer lined up in a half-moon circle, then they started singing.

"What are they singing?" Medusa asked Dian.

"I am a trønder I, and my God, how tough I am."

The moose standing in the sunset started to move to the music, so did the black angels. They moved their arms with the wings half extended while wiggling their hips. It was a strange mix of moose and angels. God, Oak, Falk and Hauk snuck into the chorus.

Dian started laughing and Lusifer could see that she forgot everything bad that had happened. After they had finished singing, they decided to return to the Hidden Place again.

Erik the Red came and met Dian and Lusifer as they approached the wrought iron gate. He was wearing a green shirt.

"You've changed," said Dian.

"I have more than one shirt," said Erik the Red, staring at her, then he stared at Lusifer. Dian thought it could take a while, so she left them. They were still standing still when Dian went through the double gate.

Gilde had discovered Blanca, he only hoped that Volven was busy dancing with Heimdal. Gilde tried to dance as much as possible behind the trees. The Hidden Place was a strange place, it was hidden at the same time as it was open to everyone. The only thing that set it apart from the rest of Falkland, was the wrought iron gate with the three thistles.

The Sun Cross came from the Hidden Place, it was the oldest symbol of the sun, it was used for increasing growth. Dian had used it to destroy the core of evil that lay within Croft Town, she had sent the Sun Cross back at full speed when she passed the town. It was time to give it back to the world again, but Dian didn't have a clue how to do it.

Originally it had been blue and gold, Dian had seen it painted on the wall at the back of Greyfriars Kirk in Edinburgh. She suddenly knew what was going to happen, a golden Sun Cross would rise from the pond. It was the fourteenth of April, exactly one month after the big battle in Edinburgh.

Gilde played a love song, "Alone Again Or". Markus thought the song was a bit tame, so he equipped the black angels with fifty box guitars and fifty trombones. Gilde wanted to dance with Blanca again.

Volven had seen Gilde sneaking off behind the trees with Blanca, suddenly she was standing right in front of him, Gilde didn't have a choice but to dance with Volven instead.

Lusifer came walking through the gate.

"What happened?" asked Dian.

"Nothing, we just got tired of staring at each other."

Markus came and asked if there was a song Dian would like to hear.

"White Foxes," Dian said promptly.

Markus changed the colour of the sky, it became pitch black. All the lights shone in white. Large snowflakes began to fall from the sky slowly.

Snowflake had woken up; she was standing next to Lusifer.

"Nice?"

"It is very nice," said Snowflake, touched.

"Don't be so moved now," said Lusifer and smiled, you are the Snowflake.

"I know," said Snowflake, even more touched.

One of the clocks was almost 12.12. It was time to get the Sun Cross out of the pond. The two clocks nearby were both wrong, one clock went three minutes faster than the other.

The golden Sun Cross rose from the pond, the sky and the pond were blue, and the snow was gone. It went back to the pond again. Dian picked it up from the pond once more, this time it was much bigger and more powerful, it tore loose from the pond and went upwards. Then it was dragged back to the pond once more.

The last time Dian picked up the Sun Cross, the other clock showed 12.12. This time it lay like a great Sun Cross across the sky. The four arms sent red clover leaves over the Hidden Place. The atmosphere turned golden and reddish pink, everything calmed down and became peaceful.

Blackbird had demanded that they changed the tablecloth to black.

"Why did you change the tablecloth?" asked Dian.

"I have to do something sensible too," Blackbird replied, sour, "since you are getting the Sun Cross out of the pond all the time."

Dian just rolled her eyes.

"We have to get Blackbird something useful to do," she said to Lusifer, "he can't keep changing the tablecloths all the time."

"I kind of liked that the tablecloth changed from purple to black," Lusifer said quietly.

They decided to go back to Midas' Palace, it started to get cold. Erik the Red and Beatrix entered the stage just as they entered the dance hall, and soon they could hear "Islands in the Stream." The floor was transformed into water with many small islands. Along the walls, the geysers rose through the roof.

Volven couldn't help herself, she sent Tue up on a geyser, he was thrown from geyser to geyser, but this time he thought it was funny.

Tue's owl fluttered feverishly around.

Dian and Lusifer went back to their house to sleep for a few hours. When they woke up, some of the black angels stood around the bed. Sus said it was time to get up.

Dian was about to put on the same dress as the day before, but Medusa stopped her.

"Present from Flora," she said, and gave Dian a golden dress.

The dress could change from golden to silver, depending on the light. Lusifer got a golden shirt and silver pants. Medusa gave Dian a pair of golden boots, Lusifer had his yellow shoes, nobody tried to make him wear any other pair.

Sus had made a wreath of black feathers for Lusifer, and Medusa had made a wreath of snowdrops for Dian.

"Do you mind if we change?" Dian asked Medusa.

"Not at all," Medusa replied, laughing. "Everything is turned upside down anyway."

The snowdrop wreath looked much better on Lusifer's black hair. Dian's wreath was made with feathers from the magpies, crows and swallows. Blackbird and Snowflake stood waiting for them outside. The whole street started playing as soon as Dian mounted Blackbird and Lusifer flew on top of Snowflake.

The black angels stood in the front row and played drums. It was one year and a half since they had played drums on Machrie Moor. This time the leather balls on the drumsticks were removed, only the sharp sound was left.

Heimdal sat at the end of the street and played a large golden harp, none of the others wanted to play the harp. On one side of him stood Blanca playing the saxophone, and on the other side stood Beatrix playing the horn. Gyda played double bass, while all sixteen trolls played the trumpet. Flora and Oak blew out long tones from the trombone. Haug, Håkon Håkonsson, Myrt and Mort played the violin.

Erik the Red had chosen oboe, and God handled the bassoon. Medusa played the transverse flute while Sus played the little piccolo flute. The cellos were ruled by Lukas and Angus. The music echoed from both sides of the street, all the way from Falkland Palace and up to the Hidden Place.

Blackbird and Snowflake jumped over the gate by the Hidden Place, and continued galloping until they came to a large table shaped like a ring.

The table was full of food and drinks. The tablecloths had changed to silver and gold. All the lights were ice blue, the sky changed from light blue to golden.

The sun was big and pink above the Hidden Place, while the illuminated moon stood large and blue on the other side, hovering over the moors.

All the planets had come to visit. Saturn stood above the table; the other planets stood in a large circle in the sky. The Sun Cross had become a zodiac sign, it appeared low in the sky on top of the hill. Blackbird and Snowflake jumped in the middle of the ring and looked towards the pond where the rainbow made a large arc. The phantom image of the two unicorns chained there was gone forever.

"Do you want Lusifer?" Blackbird asked Dian.

"I do!"

"Do you want Dian?" Snowflake asked Lusifer.

"I do!"

Blackbird and Snowflake jumped over the ring again, and set off at full gallop down the street, and up again to the long grass slopes around the Hidden Place, and then down and up the street again, time and time again.

The time was 14.45 on the sixteenth of April 2015. 144504162015

001112444556 231321 111111 6

112233

222

When they came to the end of the street, Lusifer and Dian spread their wings and flew away, while the sound of "Bolero" by Ravel died out.

They turned and saw Blair and Andrew slapped two large copper lids together at the end of the song.

The wedding had lasted just as long as the song. Sixteen minutes and fifty-two seconds.

Snowflake and Blackbird galloped back without Lusifer and Dian. They passed God's window on their way to the Hidden Place; Raven's toys were exchanged with musical instruments.

The guests sat once again around the round table, eating and drinking.

"Do you think they will return?" Medusa asked Sus.

"Not tonight, maybe tomorrow," Sus said, but he had his doubts.

52

Lusifer was so angry with Dian. He wanted to give her everything before she knew she even wanted it. Dian had told him what she wanted, and he couldn't stand it.

"I was going to give it to you, had you only waited a second," he said.

"I didn't know," said Dian.

"I know everything about you," Lusifer said firmly.

"You don't," said Dian.

That was enough to hurt his ego, Lusifer went furiously away. He went to Sus.

"What's the problem?" asked Sus.

"Dian said what she wants."

"You wanted one who was equal, didn't you?"

"You know I did, but I want to give Dian everything."

"Nobody wants everything, go home and stop being so childish."

Lusifer went home to God and Gyda.

"What's the problem?" asked Gyda.

Lusifer told them about his problem. Gyda kicked him out and slammed the door behind him.

"Why did you kick him out?" asked God.

"I can't stand listening to nonsense," said Gyda.

Lusifer met Medusa and Blair on the square. Blair looked at him behind Medusa's skirt, she reminded him of Dian as a child. Lusifer remembered Dian in the thick yellow bubble suit she could barely walk in, with a teardrop-shaped white cap.

Lusifer felt stupid, he didn't really have a problem. He went home. He didn't have to say anything, Dian kissed him and Lusifer forgot what he was cross about.

If his ego got in the way again, he would think of Dian sitting on top of the snowdrift. Lusifer always laughed when he saw Dian safely on top of the snowdrift, and the yellow snowplough drove past at full speed. Dian had laughed too, but Lusifer hadn't thought she had seen him.

53

Dian was close to a collapse. The brain began to short-circuit, her mind was in free flow, she couldn't think clearly any more.

Lusifer saw that Dian's eyes began to flow, he sent for the best. They came and cooled down her brain, but it wasn't enough. Dian was a hair's breadth from a total collapse. They had to find out what would make it turn quickly, they could only cool her brain for a short time.

Dian tried everything, she sent formula after formula around herself, but nothing helped. She began to think it wasn't so bad if the brain collapsed, she would still have the memory of Blackbird, who looked like he had fallen from the moon when he heard her fart.

It was the memory that saved Dian from a total collapse, she had to laugh every time she thought about it, her laughter sent out the chemicals the brain needed. She was allowed to rest for twenty-nine hours, then her brain was back a hundred times stronger than before.

54

God took a walk up to Oak, he found him in the garden. Oak stood and looked despairingly at the weeping purple willow he had planted in honour of Purple.

The leaves hung down, all the magic in the world couldn't change the willow from mourning.

"Are you grieving, Purple?" asked God.

"I can't believe it would go so wrong."

"Maybe you should think about what you have instead of what you have lost."

"I can't stop thinking I could have done something different."

"That's what everyone thinks, but that's not the problem."

"I know, but I think so anyway."

Flora came out to them in the garden, she was not her usual self any more. Oak's grief had left its mark.

"How are you feeling?" asked God.

"Not very good, I don't know how to comfort Oak anymore."

"Oak," God said hard. "You still have Angus and Dian."

"Purple had too much of Hazel in him," said Oak. "She was running away as soon as an uphill came, as did Purple."

"If you don't stop grieving, you will lose the two you have left," said God.

"Plus me," said Flora.

Oak looked at her astonished.

"I mean it, enough is enough."

It looked like Oak suddenly woke up, he looked at the weeping purple willow in the garden.

"I don't know what to do," he said.
"You do what everyone has to do every single day," said God.
"You have to repair yourself."

55

The time had come to start the third circle of light above Inis Shroin. It was a super moon, spring equinox and solar eclipse at once. The night and the day were equally long, and the earth, the sun and the moon stood aligned with the moon closest to earth. A robin showed Dian the little space she had to stand on.

Each garden should have its own robin, thought Dian.

At exactly 09.36 a.m. on Friday the twentieth of March Dian stood in the place the robin showed her. The solar eclipse was happening above the island Inis Shroin.

"Up, down, south, east, north and south," said Dian while she thought of silver.

Nothing happened. Everything was as usual, except that the moon stood in front of the sun and made some miserable brownish colours in the already grey weather. Dian was sure the circle of light hadn't started. Raven came and sat down next to her on the bench in the garden. They looked at Inis Shroin.

"You're right," said Raven. "The circle of light doesn't move, it stands still. The solar energy and the lunar energy must be used simultaneously in order for the circle to move around the island. We thought we could get Purple to help you, but he lost faith, therefore you have to take over the solar energy."

The gannedruids had calculated that it was possible if Dian changed all her senses, but there was a huge chance that Dian would be destroyed from the inside, by possessing two such powerful energies.

"You must change your senses in order to withstand the solar energy," said Raven.

Dian sent full spectrum into her cells, then light green, pink and orange. The first sense was changed from grey to white. Second from brown to dark green. Third from beige to light green. Fourth from red to yellow. Fifth from turquoise to blue. Sixth from blue to red, and seventh from silver to gold.

The time formula was protected with purple, and time itself with red. The heart was protected with white with a pink and red thread around. The hands got an orange colour in the palms with a silver thread around. Finally, Dian made a maze inside her brain, then she made silver threads inside the maze.

Three fives were given to her from the druids. Dian used the first five to move the solar energy from Purple to herself. The second she used to get a formula to move forward and backward at the same time. The third she used to make her brain strong enough to receive the solar energy times a hundred.

The black angels collapsed one after another, the tension was too high. They didn't see when Dian got the solar energy. It was the silver threads in Dian's brain which saved her when the solar energy entered her body.

Later that evening Dian got a feeling that she should start the circle of light again.

She thought of some numbers she had noticed in March 2012, she didn't notice neither numbers nor formulas at that time, but two things had happened that made her remember the numbers. A friend paid at a cafe and Dian saw his pin-code, it was the same pin-code she had.

The night after, she was thrown out of the hotel in Oslo where she was staying. Dian had gone downstairs to talk to the receptionist in the middle of the night, she couldn't sleep. He threw her out because she talked too much. Dian came from

Verdal, there it was common to talk to everyone, obviously that wasn't the case in the capitol.

The room she stayed in, was number 703, and the room she found in another hotel was room number 602. Dian wrote down the numbers and saw that it wasn't the actual numbers she should use, it was the numbers in between.

She sent 3489 to the right and 9843 to the left. 543 to the left and 6543 to the right.

Soon after, a strong crackling red, orange and yellow explosion appeared. Afterwards the colour blue, turquoise, green, red, purple and yellow appeared around Inis Shroin and the firth. The colours crackled and splashed both in the firth and up to the sky. Dian looked at it with her eyes wide open, the start of the light circle wasn't at all what she had imagined beforehand.

She had to protect the sky, the firth and Inis Shroin with a brown colour. She had seen a picture at the waiting room on the ferry berth. It was a brown sky, a brown sea and a brown island. After Dian had put brown as protection around the island Inis Shroin, there was a new colour show again, this time in turquoise, blue, gold and silver.

Dian sent scarlet to the left and scarlet to the right. Finally, she sent a horizontal eight around to the left, so the circle of light would last forever.

543 was sent to the left to pick up the time that had passed since the eclipse, and 6543 was sent to the right to start the light circle. The numbers crashed in order to pick up the time backwards, and then move forward again. Dian sent the same formula around once more, this time she sent number nine around to the left, and number six around to the right, they crashed with each other, and sent the solar energy up and down. The start of the circle of light was on the sun's day at 6.15 p.m. 03.22.2015.

It was now the big test began. Dian had to trust that she had managed to start the circle of light until the time was 2.22 p.m. the day after, otherwise everything would have been in vain.

Dian had begun to wonder when the circle of light had started with a red and yellow-orange explosion instead of a white beam of light. Either everything was completely ruined, or it had gone well.

She could feel the turmoil from the seventh heaven, but everyone had collapsed, there was no one she could ask. God knew that Dian looked straight up into the seventh heaven. It had to be completely dead, it was important that she didn't pick up anything. Dian decided she wanted the time and the date to be 44458. It was, and Dian knew she had succeeded. The numbers had helped her one more time.

The next day she went to Brodick. She sat down on a bench and looked out over the firth. A seagull came up behind her and stood completely still. Dian had a long talk with the seagull before it was time to catch the bus back home.

"Do you know what time it is?" she asked a woman at the bus stop.

"2.22," replied the woman.

Dian suddenly understood why the seagull had been so eager to talk to her, it was a test that ended when the clock struck 2.22. If she didn't believe the third circle had started, it would go in reverse.

"You know it shouldn't have worked," said Lusifer to Raven.

"I know," said Raven. "When I was in Verdal, it was so strange there. I bet my wings that there's something in the water."

"We will take another trip to Verdal when all this is over," said Lusifer and laughed.

"I made a present for you," said Raven.

Lusifer unwrapped the gift, it was a humming top.

"It's you," said Raven. "You can try to hold it down, but it pops up time after time."

Lusifer was so touched that he had to wipe away the tear that was trickling down his nose.

56

Dian went up to the seventh heaven. Lusifer stood leaning against a pillar with his back to her. He talked to Bonnie who was visiting, she usually lived on the other side of the ocean. Bonnie stood leaning against the pillar with the night sky behind her.

Dian thought they looked like a jewel. On one side of the pillar Lusifer in black with his yellow shoes, and on the other side of the pillar Bonnie in her long dark purple dress.

"Hi! What are you doing here?" Raven asked. He had come up behind her without Dian noticing.

"I couldn't help myself, but now I have to go, I'm not supposed to be here."

Raven nodded, and Dian disappeared back to earth.

Dian asked Gyda if she could close the sky, it was too difficult to stay on earth when she knew about the seventh heaven, how easy it was to get up there.

Gyda didn't tell her that it was impossible to get up there for anyone other than the black angels, it was only Dian that had managed to. Gyda asked Dian if she wanted to go up one more time before she closed the seventh heaven for her.

When Dian came up, she could see that the rest of them were all dressed up, she felt a bit out of place.

"You can borrow a dress from me," said Bonnie.

Dian chose a long turquoise dress with green stones from the shoulders down to the hands. She met Raven on her way into the great dancehall. Dian couldn't breathe, she had to sit down in the long open hallway with a view to the stars. Finally, she lay down on the floor, she felt that her heart was growing. Raven got scared, he ran to fetch God.

"She must return to earth immediately," said God.

Dian had just as much trouble with her breathing on earth, but after a couple of hours her heart settled. Raven was sitting at the foot end of the bed.

"What's your surname?" asked Dian.

"Crow."

"Who would have thought," Dian said with a smile.

Raven flapped a little with his wings. "Do you want to fly?"

"In your dreams!"

Raven laughed. "Maybe you will learn how to fly one day."

"Right now, I have enough trouble staying on earth."

Dian told Raven that she had found the halving formula and the doubling formula the night before.

When she sent 333 to the left and 666 to the right with the number nine in the middle, it was Raven, Lusifer and Bonnie who showed up. When she used the halving formula 33 to the left and 66 to the right, there were only two people left.

"You and Lusifer," said Raven.

"Lusifer has been there the whole time," said Dian. Raven nodded and looked inquisitively at her.

"Do you think it's strange?"

"Not very," said Dian.

The black angels hadn't taken the chance to introduce Lusifer to Dian prematurely, they were afraid she would think the same as the rest of the world, that he was a demon.

Therefore, they had introduced Dian to the playful side of Lusifer first, who was Raven. They could see that Dian was amazed that Raven didn't join them when they were snowboarding on top of the Lyngen Alps. They realised the time to present Lusifer to Dian had come.

Lusifer thought it was scary what Dian could read from all the number combinations. She had told them that Bonnie had number seven, just like herself. Lusifer had gazed at the others, but they had just shook their heads. Nobody understood how Dian had found out that Bonnie had number seven.

57

Dian sat on the working bench in God's workshop, he was making a cuckoo clock.

"You can make yourself with tousled hair," said Dian.

"Who comes out of the cuckoo clock and says Cuckoo! Cuckoo!" said God and smiled, "that would be the day."

"What did you think of me as a priest?"

"You were amazing."

"I have never had so much fun on earth before."

"You looked fabulous in your beige suit."

"It was the worst suit I could find," said God and laughed.

Dian started to laugh too. "You wore your beige suit like a peacock, I always stopped and looked at you when you walked the streets around your church. I remember one time I sat at the neighbouring pub drinking beer, you came inside and asked the owner if you could put up a bill sticker on the window. The owner said you could hang it in the hall by the toilets, she didn't want to block the light."

"Then I trampled furiously around the room while cursing," said God smiling at the memory.

"I couldn't stop laughing," said Dian.

"I complained how expensive the cakes were," said God, "then you stood up and yelled at me that the congregation had baked for me all my life, that I never had to pay for any cakes."

"Then you roared across the room how much you liked that I said what I meant," said Dian and laughed. "After that you stopped talking to me, except when you said some really embarrassing sexual stuff."

God laughed and said, "I couldn't help myself. You had your eyes wide open wondering if I existed for real."

"But you didn't," said Dian and smiled at him.

"No! I just went into the priest, I thought, took the whole cake."

"It was a good choice," said Dian.

"It was, wasn't it," said God and laughed. "I liked Verdal, people said all the time: Are you sitting here alone, come and join us, you mustn't be alone."

"I was amazed that anyone would talk to you," said Dian.

"I got yelled at a lot. They told me to keep my feet on the ground," said God and laughed.

"That's Verdal for you," said Dian and laughed too.

"Join me in the garden for a walk," said God. "I've got a new tenant."

Dian looked through the purple windows of the miniature house in the garden, but she saw no one.

"We have to wait until he decides to come out," said God. "Come back tomorrow morning, we usually drink coffee together."

58

"How old are your children now?" Lusifer asked Sus.

"They turned five the day after they were born. Next year they will be ten, the year after fifteen, then it's time for them to move out."

"So, they live at home for three years?" asked Lusifer.

"Something like that."

"There's one thing I have realised living on earth, your kids can't be ten next year, they must be six."

Sus smiled and said, "Good you realised, it could have been really embarrassing."

Lusifer just laughed.

"How did the flight go down to the earth's inner core?" asked Sus.

"It went well, Dian was half asleep."

"And yet she managed the most difficult flight of them all. How did she manage?"

"She put her wings tightly around her and twirled down the spiral at full speed."

"The spiral is long," said Sus.

"Dian was half dizzy, she didn't think. Most people think a distance is a distance, but it takes much longer to fly down to the inner core of the earth than it takes to fly to the outer bulwark, yet it's a million times longer.

We flew to the underground water and swam under some rock formations that stood in the water. The path that led to the next water was full of wraiths."

"The huge wraiths with scaly faces?" asked Sus.

"That's the ones," Lusifer replied. "Anyway, we arrived at the small lake in the middle. I had to tell Dian all the formulas, she was still not fully awake.

I told her to use the blue colour, full spectrum and the DNA-link. Finally, I told her to use dust."

"You had figured it all out," Sus said.

"Not enough, when Dian asked whether she should use magic dust or star dust, I didn't know so I told her to use all the dust she had. And that's where it went wrong, Dian should have used the magic dust, but it wasn't a big disaster, the only thing that happened was that it got much brighter."

Dian came out on the terrace where they sat.

"It was a pity you didn't get to see the flight up from the inner core of the earth," said Lusifer.

"I fell asleep, didn't I?"

"You did, Jordi is still offended that you fell asleep."

"Isn't he Volven's twin?"

"He is, but Jordi was born last, so he doesn't have much to say."

"No one has much to say when it comes to Volven," said Dian. "Are you done flying down to the earth's inner core?"

"I don't dare to any more, I've been there five times already," said Lusifer.

"I saw what you were most afraid of when I sent your formula around you."

"You found my formula?"

"A patch hung on a rhododendron close to your tree and mine, with the letters and numbers HC 202. It wasn't very difficult to find."

"It's not difficult if you know that H stands for Heaven, and my surname is Crow."

"I saw you were stuck in the spiral, and a long worm head came in from both sides and ate you alive."

"Her name is Ellie, the spiral had to be cleaned up every time anyone got stuck."

"What can make you get stuck?" asked Dian.

"Alas! I forgot to tell you beforehand," said Lusifer. "You get stuck if you think one thought inside the spiral."

"It's so strange," said Sus. "You have to wrap your wings around you, spin around with your head first, and not think otherwise you will be eaten, who comes up with something like that?"

Lusifer just grinned.

"I'm not surprised," said Sus, "and that surprises me."

"Fortunately, it's over," said Lusifer.

"What's Ellie eating now, when no one needs to use the spiral anymore?" asked Sus.

"Ellie's got a taste for delicious vegetables. Jordi cultivates many strange ones. There was some mix up with the colours since Dian was so tired. Jordi brags to Volven that he has green strawberries and pink pears. I told Dian to send full spectrum the wrong way, I hadn't memorised the formulas properly."

"Let's hope Ellie loses her taste for meat," said Sus.

"Jordi wants me to tell you how offended he is because you fell asleep," said Lusifer to Dian. "He told me how much he had done that day without falling asleep."

"What had he done that day?" asked Sus.

"He had hung the laundry; it was five green pants and twelve blue sweaters. After that he had picked some potatoes. I said that Dian had also hung a laundry that day, but then Jordi started scolding me, telling me how little people managed to do before they fell asleep."

"How was the flight up again?" asked Dian.

"It's a landscape with light blue air between large giant mountains that goes all the way up. You can suddenly see a white foxglove or a yellow mullein on a mountain ledge, it's magical."

"Didn't you get tired?"

"I did, but Jordi has made red transparent benches hanging in the air on the way up, so it's possible to get some rest."

"Did Ellie fall into the earth's core in the crack where Loch Ness was formed?"

"That's what happened."

"What were you two doing down there?" asked Dian.

"I gave them an ultimatum. Those who wanted to continue being evil would sail in their own sea."

"What happened next?"

"I said that all who wanted to be good, should refrain from taking their morning bath that morning. Then me and Sus sent electricity into the water, they were all killed. Jordi was very dissatisfied that the water was full of dead bodies. I promised to take you down to clean up."

"And what did he say?"

"That would be the day!" said Lusifer and smiled.

"What really happened between you and Erik the Red by the Hidden Place?" asked Dian.

"Beatrix passed by with her long and green tight-fitting dress and her long fluttering hair. She gave Erik the Red a mischievous look, he forgot I was there, and followed Beatrix instead."

"I've heard they moved to Greenland," said Sus.

"They did, Erik the Red wanted to move to Island, but he didn't have the guts to fight Volven," said Dian.

"Beatrix is the one who has the powers," said Lusifer.

"That is how it is between Blanca and Heimdal as well, he is the one with all the powers," said Dian.

"Blanca wants to have powers, but she is content with the fact that Heimdal has more powers than both Tor and Odin combined," said Lusifer.

"I heard that Blanca met Heimdal on the small mountain where the first light circle was started," said Sus.

"Blanca lived there. Beatrix was married to Blanca's son, he died, so that's how she ended up here," said Dian.

"Blanca and Heimdal have moved to the beginning of the rainbow," said Lusifer.

"Heimdal didn't want Blanca to be more preoccupied with the cauldron of gold, than with him," said Dian.

"Wise thoughts," said Lusifer and laughed.

59

Oak didn't manage the grief when Purple disappeared, he moved to a small hut deep in the mountains far away from people.

"Take the weeping purple willow with you," said Flora when he left.

She had nothing more to give him, she had tried everything. God had told Oak that there was no reward in heaven if he mourned himself to death. Oak failed to let go of the thoughts, that at some point it had been possible to help Purple.

Flora breathed a sigh of relief when he left, she chose to live as usual, Flora was Flora. Markus knocked on her door the very next day.

"Do you know what's happened?" he asked.

"I'm not quite sure what you are referring to."

"All the black angels are living on earth now, and Dian is done with the formulas."

"It is important to stop in time," said Flora. "What happened?"

"Palle Pellegrino put his foot down."

"The one and only Palle Pellegrino," said Flora thoughtful.

"The oldest spider in the world."

"I thought he barely existed," said Markus.

"It's no wonder, he hasn't shown himself during the last four hundred years. What did he say?"

"Palle Pellegrino said that if Dian said one more formula that changed the world, all the formulas she had done up till now would collapse. Dian doesn't want to have the lunar or the solar energy any more either."

Flora breathed a sigh of relief and said, "I was worried for a while, Dian sleeps too hard, when she's half asleep she could have done anything."

"That wasn't what I came for," said Markus, "I came to ask for your hand."

"I have always said that if a man is younger than Angus, then he's too young for me. It's a shame you're not a year older."

"I can change my age." Markus transformed himself into a middle-aged man.

Flora became dumb, *Markus was so nice and so...* she didn't find the words, but she had a feeling she didn't need any words.

60

"Today," said Lusifer, "shall I show you something new. You lay down and take away all your thoughts about what awaits you." Dian did as he said, she wiped away all her thoughts. He came and lowered his body light as a feather over hers. She could feel her body become light as a butterfly. Lusifer came inside her with light wingbeats.

"Think of something cruel."

Dian thought of Ellie. The inside of her body turned into a black swamp.

"Now comes the big bad wolf," said Lusifer and grinned.

Dian felt she began to change; she became light blue. She was full of butterflies; they flew wildly around in the depth.

"Let them out," said Lusifer. Dian let all the butterflies out.

"So, that's why you wanted me to turn on the radio?" she asked.

"I didn't want the whole of Falkland to hear what we were doing."

"I bet Sus is standing in the garden laughing."

"That's how he learns, Sus needs to since he's the leader of the black angels now."

"And you are?"

"Right now, I'm your lover. We are not done yet, imagine that there are more butterflies trying to get out."

Dian saw a golden butterfly, the next one was silver, then came a blue, and finally one in copper. There was no light flapping of the wings any more, they had turned into heavy and powerful flaps.

"Now the last one comes," said Lusifer. Dian could hardly breath. Lusifer's body was not light as a feather any more, it was massive. The last butterfly sat far inside. Lusifer worked hard to let Dian release it. She wondered if the radio was turned on loud enough.

"Stop thinking," said Lusifer.

Dian stopped thinking, and the butterfly left her body, it was pitch black. "You're not just a lover, you're a man, a black angel and whatever," she said, and fell asleep like a stone.

"Would you like to go to Island?" asked Lusifer Dian the next morning.

Dian stretched and nodded. She barely managed to get dressed and get outside before Lusifer lifted from the ground. They flew above Vatnajökull, there were only two black angels left at the Mercy Seat, the others were born again.

"Why are they still there?" asked Dian.

"They are born in the constellation Pisces," Lusifer replied. "They never managed to decide where to go or who to be."

"I'm excited to meet the five star trolls," said Dian. "Have you heard the names they've been given?"

"No."

"It's Sunshine, Moonshine, Stardust, Milkyway and Heaven."

"Milkyway," said Lusifer in disbelief. "Is that supposed to be a joke?"

"It's a girl with white hair. Gilde was completely sure she had to be from the Milky Way."

They landed by Volven and Gilde's house. Volven came running and hugged Lusifer hard to her bosom and kissed Dian on the cheek.

"Gilde!" shouted Volven. "Important people in the yard!"

Gilde came around the corner of the house with an axe over his shoulder. He did the opposite; he hugged Dian and barely touched Lusifer's cheek.

"Welcome! And thanks for last time! Never had so much fun before."

"No?" Volven asked and looked angrily at Gilde. "Hiding behind the trees with Blanca at your age."

"My age," said Gilde upset. "My age is indeterminate."

"Exactly, you have looked the same for hundreds of years. Those who had fun were me and Lusifer, in the side streets of Edinburgh. When you were Raven," Volven said and looked at Lusifer.

"Now it's easy keeping track of Raven, we are one," said Lusifer.

"Good for you," said Volven. "It must have been awful for you when Dian was with Raven."

"Don't be stupid!" said Gilde agitated, "Raven was him, remember? What was awful was when Dian was with Purple."

"Enough about Purple. Come and eat!" howled Volven in the four directions of the sky.

"Immediately sixteen small trolls sat around the long wooden table." Dian and Lusifer sat down at the end of the table with the five star trolls. Lusifer saw immediately who Milkyway was. She had long white hair and light blue eyes. The four other star trolls were boys with brown hair down to their shoulders and green eyes. Milkyway moved closer to Dian on the bench and blew on her porridge.

"It was you who took us away from the outer bulwark, wasn't it?" she asked.

"It was, do you remember what happened?"

"No! Volven told me. When you came along, I would understand who you were, and I did."

"Who did she say we were?"

"She said one of you had the highest white, and the other one the highest black, and together you were one."

"That's a good description," said Dian. "I would have guessed who we were too."

After they had finished eating all the porridge, they went to swim in the hot spring next to the low and round house. It was built in a transparent turquoise stone and almost impossible to see, it slipped into the landscape.

The small trolls slept in boxes attached to the round wall at different heights. The house was a single large room, with a kitchen made from driftwood with open shelves at one end. At the other end of the room stood a huge sofa in a semicircle, it had the turquoise blue colours of a blackbird egg splashed with brown-grey dots here and there.

The big table in front of the sofa looked like a robin's egg in white and beige. A fireplace hung down from the ceiling and looked like a solid white egg. The only other room was a bathroom, it was built as a second globe. Gilde had made a sun that shone into the bath no matter what time of day it was. The bathtub was round and yellow, and big enough for sixteen small trolls. The water was always warm thanks to the artificial sun which collected solar energy. When the weather was good, they bathed in the hot spring outside.

"Where would you like to sleep?" asked Volven.

"We'll sleep outside underneath the stars," replied Lusifer.

Volven collected some sheepskins and blankets. She gave Dian a turquoise flannel nightgown, and Lusifer a dark blue one. Lusifer had to read a fairytale for the trolls, he read the fairytale about the little blue bird who didn't want to sing.

When everyone had fallen asleep, he came out and sat next to Dian. They put a blanket around their shoulders and looked at the dark blue sky, and the even darker mountains with the turquoise hot spring in front. Volven had spoken to the northern lights, they were neon green.

61

It was Timmy Willie who had moved into God's backyard. Dian met him early one morning.

Timmy told her that one day he had crawled into a basket that was going to the city. He met Johnny Town Mouse who tried everything to make him happy. He gave him bacon, that Timmy didn't like, he was used to eating vegetables. Johnny showed him the best sleeping place, which was a pillow with a hole, but Timmy smelled the cat that lived in the house, he didn't dare to sleep there. He got thinner and thinner, finally Johnny asked what was wrong.

"I long for home," Timmy replied.

"You know you can crawl into the empty basket; it goes back to the country on the lorry," said Johnny.

The next day Timmy was on his way back home. Johnny Town Mouse came to visit him a few days later, and Timmy welcomed him with open arms.

"What do you do when it rains?" Johnny asked.

"Then I sit under a leaf looking at all my flowers."

Johnny thought it was awful in the countryside, it was too quiet for him, it wasn't long before he returned to the city again.

"It sounds like a story Beatrix Potter could have written," said Dian.

"Maybe she did," said Timmy secretive.

62

Listen to this poem written by Percy Shelley," said Lusifer to Dian.

> "The fountains mingle with the river
> And the rivers with the ocean,
> The winds of heaven mix forever
> With a sweet emotion;
> Nothing in the world is single;
> All things by a law divine
> In one another's being mingle…
> Why not I with thine?
> See! The mountains kiss high heaven,
> And the waves clasp one another;
> No sister flower would be forgiven
> If it disdained its brother;
> And the sunlight clasps the earth
> And the moonbeams kiss the sea…
> What are all these kisses worth
> If thou kiss not me?"

Lusifer had not seen that Dian was asleep. He lay down next to her and put his wings around her and fell asleep just as heavily as Dian always slept.

    Soon after, God knocked on the window downstairs. Lusifer went down the stairs to let him in, Dian was right behind him. God looked like he was thirty years old.

"Holiday?" asked Dian.

"Holiday," God answered.

"Does the holiday involve any young gorgeous ladies?" asked Lusifer.

"It involves seven sisters."

"Sounds like a good plan."

"Doesn't it though? I just wanted to say hello before I left."

"Don't do anything I wouldn't do!" shouted Lusifer after him.

"Cryptic!" said Dian.

"Very," said Lusifer and kissed her.

"So, the mountain range in northern Norway is named after the seven sisters?"

"It was God's idea; he was afraid he would forget how nice they were."

"I guess God loves the reverse formula."

"He loves it, it's probably them he intends to use it for."

"Whom?"

"The seven sisters."

63

Storm and Sus came and wanted Dian and Lusifer to join them. Sus wanted to compete with Dian, he was tired of winning over the rest of the black angels all the time.

"Let's try to crash into Inis Shroin," said Sus to Dian.

They got up on their boards, bent their knees and got their wings in the right position.

"Go!" said Storm.

The wind got hold of their wings and they were on their way.

"They're going to crash into the island," said Lusifer.

"Sus has a plan," said Storm, "but Dian needs to figure it out fast." Sus and Dian hit the island at full speed at the same time, both managed to make the board fly up the mountainside.

"How the hell did they manage?" said Lusifer.

"Let's try," said Storm.

They lined up on their boards and flew over the waves. As they approached the island, they both collided with the mountainside. Sus and Dian stood and watched them on top of Inis Shroin.

"It will probably take a while before they find out what to do," said Sus. "What about a trip to Falkland to see how Blackbird and Snowflake are doing meanwhile?"

Dian agreed, it had been a long time since she had seen the unicorns.

They landed on top of the Hidden Place, and strolled down the hill to where Blackbird was grazing together with Snowflake.

Blackbird was fully grown now, he was glistening black and held his head high, the long mane blew around his neck.

"He looks great," said Sus.

"Very," said Dian, "hope he hasn't become conceited."

"Where's Lusifer?" asked Snowflake.

"He's busy," Sus replied.

"With what?" asked Snowflake.

"Scratching his head."

"I wish you could fart for us again," said Snowflake, looking at Dian.

"I can't fart loudly on command," said Dian, "but I'll let you know next time."

"Let me know too," Sus said grinning.

"There will be four of us," said Blackbird.

"Great!" said Dian. "You're invited to a fart party."

"With cake," said Sus.

"I can't bake all the time."

"You can put the cake in the freezer."

"And otherwise?" Dian asked Blackbird.

"Otherwise, I'm a fully grown stallion."

"And you like being a fully grown stallion?"

"Like it? Love it! And you are not too bad, considering you're the one who's supposed to decide what I should do, when it suits you."

"You're not very happy about that?"

"I don't feel very important, you can decide over the only stallion in the world which is a unicorn, and what do you do? We could have achieved great things together."

Dian and Sus exchanged glances.

"Has nobody told you, without you and Snowflake, there wouldn't be neither faith, hope nor love in this world," said Dian.

"That's why everyone cried so much when the two unicorns were caught again. If they hadn't been freed, you and Snowflake wouldn't have been born, Lilith's curse made it impossible."

"What do you mean?" asked Blackbird.

"No unicorns could be born again before the two black unicorns were set free."

"You're saying I'm doing an important job just by being alive?"

"Exactly!" said Dian.

Blackbird just looked at her thoughtfully. After a while, he said, "So my job is the most important one in the world?"

"You and Snowflake have the two most important jobs in the world," Dian replied.

Blackbird was pleased with the answer. He lifted his hooves high and trotted over to Snowflake.

"Thanks," said Sus. "Now I don't have to listen to Blackbird's whining every day."

They flew back and saw that Storm and Lusifer still hadn't figured out how to get the board up the mountainside.

"Join us and see how it's done," said Sus.

Lusifer stepped onto Dian's board, and Storm stepped on to Sus' board. They flew over the waves and straight up the mountainside.

"So that's how you did it," said Lusifer.

"What?" said Storm. "I didn't get it; I closed my eyes."

"They took a hand underneath in front of the board just when it was about to go up," said Lusifer.

"Brilliant, next will be the two of them going straight through the island," said Storm.

Sus and Dian exchanged glances, they already wondered how it could be done.

64

Dian went to visit Timmy Willie.

"Have you found any new formulas lately?" he asked.

"I have found two."

"Let's hear!"

"The first one is a formula of truth."

"How did you find it?"

"I have the seventh hour, I put it together with the twelfth hour. 712 to the left, and 217 to the right, but this formula shan't be passed around, it shall stand still on each side."

"Very interesting, and the second?"

"The second is how I shall be able to count fast to a thousand."

"What do you need it for?" asked Timmy.

"A volcanic eruption," Dian replied.

"A volcanic eruption," said Timmy. "You don't happen to be talking about a very passionate guy?"

"I don't survive counting the normal way to a thousand," said Dian.

"How do you count to a thousand fast?"

"I set up the truth formula and count to ten, then all the numbers are present, then I add two zeros, and within a second the series of numbers has become a thousand and two."

"Not a thousand?"

"No, strangely enough, it wants to be a thousand and two. If I add another zero in the number row it will be a thousand and three etcetera. I thought I could stop the number row by using number one, but it doesn't work, it stops at the same time as it formats itself."

"What!" said Timmy. "Explain."

"If I say number one before the number row has managed to become what I want it to be, I'll get a lot of number one on each side, then a zero on each side of the number one I'm stopping the number row with."

"And then what happens?" asked Timmy excited.

"The zero on both sides begins to roll over the number one which stands on each side and creates new numbers."

"What?" said Timmy again.

"All numbers have either a round shape or a line."

"I understand," said Timmy. "What's my number by the way?"

Dian wrote down his name.
TimmyWillie tiiimmywlle 1321121-111211-312-111

"Three," she said.

"Three," said Timmy Willie thoughtful.

God came out into the garden at the same time with coffee. "What are you talking about?" he asked.

"We've talked about numbers," said Timmy, "but we're done now." God breathed a sigh of relief. *Thank God!* he thought.

"Does it mean that I have the third hour?" asked Timmy.

"It does," replied Dian. "We are done now," she said dryly to God, "you don't have to disappear into the thin air."

God was a bit ashamed; he knew the numbers had helped the earth to come up to the next level. He was just allergic to numbers, just like the rest of the black angels were.

God went in to get some dry biscuits he had baked. Timmy Willie hurried to ask about the DNA-link.

223

"It was originally a golden triangle, two silver eights and a silver zero," said Dian.

"How come you use two silver eights?" asked Timmy.

"At that time the earth had reached its new level. The zero got another zero on top and became number eight."

"I understand," said Timmy Willie. God came outside again.

"Now we have to talk about something else," Timmy said in a low voice to Dian.

The biscuits looked like glue and cardboard, but they tasted surprisingly good.

"You don't care much about how the biscuits look," said Dian.

"I don't, as long as they taste good."

"I have learned how to count fast to a thousand," said Dian to Lusifer.

"How?"

"I'm just taking a series of numbers." Lusifer moaned loudly.

"I'm just kidding."

"I hate when you say you're just taking a series of numbers."

"I know," said Dian, "that's why I say it." Lusifer kissed her so she would stop talking about numbers.

That was a hell of a formula, thought Lusifer after a while. He had never given up first, but this time he had become completely pumped. He didn't want Dian to know that she had found a formula that interested him. She had counted to a thousand three times. Since the number became a thousand and two the first time, the end result was a thousand and six. *We'll see who lasts the longest when I use the formula as well,* Lusifer thought and fell asleep.

Dian thought about what had happened over and over again. It started with a volcanic eruption with a calm water afterwards, the rings spread in the water. Then came a waterfall which led down to a new still water, where the sun shone between the trees. The water was turquoise, in its depth lay an emerald.

Dian loved the ripple effects. The still water always came after a new waterfall where the sun shone. Dian could have kept on going, but Lusifer needed a break.

The act itself evoked a memory in Dian that she had forgotten. It was the year 1032 on the beach with a view to Ailsa Craig. The unicorn had run off along the beach with Dian behind, trying to run fast in her wedding gown.

The guests sat and ate without a thought, they were hypnotised. The unicorn stopped. Dian saw a black angel stroking it over the muzzle.

"Who are you?" she asked breathless.

"I've been waiting for you," he said.

He walked over to her and pulled off her pink wedding gown. Dian looked into his suggestive grey eyes, and began stroking his raven-black hair, that went down to his shoulders.

He laid her down on the beach and got undressed. Dian couldn't wait, she pulled him towards her while she kissed him fiercely. He showed her the water and the green emerald, while the tide drew closer and closer. Dian wanted more of him, but the guests couldn't be hypnotised much longer.

65

"Dian has made a new friend," said Lusifer to Storm. They sat on Lusifer and Dian's terrace.

"Hope you don't get jealous," said Storm.

"It's a mouse who's interested in numbers. What was it Timmy wanted when he dropped by just now?" Lusifer asked Dian.

"He wanted to borrow a cup of sugar."

That wasn't what Timmy had come for. He wondered why no one could look into the future when Dian used a formula. Dian had answered that there were too many pieces that had to fall into place. It was like a domino effect, the first number overturned the first piece, and then millions of pieces collapsed. The black angels managed to look into the future when it came to ordinary things, because there were so few pieces that needed to fall into place.

Timmy understood what she meant, he had gone back to his garden, where God waited with freshly baked biscuits and freshly brewed coffee.

Dian went inside to get three glasses of whisky.

"We are talking about Ormen Lange," said Lusifer when she returned. "Maybe we should build it," he said to Storm.

"I talked to Håkon Håkonsson at your wedding," said Storm. "He said there was something wrong with Ormen Lange. The ship was wobbly and capricious. Suddenly it could fly, no one had any control over it. The Vikings always thought they had eaten too many liberty caps when it lifted from the sea. Håkon gave me some information about the ship, I still got it." Storm took out a note from his pocket.

"The ship was built in the year 996, it was fifty-five metres long and six metres broad. The sail was two hundred m² and was built for a hundred and four rowers. Håkon believed that the numbers were almost correct, but not completely."

Storm and Lusifer looked at Dian.

They didn't know if they could ask her to look at the note, since they had escaped every time, she talked about numbers. They sat for a long time staring at her.

Lusifer knew that Dian wouldn't say anything first. Finally, he asked, "Do you mind?"

"Of course not!" Dian replied and took the note from Storm's hand. She wrote down some new numbers and said, "Go back to the year 969 when you build it and make the ship sixty-six metres long and five metres broad. Get hold of a hundred and two rowers and make the sail two hundred and twenty-two square metres."

Storm and Lusifer looked at the numbers, then they looked at each other and shook their heads.

"Do you mind?" asked Lusifer again and gave Dian the note back.

"Ormen Lange was originally built in the year 996, that's why it was unstable. If you build it in the year 969, you get a steady ship with the number nine on both sides. Sixty-six metres long instead of fifty-five metres.

Number six stands for speed, the ship was six metres broad, but no one needs speed out to the sides, therefore it's wiser to make it five metres. A hundred and two rowers instead of a hundred and four. Two hundred and twenty-two stands for peace, but it also stands for three pairs of wings, which causes unrest. It will be the perfect sail."

"Cheers to the new Ormen Lange," said Lusifer and raised his glass, Dian and Storm did the same.

"Ormen Lange was built after a ship named Ormen," said Dian. "It had a gilded worm head and a gilded tail. Olav copied it on to Ormen Lange, before he tortured the king who owned Ormen to death."

"Charming story," said Storm, "I liked the part about the gilded head and tail though."

66

Gyda was sick of being alone, she went to the little hut deep in the mountains and knocked on the door. Oak opened with more tousled hair than ever; his hair stood in all directions. Gyda had never seen anything so magnificent, she was glowing, Oak hardly recognised her.

"Come in!" he said, "I haven't seen anyone for weeks."

Gyda didn't have to be asked twice. She walked slowly past him as she tossed her long hair and moved her hips. Oak looked at her in astonishment.

"What's going on? Aren't you with God anymore?"

"God is enjoying himself with seven sisters."

"I understand, and that's okay with you?"

"If you want me, then it's okay with me."

"I'm not saying no thanks, not because you're the only woman as far as the eye can see, but you look magnificent."

"You too," said Gyda and approached Oak with her hips moving from side to side slowly.

Oak couldn't speak, he felt like a stone, he couldn't move either. The clock in the living room struck twelve and the cuckoo said: Coo! Coo!

Oak started to laugh. *That's exactly how I feel*, he thought, *but it's okay to feel completely coo, coo sometimes, then I'm alive at least.*

"Let's dance," he said. "What would you like to hear?"

"Total Eclipse of the Heart."

"Let's have a total eclipse of the heart," said Oak and stroked a hand through his tousled hair.

Gyda couldn't take it anymore. She ripped off his shirt and trousers.

"Finally, I'm gonna have what I have wanted for two thousand years."

"You must be joking!" said Oak. "What's so special about me?"

"Your tousled hair," groaned Gyda. "Stop talking!"

Oak stopped talking and concentrated on what he was doing instead.

67

"Have you figured out how to ride straight through the island?" Sus asked Dian.

Dian didn't answer, she was concentrating. Sus and Lusifer sat on the kitchen counter while Dian made pizza.

"You shouldn't just follow the recipe," said Sus. "You are supposed to actually use the ingredients listed."

"Shouldn't we try to ride through the island?" asked Dian.

"You can try first," said Sus.

"You don't know what to do."

"I can look at you first."

"Coward!" said Dian.

Lusifer laughed, he could see that Sus didn't have a clue how to do it.

"Okay!" said Sus.

They went to the island Inis Shroin and lined up on their boards. Dian had changed her hair and eyes into bright yellow, her wings were dark blue. Soon after she was alone on the other side. Sus had a huge bump on his forehead.

"Let's try again," said Dian.

"Okay!" said Sus. This time he changed his hair and eyes to bright yellow and changed his black wings into dark blue. They got through to the other side at the same time.

"Want to join us?" Dian asked Lusifer.

"Bright yellow hair doesn't suit me," said Lusifer.

Sus and Dian looked at him, and Lusifer realised he didn't

have a choice. All three of them lined up on their boards, but it was only Dian and Sus who got through to the other side.

"What happened?" Dian asked Lusifer.

"I heard a nice song while I rode over the waves, so I had to dance a little on the board."

"What song did you hear?"

"Breathless."

"You became breathless because you hit the rock wall more likely," said Sus.

They tried one last time, this time three of them were on the other side.

68

God stood on the little stone bridge by the Hidden Place. He threw a small stone and saw how the rings spread further and further out. Lusifer came and stood beside him.

"Love trouble?" he asked.

God just nodded and threw another stone in the pond.

"Maybe I can help you," said Lusifer.

"What can you do?" said God with despair.

"I know how you can get Gyda back." God threw another stone into the water.

"Sing her favourite song," said Lusifer.

"And you will sing the chorus?" Lusifer nodded.

"The chorus is actually the most difficult on that song," God said.

"You created my voice," said Lusifer, "so it shouldn't be a problem."

"What happened to the angel choir by the way?"

"It was too difficult to sing when there was so much evil around."

"Maybe now is the right time," said God.

"Maybe it is," said Lusifer, thoughtful.

69

God was sinking deep into his thoughts. Timmy Willie appeared.

"What is it?" asked Timmy.

God woke up and looked, astonished, at him.

"What is it?" asked Timmy again. "Is it the last days' events?"

"You can safely say that," God replied. "I'm more shaken than I've ever been before."

"Tell me about it," said Timmy, "but get some coffee and biscuits first."

"Good idea," said God and fetched coffee and the biscuits he had decorated with icing and violets, Sus had taught him.

"They look magnificent," said Timmy.

"Good!" said God. "I can still learn."

"If you stop learning, you can just lie down in your grave," said Timmy.

"That would be the day," God said and laughed.

"It can still happen," Timmy said. He sounded like an old man.

"It could have gone so wrong," God said.

"Yes!" said Timmy. "But it didn't."

"But it could have, the chances were so high that it would go wrong and so microscopically small that it would go well."

"It went well," said Timmy. "If you tell me everything, then maybe it will dawn on you that it went well."

"Good idea," said God, "but I don't know where to begin."

"You can start by telling me why Lusifer tried to strangle you."

"He never managed to, but it was fun that he tried."

"You don't mean that," said Timmy.

"No, I don't," said God seriously, "it was horrible."

"Tell me now," Timmy said impatiently.

God nodded and began to tell, "It began in the days when a decree was issued by Emperor Augustus."

"Stop!" Timmy said angrily to him. "Tell me now."

God looked at him and said quietly, "It could have gone so wrong." Timmy got up and left.

"Come back," God said, "I'm ready now."

Timmy returned and sat down and poured himself a cup of coffee and supplied himself with a biscuit.

"Lusifer tried to suffocate me, because I got Dian to send Storm into the funnel."

"Why?"

"Storm tried to kill Dian."

"What?" roared Timmy.

"And afterwards, Dian was killed by Purple."

"Give me a break!" Timmy said.

"It's true."

"How is it possible? Dian sent Purple into the funnel."

"Dian saw that Lusifer tried to strangle me, and she understood it was because he had lost Storm, she decided to go into the funnel and bring him back."

"Couldn't she just use the reverse formula?" asked Timmy.

"That's the thing. Purple always got out of the funnel because he knew the reverse formula. That's why Dian made a ball of light at the entrance of the funnel, so he couldn't get out, even though he used the reverse formula.

We saw that Dian was on her way towards Purple, we flew as fast as we could after her towards the funnel, but we arrived too late.

At the same second as Dian removed the light ball to get Storm out, Purple stuck her with a long knife. The light ball bounced back in front of the opening after two seconds, and had she fallen forward before the opening was closed again, then we would never have gotten her back."

"What happened?"

"Lusifer had two seconds before the opening closed, he plunged forward and pulled her back by the hair."

"It's not the first time he has saved her by pulling her hair," Timmy said, laughing.

"Let's hope it's the last time. Dian was fortunately on the right side of the funnel so I could use the reverse formula. When she woke up, she said we should be quiet. She went inside Storm's mind and told him to throw a stone, so Purple was distracted long enough for her to get him out."

"And it worked?" asked Timmy.

"It worked."

Timmy thought for a while before asking, "Why did Storm try to kill Dian?"

"All the formulas Dian has done are linked together, that is why we have been telling her lies all the time, otherwise she would have been so nervous that she wouldn't have used any of the formulas."

"It was really hopeless," said Timmy thoughtful.

"It wasn't hopeless," God said, "it was impossible."

"Was there a reason to kill her because it was impossible?" asked Timmy.

"If Dian hadn't managed to say the last two formulas within

a hundred millionth of a second, the world would have gotten much worse, the sun would have risen in the morning, but there would have been no light, and we would have lived in constant darkness."

"When you and Lusifer made the big plan three thousand years ago, did you think it was worth the risk?"

"We saw how much grief and misery evil created, we thought it was worth the risk, but only just."

"Storm didn't obviously."

"Storm would rather live with evil, than in constant darkness. He wasn't alone to think so, it was 50-50."

"Half wanted Dian dead?" Timmy was really shaken up now. It was Dian's own people God was talking about.

"They were scared. In order for the formulas to work, there was a time setting afterwards for the last formula. Dian and Lusifer felt in their hearts that the last formula had succeeded, but they didn't get the answer until the sun rose, not the next day but the day after. If it was light it was a success, if it was dark, it had failed and then it would be pitch black forever."

"So that's why Storm tried to kill Dian?" asked Timmy.

"It was, but the danger wasn't over because Storm failed to kill her. There was complete chaos and anarchy in Falkland, fear brought out the worst in people. Dian and Lusifer tried over and over again to say that the formula had worked, but the fear had gained too much hold of the druids and the black angels.

It wasn't just Dian who was in danger, there were some who wanted to kill the one they loved, to save them from living in total darkness."

"Couldn't they just wait and see if it had succeeded?"

"Had they waited, and it had failed, then death would have been dark too. The other spheres weren't affected in the same way as the earth. It was possible to get there if they did so before the sun rose."

"How come everybody survived the night?"

"Dian used thyme, it made everybody fall asleep, at the same time she put a protection around Falkland, so no one would come in from outside and hurt us while we slept.

Flora was the only one who didn't fall asleep, she's the one who taught Dian how to use herbs. Flora tried to kill Markus, so Dian took Markus home and looked after him until the sun rose."

"I still don't understand why Lusifer tried to strangle you."

"Lusifer understood that Storm would never try to kill Dian. Storm and Lusifer have been best of friends for more than three thousand years. Lusifer knew that Storm had to be brainwashed and there was only one who had the strength large enough to do so. It was a test for Lusifer. I wanted to see if he was willing to fight for his best friend."

"Did you really think it was funny that he tried to strangle you?"

"It was the final proof that Lusifer has a strong core."

"I understand that you were shocked in your foundations."

"Lusifer is more shocked, he was the one that had to tell Dian when to say the last two formulas. Lusifer was so nervous that day that Dian kept asking him what it was."

"What did he answer?" asked Timmy.

"Lusifer said it was the last day his DNA changed. All the black angels have received new DNA so they can live on earth now. So has Dian, so she can be with Lusifer for real."

"Since he is heavenly, and she is earthly?" asked Timmy.

"That's right," God replied.

"There is no one who has been so close to being properly together as the two of them."

"It was lucky that Dian picked up Lusifer's thoughts," said

Timmy.

"It wasn't luck, they have been training together for more than two thousand years. On the same day the formulas were to be said, Dian was cooking. She couldn't even put the peeled potatoes into the pot before Lusifer said she had to come to the living room. The same thing happened again and again. Dian tried to peel potatoes, but Lusifer shouted at her all the time.

The sun shone through the window, and Dian saw a sharp new colour every time she lay down on the couch and closed her eyes. Dian thought her DNA needed the colours from the sun to be activated."

"Wasn't that so?" asked Timmy.

"It was, but it was also so Lusifer could practise when she should say the formulas, he calculated her reaction time."

"No wonder he was so nervous," Timmy said.

"Dian didn't know the importance of what she was doing, she just thought she was activating Lusifer's DNA, when she sent the DNA-link and the love link around him. She finished by sending a lying number eight around. When number eight came to the finish line, Lusifer and the rest of us collapsed. Dian is used to us collapsing all the time, so she doesn't think much about it. As usual Sus was the only one who didn't collapse, he told Dian about the time settings, the sun had to rise twice before we knew if she had succeeded. Dian knew she had succeeded, she felt it in her heart."

"Did you have any doubts?" asked Timmy.

"I didn't, not this time. I have learned that the heart knows for sure."

"When Dian trusted her heart so did you," said Timmy. The sun came out from behind a big dark cloud.

"There you can see," said Timmy, it went well.

70

Dian met Milkyway on the square.

"Storm is my new dad," she said.

"Has he adopted you?" asked Dian.

"Volven and Gilde thought it was enough with eleven trolls, they asked if Storm wanted five star trolls."

"And he did?"

"He did. Storm gave us new names; he wants us to have a normal childhood."

"What is yours?"

"Honey Milkyway. On a daily basis my name will be Honey, and Honey Milkyway when he's mad at me."

"And your brothers?"

"Robin Sunshine, Falk Moonshine, Scott Stardust and Hauk Heaven."

"Do your brothers like living in Falkland?"

"Scott is very happy because he's in love with Blair."

"Sounds good, you will see a lot of Blair and Andrew, and Blackbird and Snowflake."

"And Timmy Willie," said Honey. "I have visited him a couple of times already, he's funny. If I need a mother, I'll come to you."

"We live just after the pub, it's a small house that shows all the colour it has had."

"I know, I saw the sign Lusifer put up to protect Snowflake. Only I realised that the sign was nonsense."

"You don't believe in the big bad wolf?"

"Not here in Falkland, perhaps in the outer bulwark like it used to be in the old days."

"Is it the old days already?" said Dian and laughed.

"I'm five years old," said Honey, "everybody will be six next year, we must normalise ourselves to live on earth."

Lusifer came and stood beside them. "Nice name you got," he said to Honey.

"Do you like it?" said Honey and blushed.

"It's very nice," said Lusifer. "Would you like to keep an eye on Snowflake when I'm not here?"

"I'd love to," said Honey and smiled at him.

Blair came and dragged her along. "Stop flirting with Lusifer," she said.

"There's something about him," said Honey.

"Stop being so silly," Blair said and rolled her eyes. She turned and shouted at Lusifer, "You have to be careful with who you are charming to."

They looked after Blair and Honey, who ran down the street.

"I understand what she means," said Lusifer. "Usually, I can't show who I am."

Falk Moonshine came over to Lusifer and asked if he knew when Storm would come home from his trip.

"Nobody knows, but I have promised Storm to stay in your house until he gets back."

"Great!" said Falk. He took Lusifer's hand and dragged him along. "I want you to see my new room. When I stayed with Volven and Gilde I slept in a drawer that hung on the wall, now I share a huge room with Hauk." They strolled down the street hand in hand to Sus' old house.

Falk ran up the stairs which went in a straight line from the double front door and up to the first floor.

Luckily there's six bedrooms in the house, thought Lusifer as he went up the broad stairs.

Falk's room had a view of the street and Falkland Palace. The whole room bathed in light. The dark brown wooden bed stood by the window and was covered with light yellow, light green and turquoise pillows. The walls were dark grey-green, and the curtains had squares in grey and green. It looked like the colours of a dark wood where the sun rays shone through all the leaves.

One of the walls was covered with dark brown shelves full of books, boats and planes. A falcon sat on top of the shelves watching them. In the middle of the wooden floor was a round table with two dusty pink armchairs. The carpet was light green with long threads of wool that stood straight up and looked like grass.

"Have you tamed the falcon?" asked Lusifer.

"I have, I open the window every day so it can fly for a while, and suddenly it comes back again."

"You like it here, don't you?"

"I do! I was wondering if you could tell me a story, if you could read only for me?"

"Which one would you like to hear?"

"Guess!"

"The little blue bird…"

"Correct!" Falk shouted happily and sat down on the bed.

He clapped his hand on the mattress. Lusifer sat down next to him. Falk was so pleased, he could hardly sit still, he was about to hear a story only for him.

71

Elwin and Lennie ran the pub in the middle of Falkland. The pub was in a small side street, with a small park in front. On the lawn stood a bench under a large oak tree. Most sat on the street outside the pub when the weather wasn't too bad. During the day the pub was a cafe, Sus delivered cakes and God biscuits.

They served only Scottish ales, whisky and rum, coffee and cakes, but since everything was of the best quality, nobody missed anything.

Lennie and Elwin were the only black angels with long hair to their waist, the rest of them had hair to their shoulders. Elwin's hair was dark grey, and Lennie's hair silver.

Dian and Lusifer sat and drank coffee with Elwin and Lennie when Lukas came by.

"I miss Raven," said Lukas to Lusifer.

Most people missed Raven, but Lusifer had taken back all his parts, no one saw Raven any more.

"Can't you make Raven a separate person again?" asked Dian.

"I've been thinking about it," said Lusifer. "Raven is funny, I'm more serious."

"You're funny enough," said Dian.

"I will ask God for help."

"Maybe Raven can stay with Sus now that Medusa has travelled back to Greece," said Lennie.

"It was probably too cold for her here," said Elwin.

"It wasn't just that, Sus lost interest in her," said Lusifer.

"What will happen to Blair and Andrew?" asked Dian.

"They'll stay, Sus will need some help with them."

"Markus needs a place to stay too," said Dian.

"I heard Oak came back and took Flora by storm, he left the weeping purple willow on the mountain," said Elwin.

"So, Raven and Markus are moving in with Sus," said Lusifer.

"I think it will be one more," said Dian.

"Who?"

"Angus, Angina was too attached to her father. Angus felt he was playing second fiddle all the time."

"Four bachelors, that sounds like great fun," said Lukas, he almost sounded envious.

"The best part is that Sus doesn't have to worry about anything," said Dian. "Raven makes toys for Blair and Andrew, Angus teaches them how to tame oxen, Markus how to play different instruments, and they already know how to bake."

"Sounds like they have everything they need," said Lusifer.

"Nice concert you held," said Lennie to Lukas, Lusifer and Elwin.

"God wanted me to start the angel choir again," said Lusifer.

"You didn't bother with too many angels," said Elwin.

"No, it's just the closest ones."

"Except Storm and Jesus," said Lennie, "it isn't everyone who has received a nice voice from God. I've heard that Oak is God's little brother."

"That's right," said Lusifer, "you can tell by their tousled hair."

"Why have they hidden it?" asked Elwin.

"Oak and God had a fight a long time ago, they both wanted to be with Gyda."

"That can't be it," said Lennie.

"God won and Oak gave up because his son would get the solar energy and be with Dian for the next two thousand years."

"Even though you and Dian were made for each other?" asked Lennie.

"That's what happened."

"Any chance of me borrowing your diamond dress and shirt?" Elwin asked Lusifer.

"Anytime," said Lusifer.

"You will look good in diamond clothes with your long hair and a hawk on the shoulder," said Dian.

"We'll just stroll up and down the street," said Lennie and laughed.

"We are actually going to get married," said Elwin.

"How come you're not married?" asked Lusifer.

"The bairns came too fast," said Lennie, "and afterwards we forgot. We're having a simple wedding."

"That's what they all say," said Lusifer and laughed, "it's going to be a full party anyway."

"Aren't you tired of all the formulas?" Elwin asked Dian.

"I'm starting to get used to everyone collapsing, that I'm the only one who thinks it's gone well."

"That's why I'll ask God to bring Raven back to life," said Lusifer. "He was the only one who believed when no one else did."

"God doesn't think it's going well, and neither do you," Lukas said astonished.

"We're struggling this time," said Lusifer.

"But you are completely calm," Lennie said to Dian.

"I feel in my heart that it went well."

"More coffee," said Elwin and smiled at her.

He admired Dian for the calm she had every time everyone lay strewn around her.

"You said we got the diamond clothes in beforehand because we succeeded," said Dian to Lusifer.

"The star people thought you and I should have the diamond clothes now because no one knows what's happening next. We are going to have a concert by the pond to celebrate. Are you coming?" Dian nodded.

"The concert begins at eight p.m. Time to leave," said Lusifer to Lukas and Elwin.

Dian and Lennie sat outside the pub until it started to get cold, then it was time to go to the Hidden Place. The choir stood in a semicircle by the pond.

Angus came and asked Dian if he could give her a hug. "I've never squeezed a diamond dress before," he said.

"You may!" said Dian.

"I never thought you were going to wear a tight-fitting diamond dress and silver boots."

"It feels like I'm naked since the dress is elastic."

"Naked underneath maybe," said Angus and laughed.

Dian smiled at him and said, "It keeps everything in place without tightening, it's temperature regulating and keeps me warm no matter the weather."

Angus bowed his eyebrows and asked if he could borrow it.

"You can borrow Lusifer's shirt and trousers instead."

The concert was about to begin. God and Oak stood on the left side, Midas, Lukas, Elwin, Markus, Lusifer, Sus and Raven stood in the middle with black large wings and black clothes. Only Lusifer wore diamond clothes. Falk and Hauk stood to the right, they were the only ones except God and Oak who didn't have wings.

"This is a day of joy," said God, "I have finally managed to persuade Lusifer to start the angel choir again. It's not a pure angel choir any more, Oak and I have joined, so have Hauk and Falk.

We are not quite sure what the choir will be called, if anyone has any suggestions we will gladly accept.

The reason I'm talking and not Lusifer, who is the leader of the choir, is that the first song we are singing, which is the finest song we know, is made by a man I think looks like a crow, maybe he's one of us who knows."

God smiled and looked down for a while before continuing. "You know me, I'm not a good speaker, I talk about something else all the time. Where was I?"

"The song is dedicated to," said Sus.

"Right, right," said God slowly. "It is dedicated to Lusifer and Dian because they managed the penultimate formula. We have to celebrate beforehand in case everything goes to hell, we don't know until tomorrow morning at seven minutes to seven.

As you can see, I've brought Raven back to life again, he's the only one who thinks Dian has succeeded once again. Welcome back Raven!"

Everyone clapped and Raven bowed.

"Do you think Dian has succeeded once more?" asked Angus.

"I don't," shouted Raven and flapped with his wings. All fainted except Dian and Sus.

"I was just kidding!" said Raven, but it was too late.

Dian, Sus and Raven sat down at one of the tables. Sus poured whisky for himself and Dian. As usual Raven wanted brown rum.

"When do you think they will wake up again?" Raven asked Sus.

"Lusifer usually wakes up after half an hour, but I don't think he will this time. The others take considerably more time."

"We will be wasted," said Dian.

"Skål!" said Sus. "For us keeping the fort as usual." They held three glasses high up in the air and toasted.

The concert didn't begin until five in the morning, just before the sun rose. Then Raven, Sus and Dian lay and slept with their heads on the table and three empty bottles in front of them.

72

Elwin and Lennie wouldn't join the black angels any more, they thought two thousand years was enough. They enjoyed running the cafe and pub instead.

"What do you think we should do at our wedding?" asked Elwin.

"I want a procession up to the pond. It has become a tradition for the black angels to stand on each side of the road playing. What do you think they should play?"

"Spellbound," said Elwin.

"I'll let Lusifer know so they can rehearse," said Lennie.

"What about Snowflake and Blackbird, should they gallop or walk?"

"They can do the walk where they lift their feet high up in the air, while bending their necks."

"Everything is going to be fine," said Elwin. "We need to celebrate again since the last formula went well."

"I heard that Lusifer slept in Dian's bed on Arran for twenty-four hours afterwards, he was completely worn out."

"It's no wonder, it was his responsibility to give her the formula, and make sure she got to the finish line at the right time."

"What about the rest of the music?"

"Eloise"

"You think Midas should sing since he's with Eloise?"

Elwin nodded. "And of course, we would need some drums, I love drums."

"The black angels can play the drums while everybody sits down to eat."

"The tables and benches can look like they've been carved from ice, and the tablecloths can be made of icicles."

God came strolling with his daily delivery of biscuits, he sat down at the table.

"Good concert you held," said Lennie. "It was fun to see that you and Oak had rehearsed the same dance steps as Hauk and Falk. It worked well with all the black angels going berserk in the middle, and the black angels who didn't join the choir, played drums and guitars."

"Is it any song in particular you were thinking about?"

"Ruby Don't Take Your Love to Town."

"Yeah, that one worked well," said Elwin.

"It was actually a lot of fun," said God. "It was just a shame that Sus, Raven and Dian slept through it all."

"You have been given a new assignment," said Elwin, "we are getting married."

"What song did you have in mind?"

"Spellbound."

"I think we will be both entranced and mesmerised by that song," said God.

He opened the box of biscuits and offered them one. Lennie brought him a cup of coffee.

Dian came strolling and God clapped on the bench next to him.

"Awake?" asked Elwin. Dian nodded.

"Hangover?" asked Lennie.

Dian nodded again and sat down next to God.

Lennie fetched another cup of coffee and God offered her a biscuit.

"There's something I didn't tell you yesterday," he said.
"What?" asked Dian.
Lennie and Elwin looked curiously at God.
"It is, well you know?"
"No!" said Dian.
"It so happens that the diamond clothes you got, they have never been made or given to anyone before, it's a very special gift."

Dian waited, and Elwin and Lennie were dying of curiosity.
"It's like… you got such a great gift."
Dian waited for him to say more. Elwin and Lennie began to twist on the benches.
"It's like…" began God once more. "It's a very, very special gift. As I said: The star people have never made clothes from star diamonds before, so then it is clear that…"

God opened the biscuit box and offered everyone another biscuit. Lennie fetched more coffee and Elwin turned around and hid that he was yawning. Dian ate the biscuit and wondered what God was going to say next.

"A great responsibility comes with the clothes."
"Can we borrow them on our wedding day?" asked Lennie, "or is it dangerous?"
"It's not dangerous," God replied.
"What's so special about the clothes?" asked Elwin.
"They are not like other clothes," God replied.
"That, I have understood," Elwin said dryly.

Lusifer came and sat next to Lennie on the other side of the table. He was wearing the diamond clothes, so was Dian. It was as if the clothes were communicating with each other.
"Coffee?" asked Lennie.
"That's exactly what I need. What are you talking about?"

"I have no idea," said Elwin, he began to get seriously impatient. He didn't understand why Dian didn't shake God to find out what he knew, but Dian had become accustomed to them always saying a to her and never b.

Elwin asked Lusifer if he knew what was so special about the clothes.

"They talk and feel, they know where the other is and what is about to happen. The clothes are mind readers on a high level. I actually think they can alert you if there is danger on the move as well."

"That's what I was going to say," said God. "If there is danger on the move, the clothes will get warm."

"That is spectacular!" said Elwin. "Not only do they look good, but they're smart as well."

"And they are self-cleaning," said Lusifer, "they also make you light in mind and light in body."

"Would you mind lending them to me right now?" Lusifer nodded and entered the pub with Elwin.

"And you, Lennie?" asked Dian.

"I thought you'd never ask," said Lennie and got up.

God was left alone outside, he wondered how it was possible to make something so wonderful. Lennie and Elwin came back a little later, God gasped at the transformation that had happened to them. They shone like the sun and the moon.

"Wow! I have to say," said God.

He felt a feeling he had never known before; he wanted the diamond clothes. He looked down as he asked nonchalantly, "When is the wedding by the way?"

"Tomorrow," Elwin replied.

"Do you think we can borrow the clothes for so long?" asked Lennie.

"I don't think Dian and Lusifer will mind," replied God, and sent the biscuit box around once more.

"I think I have found a name for the choir," Lusifer said when he and Dian came outside again, wearing some of Lennie and Elwin's clothes. "I spoke to Angus yesterday, he wanted to join."

"Can he sing?" asked Lennie.

"Angus sang before he learned how to speak," said Dian. "He sang to Purple when he was a baby so he would stop crying."

"He is very good," said Lusifer, "almost as good as me."

Elwin laughed and said, "It takes a lot for you to say that, at least I haven't heard so during the last two thousand years."

"What was the name you thought of?" asked Dian.

"I counted the choir members and there are twelve of us."

"The Disciples?"

"Right, what do you think?"

"Maybe it could work," God said, "we can try the name and see how it goes."

"I like it," said Elwin, "especially since Jesus is not in the choir."

"Crow's Choir," said Dian.

"I like that much better," said God, "I'm tired of disciples." Lusifer laughed and said, "The choir of crows."

"The Crow Choir," said God and smiled, "it really is the choir for crows."

73

Blair and Honey were standing on the stairs when Dian opened the door the next day. They wondered if she would join them, they wanted to go to Edinburgh for some shopping.

"No!" Dian said immediately. She called out to Lusifer and asked him if he wanted to go shopping.

"I'd love to," said Lusifer. "When do we leave?"

"The train leaves in twenty minutes," replied Blair.

"We'll get Storm and the rest of the boys too. You can pick up Andrew, then you can meet us at the train station," said Lusifer to Dian.

Dian flew up to Sus' house and knocked on the door. Sus and Andrew opened it. Dian asked Andrew whether he would go to Edinburgh with Storm, Lusifer and the other bairns. Andrew jumped up and down with joy.

"You didn't want to?" asked Sus.

"You know I hate shopping just as much as you do. I'll deliver Andrew on the train station, then you and I can fly to Taos."

"Do you think I should bring cake?"

"Always bring cake," said Dian.

Andrew lay down on her wings and they flew to the train station. The others were already there waiting, none of the children had been to Edinburgh before. Andrew jumped off Dian's wings, and she flew back to Sus. He stood ready with the cake in his hands, it was a tall one.

"You intend to offer the whole tribe in Taos some cake?"

"It should be enough," said Sus. He lifted slowly from the ground with the cake in his hands.

"We can't fly fast; I've never flown with a cake before."

74

"You must be joking!" said Dian angrily.

"No, I'm not," said Lusifer. "Sus won't learn it from me, you are the only one he's listening to."

"I don't love him, he's my best friend."

"You only have to do it once, he learns fast."

"Why?"

"Sus is the new leader of the black angels. The leader has always been the first lover."

"It has only been you."

"It has, but now it's tradition. Everyone who is the leader of the black angels, becomes the first lover for all eternity. Sus hasn't managed to crack the code yet."

"After all he's been looking at us."

"It hasn't helped. You have to explain and show him."

They went home to Sus. He barely managed to open the door before Dian dragged him behind some large trees which stood right by the pond.

Lusifer was peeking behind one of the trees. Dian wore the diamond dress, Sus didn't need to be persuaded, he could hardly restrain himself.

"Listen up!" said Dian. "I lie down on the grass, you let your hands slide up under the dress and caresses my breasts slowly, then let your hands slide down on my hips, still slowly, then you'll come as slowly as you can. You should feel every inch of both me and you. Once you have done it twice, you can do whatever you want."

"No underwear?"

"Nope."

Dian lay down on the grass, Sus had to resist the urge to do everything at full speed. He didn't know what to do to control himself. Then he noticed Lusifer behind a tree.

I'm gonna show him, Sus thought.

He began to stroke his hands underneath Dian's dress; he could feel everything times a hundred. Sus did it so slowly that he hoped time would stop. He could feel that Dian wanted him too. When his hands were on their way down to her hips, he almost exploded, but he forced himself to do it slowly.

Sus could feel that Dian was struggling too. She kissed him, her tongue was deep inside his throat. His emotions went crazy, but he was still in control. After the second time, they were both worn out by the emotional strain.

"I understand what you mean," Sus said when they lay on their backs in the grass after a long while, completely shattered. "The big question is who I should be with."

"It won't be me."

"Too bad, we would have been so good together."

Lusifer came out from his hiding place, and Sus walked slowly home in deep thoughts.

75

Lusifer complained to Lennie that Dian had thrown him out.

"What happened?" asked Lennie.

"I tested her," Lusifer replied.

Elwin came and overheard what they were talking about. He started yelling at Lusifer, "You must be out of your mind! No one has been tested so much in such a short time before. You even said you were tired of God's testing, but you got tested during three thousand years, Dian has been tested just as much during the last three months."

"It has been necessary," said Lusifer.

"I know," said Elwin calmly, "but I strongly doubt that the test you used was necessary. What was the test by the way?"

"I wanted to see if she loves me," Lusifer said quietly.

"Everyone can see that she does."

"I got her to be with Sus."

"You did what?" roared Elwin. "Have you completely lost it? You've never been so happy before."

"I know," said Lusifer and looked down. "I got scared that it wouldn't last."

"No need to be scared anymore," said Elwin. "It won't last the way you behave."

Lusifer laid his head on the table and closed his eyes.

"Do you want the whisky that is seventeen or eighteen years old?"

Lusifer looked up and saw that Dian had put two glasses in front of him.

"That one is seventeen," she said pointing at one of the glasses.

"Which do you like best?"

"The seventeen."

Lusifer took the other glass and toasted with her. He didn't know what to say.

"It's over," said Dian, "we forget what happened and start over again."

Lusifer took a deep breath, and suddenly he collapsed.

"And here we go again!" said Elwin and laughed.

"You have to get tired of all the collapsing every time the tension gets too high."

"The good thing is that now I can drink two glasses of whisky," said Dian, and put her hand around one of the glasses while she swirled the whisky around.

"Not just the two of them," said Elwin and fetched the bottle with the rest of the seventeen year old whisky from Arran and toasted with her.

"I have been listening to Lusifer for more than two thousand years, you don't have to wonder if he cares or not."

Dian smiled at him and clinked her glass against his. Before Lusifer collapsed, he had heard that Dian said it was over. His heart had started beating so fast that he had collapsed at once. Raven came walking and asked what they were toasting for.

"We're toasting for Lusifer," said Dian.

"No need by the look of it," said Raven. "Toast for me instead." Elwin laughed and fetched a bottle of rum.

"What's going on here?" asked Lukas. He had followed Raven.

"No idea," said Raven.

"What's wrong with him?" asked Lukas and pointed at Lusifer.

"Who cares," said Raven.

"Have a glass, Lusifer will probably wake up at some point, then he'll have missed once again that I'm drinking and enjoying myself with Dian."

Raven toasted with Dian and laughed. Lukas laughed too; he was just happy his best friend had returned.

76

Lusifer stood on the small bridge by the pond. God came and stood beside him.

"Love trouble?" asked God. Lusifer nodded.

"You helped me last time," said God, "now I will help you."

"What can you do?"

"I'm God, there's a lot I can do, but right now I'm gonna help you as your father."

Lusifer wiped away a tear and God began to speak.

"Yesterday it was Dian who took you back, now it's you who will take Dian back."

"I know Dian is thinking of Sus, but that's only because she wants to be finished with him. She told me she wanted to be eaten alive by Ellie if you disappeared."

"It sounds like a declaration of love," said Lusifer.

"The testing of you and Dian is over, go home and enjoy life. You look gorgeous in your diamond clothes by the way, is there a chance that Gyda and I can borrow them?"

"Do you have any plans?"

"We were going for an evening walk up to Oak and Flora. Gyda wants to show up one last time for Oak I think," said God and laughed.

Lusifer took off his clothes and gave them to God. He wrapped his wings around his naked body and strolled down the road. "I'll send the diamond dress over with Dian," he said without turning.

77

Raven was right, thought Lukas, everything was turned upside down. The tin soldier had managed to stand in the boat to the first tree, and Lukas had cleaned Raven's house.

That was before God and Gyda moved in, and Raven moved out. Lukas had never thought that he would have a girlfriend, and Raven would be a bachelor. The most attractive except Lusifer were bachelors, there were four of them, and they all lived in the same house.

It didn't seem like they were stressed out about it, they actually seemed happy. Everyone thought as long as you had a girlfriend everything was fine; Lukas would have exchanged Dine for Raven anytime.

Raven came strolling and asked if Lukas had any coffee.

"Give me two minutes," said Lukas.

Raven had passed his old house on the way to Lukas. God was drinking coffee in the garden with Timmy Willie wearing Lusifer's diamond clothes. Raven looked at the house he had been involved in refurbishing across the street. The radio was on loud, there were no visiting hours there.

Lukas was always happy to see him, no matter when he appeared. They didn't talk much, sometimes they just sat in deep thoughts, but it was always good to be with Lukas. Raven enjoyed living with Sus, Andrew, Blair, Markus and Angus too. He had seen how much Sus struggled after he had been with Dian, he told Lusifer to erase Sus' memory, it had helped, Sus was himself again and he and Dian were once again just friends.

Lukas came out with freshly brewed coffee, and Raven asked if they should start a company together.

"What kind of company?" asked Lukas.

"We meet up daily, drink coffee and find out," Raven replied. "Excellent idea," said Lukas and lit his pipe.

78

Lusifer needed to rearrange his memories. Dian had to send HC 202 around him. She arranged his memories so he could manage to live with all the evil he had seen. He transformed into Satan each time he visited evil, to see what they were doing. Satan wasn't evil, he didn't have to be, his reputation was constantly updated by the Christians. And thereby they protected him from evil, so they didn't discover who he really was.

It didn't matter if they found out that he was Lusifer, what mattered was if they found out that he had a good heart. Volven was the only one who had seen straight through him, but she never told anyone.

Lusifer had insisted that he was the one who should watch Dian. He had stood in her hallway looking at all the scoundrels who gathered in her garden night after night.

Satan had a reputation as the worst of them all. He said they should wait until they arrived in Edinburgh before they attacked her, it would be so much more fun killing her at Greyfriars Kirkyard.

The scoundrels agreed, most of all they looked forward to the great gathering at the Kirkyard on the fourteenth. Satan said they had to tell everyone they wanted to come, to show up on March fourteenth. The rumour had flown around the earth multiple times.

Dian had followed Lusifer's thoughts.

"The first five digits in Pi is 31415," she said. "And that is not a coincidence."

"Still impossible to hide anything from the best nutcracker in the whole universe," said Lusifer and smiled.

"The rumour flew around the earth when the scoundrels were gathering at Greyfriar Kirkyard, and around the earth, it is three hundred and fourteen times longer than the diameter."

"Not to forget, the year was two thousand and fifteen," said Lusifer. "It is not a coincidence that the month is the start of pi, the day the next number, and the year the third."

"Why is pi so important?"

"It's endless, but it's also the number of the most important day, month and year in history.

You needed all the help you could get, why not get help from earth itself. If God killed evil a little here and there, evil would only get fragmented into many small parts and become even more dangerous. When God took his right hand down on Greyfriars Kirkyard, I stood in the form of Satan and killed those who tried to escape."

"Who came up with Satan's look?"

"It was God, he wanted Satan to look ridiculous, with a horn on each side of the forehead, and orange flames where the eyes should have been.

We laughed a lot about how stupid Satan looked. I wondered for a long time if the world would be deceived by Satan."

"What did God think?" asked Dian.

"He was sure the world wanted to be deceived."

79

"The moon is off its orbit," Lusifer told Dian, "it's about to get really dangerous."

"Can't Einstein help you?"

"No, Einstein has no idea how to get the moon back."

No one knew how to get the moon back to its orbit, and as usual the formula was time sensitive, Dian had thirty seconds. Lusifer could see that Dian knew it was urgent, but she was as calm as she always was when it really mattered.

Dian set up the truth formula so she would do everything right. The moon had been out of its orbit for 5.7 seconds each year for the past five years. She didn't have time to figure out how long that would be, so she used the reverse formula 956. The moon had gone down to the left 5.7 seconds for five years.

956 was sent to the left to pick up 5.7 seconds during the last five years, then she sent 659 to the right.

The moon went back up where it belonged, but suddenly it tore loose and was in full spin and fall. Dian went inside the moon, the moon was spiralling down again, it was on a collision course with the earth.

Dian managed to get the moon back up again. She could see the silver thread that was connected to the moon's orbit, she hung the moon on the thread, and went down to earth again.

The time was 10.43 in the evening, on the ninth of June 2015. Lusifer collapsed as usual, what was unusual was that Sus had collapsed as well. Dian wondered who had given her the information, she concluded that only one knew what had happened, and that was the moon itself. She went outside and looked up at the pale light blue moon.

"I owe you one," said the moon.

"Good, I'll see you soon," said Dian and laughed.

"I think it's so weird that I didn't understand that Sus originally was your son," said Dian. "He is the leader after you, and that says something."

"In this life he's a good friend. Storm and Sus' last name is Ark, or Arch originally, they were two of the four original archangels."

"And the two others?" asked Dian.

"Guess!"

"You and Raven. Who was Sus' mother?"

"It was Wicca. Sus has no evil in him. I had some or have some, I don't know any more. I needed to in order to spend so much time with evil."

"How did you manage to stay good?"

"I had to choose every day. Go inside my heart and see if it's good." Dian went inside Lusifer's heart. It was completely white, the only thing she found otherwise was a small black heart. She picked it up and showed it to him.

"It's the germ of evil. From that heart you can create the greatest and worst evil in the world."

"We should destroy it," said Dian.

"It can't be destroyed," said Lusifer. "That's why I'm giving it to you, so you can keep it in a safe place."

"I know someone who can," said Dian.

She held the heart in her hand, and flew up to the moon in her nightgown, it was long with white whales. Dian hoped the moon was blind.

She landed in the middle of the moon. It was one big room,

the only thing that was there, was a small frosted box. Dian lifted the lid and put the black heart in it. When she put the lid back on, lightning struck the box from the inside. The heart was broken into millions of parts and was more dangerous than ever before.

If Dian lifted the lid now, Heimdal wouldn't have time to blow Gjallarhorn to alert another Ragnarok, it would be over in a second. All the black bits turned into star dust inside of the box.

Dian went down to earth again. Lusifer asked what had happened. Dian told him, and Lusifer breathed a sigh of relief. He didn't know for sure how dangerous it was to take the black heart out of his heart, if it was stronger than Dian. If she had lost it, it would have been the end of everything.

"I have put a little grey stone in your heart," said Dian, "you won't collapse anymore."

"We'll see, you and Sus not only have a little grey stone in you, you have a lot.

It was Lilith who got the moon off course. She used a magnet; the nutcrackers had made the magnet so strong that the moon lost its grip."

"Do you know why?" asked Dian.

"Lilith has always been scared of being betrayed. The nutcrackers have always predicted that it would happen in the month of March 2015." Lusifer looked at Dian to see if she understood what he just said.

"The Mayan Indians received the wrong time," said Dian surprised.

"The Mayans managed to fool Lilith, but not the nutcrackers. They tried over and over, to tell her that the Mayans predicted the wrong year and date, but she wouldn't listen. That's why they made the magnet, those who betrayed Lilith would be killed by the moon, it was supposed to suck all the energy out of them."

"It was really dangerous for a while," said Dian.

"It was. No one expected that you had to say the formulas three more times."

"Sus told me you see Storm regularly," said Dian.

"We have loved each other for a very long time."

"I can be with Sus when you are with Storm."

"Would you let Ellie eat you alive if I disappeared?"

"I'll take it back, since you almost died yesterday, and I never know when you're going to die."

"I love you so much that I won't let Ellie eat me alive," said Lusifer and looked closely at Dian. "I don't feel like sneaking around with Storm anymore."

"I feel the same," said Dian. "Now it's just the two of us."

"It was the horrible nightgown that did it."

"Did what?" asked Dian.

"Made you so irresistible. It's like the butter package, you don't give a damn about how you look sometimes."

"So the nightgown is juxtaposed with the butter package?"

"It's the worst I've ever seen. No one wears a huge nightgown with prints of white whales."

"I could never have been a fly on the wall with evil if I didn't have the spire of evil like you had. Do you think I have a small black heart in my heart as well?"

"I'll have a look," said Lusifer.

He went inside Dian's heart. A small pink heart lay there. Lusifer took it with him and gave it to Dian.

"It symbolises those who have been evil, but has become good," he said.

"What do we do with the heart?"

"I can take it up to the moon and lay it in the box with all the lightning. When it fragments into millions of parts I will lift the lid and release them. Then those who are evil will be good if they get hold of a small part."

As soon as Lusifer was back on earth again, Purple arrived.

Lusifer poured him a glass of whisky, and they sat by the fire in two armchairs. Purple looked at the fabric, it was iguanas caught with plant stems wrapped around them. Purple took a sip and said nothing as usual. Lusifer didn't say anything either, he just looked into the flames and felt the heat from the whisky. After a while he asked Purple if he wanted to join the choir, it was time for a rehearsal.

Purple nodded, and they walked side by side, without a word up to the Hidden Place. Angus and Oak spotted Purple at the same time, none of them could believe what they saw, the old Purple was back.

God went over to Lusifer and said, "Explain."

"Dian had a little pink heart in her heart, I took it up to the moon and put it in the box where the lightning strikes continuously. When the heart was fragmented up in millions of parts, I opened the lid. The pieces fell to the ground and one of the pieces must have hit Purple."

"I'm happy for Oak's sake," said God, "but I'm not sure I'm happy for you, maybe Dian wants him back now that he's himself again." Sus came and stood next to God and Lusifer.

They looked at Oak, Angus and Purple. Oak had regained a son and Angus had regained a brother and his best friend.

"Don't tell me," said Sus. "That's another bachelor."

"Afraid so," said God and laughed.

"I'm moving," said Sus, "then Purple can stay with Angus, Raven and Markus."

Lusifer said the choir practice was about to start. Sus told Purple he was moving to Antrim; Purple could stay in his room if he wanted to. The only rule was that he was a bachelor.

"Great," said Purple. "What's the first song you are rehearsing?"

"Somebody I Used to Know."

"Who sings the female part?"

"Wait and see."

"I'm moving in with you," said Purple to Angus.

"I heard Sus ask you."

"What do you reckon?"

"As long as you stay away from women, it's fine. They have some beautiful oxen a little further inland we can go and look at."

"You should move to Oxford."

"The ford and the ox," said Angus and laughed. "Makes sense, I could bring the oxen across the river by the ford in Oxford. That's more Dian's department, isn't it?"

"Maybe it's mine too," said Purple. "Maybe I have been hiding that side of me."

That's not the only thing you have been hiding, thought Angus.

"Take your coffee with you," Dian told Flora.

Flora could hear the choir from her garden, but Dian wanted her to see that Purple was back again. They sat down on a bench overlooking the choir.

Flora started laughing when she heard God sing the female part of "Somebody I Used to Know." She stopped laughing soon after and asked Dian if it was Purple standing beside Angus.

"Purple is himself again," said Dian.

"And you will still be with Lusifer?"

"I'll never give him up willingly."

"You and Lusifer are the only two who are made for each other," said Flora.

"You know why we didn't get to be together right away?"

"I'm not sure I follow."

"Oak made a bargain with God, they both wanted to be with Gyda. Oak said fine as long as his son got the solar energy and could be with the one who had the lunar energy."

"God sold you so he could be with Gyda. No wonder Lusifer has stayed away from him for so long."

"Purple is moving into Sus' house," said Dian.

"Everything falls slowly into place," said Flora.

Dian saw that the choir practice was over, Purple headed towards them.

She got up and went over to Lusifer.

"Originally I had a different name," said Dian.

"How the hell did you find out?" asked Lusifer.

"U is the second letter in your name. Those who were decoys have u as the penultimate letter. Angus, Jesus, Markus."

"I have never thought about it, but then I don't see patterns everywhere the way you do. You should be with Purple for two thousand years, that was the deal between Oak and God. Had you had your original name, you would have figured it out right away, that we were supposed to be together."

"My name was Lucy?"

"Lucy and Lusifer, it's pretty obvious, isn't it?"

"What about Lukas?"

"What about him?"

"Letter number two is a u."

"He is Lukas Evangelium, he is the unwritten chapter."

"The invisible ink," said Dian.

"It's the story about us, we are the guardians of the universe, Lukas has been guarding it."

"Big words," said Dian.

"It's hard to explain it with small words," said Lusifer.

Dian went to the kitchen to make a soup she hoped wouldn't look like puke.

Dian and Lusifer realised something was wrong when they went to bed in the evening. Lusifer tried to put his arms around

Dian, but he couldn't.

"Purple has left a curse," said Dian.

"The little pink bit from your heart only works if you want to be good yourself," said Lusifer, "Purple just pretended."

"He's good at it," said Dian.

She decided to go and see Flora and Oak.

"Tell me how I can take away Purple's solar energy right now," she said harshly to Oak.

"What has he done?" asked Oak.

"He has left a curse in our house."

"It was too good to be true," said Flora.

"The solar energy can't be taken away from him before the twenty-second of July," said Oak, "but there is a place he could be."

"The middle star of Orion's belt," said Flora.

Oak nodded. He had had a feeling something was wrong, ever since he saw the look Purple had in his eyes when he looked at Dian, while she walked over to Lusifer.

"We need the four original archangels," said Oak.

At the same time as he said it, Sus, Storm, Raven and Lusifer stood there. Oak explained what they had to do.

"Enough is enough," he said and looked at Flora. "Now my family is you, Dian and Angus, I can no longer bear Purple."

80

Einstein sat in God's garden, drinking coffee with him and Timmy. Dian passed by on the street.

God shouted at her, "Dian come and meet my good friend Einstein." Dian shook hands with Einstein and started to laugh, *there it was again, the tousled hair.*

"You don't happen to be related?" she asked. They looked at each other and laughed.

"Einstein has given us a formula neither me nor Timmy can solve," said God.

Dian looked at the formula: mo in second x 30 in third = m in third x 6 in third divided by 100. Dian set up the formula further.

2 x 9 = 36 divided by 100 = 33+3 = 2

"The answer is two," said Dian. "What is it for?"

"It's a new and ground-breaking way to solve formulas," Einstein replied. "You realised that it didn't say zero, the circle stands for the letter o and the letter m is of course mass, you are solving a formula made by me after all.

You also understood that you had to go to both sides of = to retrieve the third number 3 so it became 9.

The third you understood was, when 100 stands under the line it stands for a half. Half of 6 is 3.

Then you understood that when it says x, it doesn't have to mean that it should be multiplied, maybe it should just stand like that. It's about seeing completely new patterns. Instead of 3+3 which is 6, it's 2-3s you saw therefore it became 3+3=2, which is the correct answer."

"Is the formula about seeing new patterns?" asked Dian.

"Everybody should have fifty-two screws loose like you have," said Einstein and laughed.

"How many loose screws do you have?" asked Dian.

"A hundred and two," Einstein replied, "but that was after I died, before I only had eleven loose screws."

"You can see it in the famous photograph of him," said God.

"How you been?" Dian asked Timmy.

"I'm excited about meeting Purple; I have never met him before. Maybe he will come and visit me, since my windows are purple."

"He has been inside your house once before."

"He has?" said Timmy surprised. "Then he knows where I live."

81

Raven flew high above Falkland and sang "Sailing".

He saw Lukas and Dine come out of their house. He dived down the street and flew low with the rest of the Crow's Choir up to the Hidden Place.

Raven was the best man for both of them, they didn't want anyone else. Sus had made the wedding cake, but Raven was the one who had decorated it with paper boats, tin soldiers and rats made of marzipan and light grey feathers.

It looked great, thought Raven, *it was all about making the cake personal.*

He and Blackbird had decided how the table should look. Raven thought water and stones would look great, the water followed the long table down the grassy slope and splashed into the pond at end of the table.

The guests sat on large logs on both sides of the table. The plates were made of wood, and the glasses looked like the drink you filled it with, you could only see the drink and not the glass, when you had finished drinking, the glass was gone.

Raven had let Flora make all the food; he was more interested in the decorations. He wondered how he should decorate so Lukas understood that he appreciated him. He asked Lusifer.

"What Lukas appreciates the most," Lusifer said, "is the paper boat with the tin soldier on board."

Raven run up to the Hidden Place. He made a whole row of

tin soldiers which stood in their respective paper boats at the top of the burn.

When Lukas said, "I do", the long row of tin soldiers passed them on their way to the pond with a long row of rats swimming behind.

82

Markus and Angus sat and ate the cake Sus had left for them. Sus had decided to stay, the bairns wouldn't move to Antrim, they thrived in Falkland.

"Are you sad?" asked Markus.

"No, it was too good to be true," Angus replied.

"I don't know if you know," said Markus, "but you have a friend in me."

"I like you better as a friend than a stepfather. You look much better now than you did as a middle-aged man."

"I would have done anything for Flora," said Markus.

"How is it to see Flora and Oak together again?"

"When you love somebody, you want to set them free."

"Skål for Flora!" said Angus and lifted the small crystal glass with hagberry wine against Markus' glass.

"Hear! Hear!" said Markus.

Hagberry wine tasted perfect alongside cheesecake.

"It's not too bad staying with Sus," said Angus.

"Best brother in the world."

"I can't say the same thing." Angus decided to forget about Purple.

"You are the best brother Dian could ever have dreamed of," said Markus.

"I have what I need," said Angus, "a family, a sister I love, and good friends, besides we live with a cake baker."

They laughed and raised their glasses and ate the rest of the cake.

83

Lusifer sat and stared at Dian. He had the same expression as when she was about to collapse.

"What is it?" she asked.

"You have no one to share everything you're experiencing with."

"I have my cat."

Lusifer laughed and said, "Is it enough that you won't lose your marbles? Elwin is still waiting for you to have a breakdown."

"I think I am extremely well planted on the ground. Maybe I'm a troll carved from a huge grey stone block."

"Maybe, but I think you should go and buy lots of sweets and watch a movie."

Nobody understood why Dian didn't lose it. She had made all the black angels, druids, God, Gyda and the star trolls earthly.

It had happened the day before they said it would. Lusifer had ordered her out to eat cake, it helped make Dian feel normal. She was going through the worst grinder that day, but as usual she knew nothing beforehand.

Dian couldn't make the slightest mistake and the formulas changed all the time. She was sitting outside the post office in Whiting Bay, eating cake and drinking coffee, looking at the sea. Everyone started to get nervous. It was almost twelve o'clock, and Dian hadn't begun to find the formula yet.

Lusifer planted a thought in her head, she had to look at their surnames.

Dian picked up a pad and a pen from her bag. She reasoned that God and Gyda's surname had to be Black, since it was Oak's, and he was God's brother. She didn't know Lucy's surname, but Dian knew she needed a surname where c stood as number two. She suddenly knew it had to be Eclipse, since it had played such a big role. She wrote down their names:

God, Gyda Crow
Sus, Storm Eclipse
Lucy Arch
Lusifer Black

She drew a line between God, Gyda and Black, Sus, Storm and Arch, Lucy and Eclipse, and Lusifer and Crow. In the surnames the c was the first letter, and it moved one letter for each surname. She looked at the surnames and wrote down the numbers and got 4745. The first names became 7487.

When she sent 7487 to the left and 4745 to the right, two treble cefs appeared, which went their separate ways, that was the formula. Dian had to draw the treble cef mentally in her head every time she sent the numbers around, often they were to be drawn in a mirror image.

The first time she said the formula in Whiting Bay was twelve o'clock. The times it was to be said was constantly changing, Dian set up the truth formula on both sides every time she said it. When it was 10.47 in the evening it was over, and Dian had said the formula sixteen times.

84

A thousand years ago, Lilith had cast a curse on the black angels. They had been swimming in the druid burn where they recharged their batteries.

After Lilith cast her curse it worked the opposite way, the burn stole their energy.

Dian used the reverse formula and went back a thousand years. She saw the black angels swimming, and Lilith who stood ready to send the curse upon them. Dian made Lilith send the curse over herself instead.

As soon as Dian reversed the curse, all the black angels went to Arran and swam in the Water of Life. The sun shone and the water sparkled, the burn was full of naked black angels as far as the eye could see.

85

Lusifer and Dian went to the horseshoe bench. The mountains around stood in a horseshoe as well, with the fjord far down below.

It was completely quiet; the sky was light grey with a narrow row of bright clouds. All they could hear was the stream trickling down the mountainside. They sat there without saying anything, they just looked at the landscape and seascape and listened to the silence. Dian looked at the steep mountainside with moss and grass.

"Want to roll down the hill?" she asked.

Lusifer looked at the rocks that lay all the way down. Dian flew to the top and placed the wings around her, then she rolled at full speed down the mountainside.

"Your turn!" she shouted at the bottom of the hill.

Lusifer placed the wings tightly around his body. It couldn't be worse than the spiral down to the inner core of earth.

"You won't be eaten!" shouted Dian.

Lusifer lay down and began to roll, he went faster and faster down the hill, it was the funniest thing he had ever done. The sun had just started its way up from the horizon.

A large herd of deer came slowly walking on the ridge of the closest mountain. The golden eagles flew high in the sky.

"You're everything I want," said Dian, "and everything I haven't thought of."

"Like deer at sunrise?"

"Something like that."

Dian wanted to stop time. She could hear the burn trickling in the background and felt the sun begin to warm. This was the best; it couldn't be any better.

"I have a feeling this isn't the first time we've been together," she said. Lusifer told her about the eighty lives she had lived with him, Sus and Storm high up on a small mountain shelf. It was steep down to the fjord.

"The four of us lived together?" asked Dian. "Who was I with?"

"You were with all three of us, but not at the same time. Storm made a watch. The figurine that looked like me stood on number nine, you stood on number six. Sus on number three and Storm on number twelve. He made moving arms on you. Every night when we went to bed, you took one hand towards one of the numbers. Sometimes you chose me too often, then Sus or Storm changed your hand, so it pointed towards one of them. I knew you liked me the most, so it didn't matter."

"What was it good for?" asked Dian.

"You loved every minute of it."

"Did none of you want to be with anyone else?"

"Sometimes Sus or Storm was with someone else when they went on a raid."

"You didn't go?"

"I wanted to be alone with you."

"What did we do with all the time we had on our hands?"

"You grew all sorts of weird things that were edible, even grapes and peaches. You planted a hedge of blackcurrants, then one with red currants and the last with hazels. The wind was sifted through each hedge, so it became windless.

Sus made all the food, he juiced and pickled and made

delicious cakes. Storm made wine from different berries and mead. You made a strong liquor in a copper still. Every full moon we drank it, while we watched the moonbeams hit the pitch black fjord far below, surrounded by the huge powerful mountains.

I made all our clothes; you grew the linen. I made dresses for you in different colours. Sometimes Sus and Storm brought silk from one of their raids. You always said they should bring coffee instead.

The beans were ground on the stone grinder Storm had made. Two large millstones lay heavily on top of each other, the stone on top moved slowly around, while the one underneath lay still, it was connected to the wheel in the river.

Storm made all sorts of things; his workshop was located by the waterfall. On each side of the house there were four broad stone stairs. You thought we should sit on the stairs and drink coffee and look at the fjord, or the squirrels."

"Was it in Istanbul they got the coffee?" asked Dian.

"It was."

"What else did we do?"

"Every morning I, Storm and Sus stood howling at the sunrise. You slept no matter what, until one of us brought you coffee in bed.

We swam in the fjord all year round, you on the other hand bathed in a large stone bowl that Haug had chiselled, it was made from green granite. Sometimes we couldn't help ourselves, then we poured a bucket of ice-cold water onto you.

Occasionally we went sailing, we had a boat from Nordland with a red sail. You and I were the only ones who bothered to row, Sus and Storm had rowed enough when they came back from one of their raids."

"Did we see any other people?" asked Dian.

"Loads, especially when the Vikings had gatherings. Our best friends were Håkon Håkonsson and Haug."

"Every time we were born again, we chose to be together, because we had so much fun."

"That's not the whole truth, is it?"

"No, we needed eighty lives together to pick up each other's thoughts within a second. When Sus shouted at you inside the bubble, then you reacted within a second when Arnold Clark came flying."

"Did we have any bairns?" asked Dian.

"We did, they all had black hair and grey eyes. In Norway at that time there was no one with black hair. The explanation why there suddenly were bairns with black hair was that a ship had sunk outside the coast with Spanish sailors, and some of the sailors managed to swim onshore."

"It was a beautiful sight with the three of you."

"I have the nicest thighs. They are round, hard and soft at the same time. You like my thighs, don't you?"

"Love your thighs," Dian replied.

"How come Storm and I can never sing no matter how many lives we live?"

"You used your energy for what you were good at."

"Tell me more about our lives high up on a narrow mountain ledge above Trollfjorden," said Dian.

"The house we lived in was completely hidden from the fjord; the whole house was made from stones we collected around the house. Storm built a stone maze underneath the house. On the outside lay a kiln, it looked like half a ball lying on the ground, the other half lay underground. The heat from the kiln went into the maze. It was possible to light the kiln from the inside of the house, during the coldest winter months.

Storm had made a sharp saw; it was attached from the workshop to the wheel which stood in the waterfall, so it was easy to saw. There were thick silky soft oak planks on the floor. Storm used blue granite which he sanded the floors with, together with soap and water. We had woven carpets and long silk curtains that fell lightly on the floor.

The only thing that was magical in the house were the stairs that went up to the bedrooms, a large white conch stood in the middle of the room, the stairs inside were made of mother of pearl. The roof was sloping and covered with glass roof tiles."

"Did you say glass roof tiles?" asked Dian surprised.

"They were so thick that they insulated much better than the roofs do today. It was a huge round hole in the middle of the floor in all the bedrooms with a thick glass we could walk on. The wall towards the fjord was made from different glass shapes. That's why no one could see the house, it looked like ice that was about to melt.

You used to ask Sus what you should do if you made a soup occasionally. Sus always asked: What does it taste like? And you always answered: Awful and awful. The answer he gave you was always the same. A pat of butter and some thyme. Then he always howled: Enough! Then you always shouted back: I haven't put anything into the soup yet. I always cooked if Storm and Sus were on a raid."

"Where did they go?"

"Scotland and Ireland. They only went to Istanbul if you started to whine about the coffee ending soon."

"Some scoundrels came to visit this morning," said Dian.

"What did they want?" asked Lusifer.

"They wanted a home, I said they could move to Loch Ness, only a few thousand returned, they said it was too cramped for them in Loch Ness, they wanted another home."

"Who were they?"

"It was the scoundrels from the underground in Edinburgh, there were millions of them."

"Where did you send them?"

"Trollsvann in Vestfold."

"That's fine, as long as you don't send them to Trollfjorden."

"Sixty lives we lived together in Trollfjorden," said Dian. "Where did we live the last twenty lives?"

"Ten on Island and ten in Ireland. No stories of shipwrecks were made up after we lived there, both Island and Ireland have always had black haired people. The house on Island was the nicest one we had ever lived in."

"We probably stayed on top of a geyser," said Dian.

"You remember?" asked Lusifer astonished.

"I begin to understand that every time I think I say something completely rubbish, it's true."

"You and Storm built the house on poles; it was a round stone house. Inside there was a large round glass wall, and inside the geyser sprang up, over the roof sometimes. It wasn't a huge geyser; it was more like a water fountain. We bathed both inside and outside. It was a terrace around the house where we sat on chairs that were light as a feather and looked like clouds. Storm made them from air.

The wooden floors had nuts in various types of wood. You decided how the table should look. It was huge and white, the legs looked like colossal icicles. Our beds were a different chapter. You slept in a grey-green leaf with bedding in gold. I slept in a turquoise wave with a dusty pink bedding."

"And the Ark brothers?"

"Sus slept in a cream cake decorated with light blue violets."

"And Storm's bed?" asked Dian.

"He slept in a bed that looked like a scarab, with yellow bedding."

"Where did we stay in Ireland?"

"You have probably guessed that we lived on the coast of Antrim. We stayed there the last ten lives, in a house that looked like a grey crow castle, with a tree in the middle surrounded by blue mountains."

"And the sea far below," said Dian.

"That's right," said Lusifer and smiled.

"I had a dream about a company called Herbert and Derbert."

"It was Sus and Storm's company.

They sold different items they had made in the square in Antrim. It was a market every Saturday. Sus made small cakes and Storm made knives and things out of wood. They sold children's clothes I had sewn, which the children had outgrown, and of course lots of vegetables, fruit and berries you had grown.

We didn't use coloured clothes any more. You wore light grey dresses, Storm brown leather clothes, and me and Sus wore brown and grey. We should learn how to pick up each other's thoughts without the help of any colours. We had a great time together; we didn't try to change each other."

86

The last life they lived together was in Antrim in the year of 1601. Four hundred and fourteen years would pass before they could be together again.

Lusifer bred white rabbits, Storm slaughtered them, and Sus made rabbit roasts. The rest of them Lusifer used to sew a white rabbit coat for Dian.

The sheep suffered the same fate, they became sheepskin jackets for Lusifer, Storm and Sus. The four Arabian horses they had, got a sheepskin under their saddles.

There were two mares and two stallions. Dian had the black stallion Blacky. Sus the red mare Honey, Lusifer the white stallion Snowy, and Storm a mare named Beauty.

Lusifer, Storm and Sus had left and gone to the sea early in the morning. Out sailing! It said on a note Dian found on the kitchen table. She knew it was the last time she would find a note where it said Out sailing!

Lusifer knew it too, but he kept it hidden from Sus and Storm. The bairns stayed with some friends.

Blacky galloped towards the steepest mountainside, Dian stopped him halfway, and turned to look at the crow castle one last time.

Sus and Storm asked Lusifer what was on his mind, they had never seen him so serious before.

"I'm thinking of the dinner that awaits us at home," he said.

"We always eat elsewhere when Dian cooks," said Storm, "that can't be the problem."

"You know it's the last life the four of us have together?" They stopped the horses and looked at him.

"What is it?" asked Sus.

"There will be big changes when we return."

They looked at him; but said nothing. He looked at them and said quietly, "Dian is dying right now."

"How?" asked Sus.

"She's climbing a steep mounting wall, a worm bites her in the foot, she falls and hit her head on a rock."

"We can prevent it, can't we?" asked Storm.

"We're not supposed to, Dian is going into the world of formulas."

Sus and Storm had lost their appetite. All three of them turned their horses and galloped towards the mountainside.

They found Dian laying on the ground. Lusifer lay her gently across Snowy's mane and held her tight while he put Snowy at a slow gallop home to the crow's castle.

Blacky stood waiting for them with his head down to the ground. Storm took the saddles of the horses while Sus and Lusifer cleaned the blood out of Dian's hair and removed her clothes. Lusifer had made a funeral dress with small moths everywhere in a peculiar pattern. He had asked Storm to make a casket in case something happened to one of them. Storm had made a casket with inlaid nuts and white lining.

They set up a marquee in the garden, they knew all of Antrim would attend the funeral. Sus made white cakes decorated with nuts still within their shells, he put four and four together like a four-leaf clover.

"Sometime in the future, we will crack nuts together," he said quietly to Dian.

"Are you going to say something at the funeral?" asked Lusifer.

"No, what about you?"

"I'm gonna read a poem. It's called Wandering Aengus."
Lusifer read the poem for Sus.

"I went out to the hazel wood,
Because a fire was in my head,
And cut and peeled a hazel wand,
And hooked a berry to a thread;
And when white moths were on the wing,
And moth-like stars were flickering out,
I dropped the berry in a stream
And caught a little silver trout.
When I had laid it on the floor
I went to blow the fire aflame,
But something rustled on the floor
And someone called me by my name;
It had become a glimmering girl
With apple blossom in her hair
Who called me by my name and ran
And faded through the brightening air.
Though I am old with wandering
Through hollow land and hilly lands,
I will find out where she has gone,
And kiss her lips and take her hands;
And walk among long dappled grass,
And pluck till time and times are done,
The silver apples of the moon,
The golden apples of the sun."

Lusifer and Dian had spent the last night together. They had slept on sheepskins covered in warm blankets in the middle of the house, where the rowan tree stood under the open sky. The stars shone bright, while the moonbeams hit the branches of the tree. Dian lay with her head on Lusifer's shoulder, none of them said anything. They awoke when the rays of the sun struck them. Lusifer kissed Dian, he forgot for a second what was going to happen that day. When he remembered, he just squeezed Dian hard, and they got up to have a last meal together.

"What do you want for breakfast?" asked Lusifer.

"Haggis, black pudding, tatties and coffee," said Dian and sat down by the table.

After they had eaten, Lusifer went away with Sus and Storm, on the table lay a poem.

The fountain mingle with the river
And the rivers with the ocean,
The winds of heaven mix forever
With a sweet emotion;
Nothing in the world is single;
All things by a law divine
In one another's being mingle…
Why not I with thine?
See! The mountains kiss high heaven,
And the waves clasp one another;
No sister flower would be forgiven
If it disdained its brother;
And the sunlight clasp the earth
And the moonbeams kiss the sea…
What are all these kisses worth
If thou kiss not me?

Dian heard Blacky neigh outside, he was ready. She mounted him and galloped towards the mountains.

87

Sus wondered if Dian wanted to compete with him. The other black angels became dizzy if they flew too fast.

Dian knew that Sus' eye colour changed to sharp yellow when he flew fast.

"Let's head for the moon," said Dian.

"Go!" said Sus and disappeared into the air.

Dian had transformed herself into a sharp yellow, she couldn't move, she understood the balance was wrong. She kept the sharp yellow colour in her eyes and hair and accelerated immediately. She passed Sus halfway to the moon. He saw her sharp yellow hair and did the same himself.

They landed on the moon at the same time. They spread their wings and flew in long semicircles down again. No colour could compare with the suns. Everybody thought the light was fastest, but it was the sunbeams.

88

God, Oak, Sus, Storm and Lusifer went with Dian when she drove to the horseshoe bench, it was one of their favourite places on Arran too. Since Dian's last visit, a lot of cotton grass and thistles had sprung up from the ground.

When they walked along the path a little sparrow chirped endlessly. God and Oak sat down on the bench alongside Dian, while Storm, Sus and Lusifer stood with their backs to them, arms crossed, overlooking the fjord.

"You know everything gets calmer now?" asked God.

"Hope so," said Dian.

Oak didn't say anything, he knew God was wrong, but he probably had his reasons to say so.

"Let's go to the Water of Life and swim," said Lusifer, "the rest of the black angels are there already."

Arran was full of ferns and foxgloves. When they arrived at the Water of Life, they all threw themselves into the water except Dian. She stood and watched a white foxglove; it stood on a slope among all the purple ones.

The ferns had reached the stage where they looked like dancing moths. She thought there was surprisingly little heather, but it was way too early for the heather to blossom, she had mixed up the seasons.

89

Purple was messing with Dian and Lusifer once again, Dian knew Oak wasn't able to do what had to be done, she decided to end him once and for all, she summoned Sus.

"Are you ready to put an end to Purple?" she asked. Sus nodded and asked what she had in mind.

"I want us to take the spiral down to the earth's inner core. I know the two of us can do it, but I don't think Purple can."

"I don't think so either," said Sus.

Dian went to Purple and asked if he wanted to take the spiral down to the inner core of the earth. Purple said yes immediately, he had always wanted to go down there, but he didn't know where the entrance was.

Sus waited for them by the entrance of the spiral. The first seventy feet down were not so cramped, it was possible to get enough speed before the spiral became too narrow.

"I'll go first," said Dian and wrapped her wings tightly, before she put her body into full spin. Suddenly she felt a thought was on its way, she decided to go up again.

Sus saw what happened, he created a grey thick smoke around the entrance, so Purple couldn't see what was happening, then he dived after Dian down the spiral, got hold of her hair and dragged her up again. When the thick smoke lifted, Purple saw that Dian was back again.

"Didn't you make it?" he asked.

"No, I felt a thought was on its way, so I decided to vacate."

Is it that easy to get up again? thought Purple.

"I'm going down," he said.

Sus had equipped him with black wings for the occasion. Purple wrapped his wings tightly and put his body into a full spin. Sus and Dian stood and watch Purple disappear down the spiral. Soon after they heard an insane cry. It was Purple, he was being eaten by Ellie.

90

Dian had done formula number one hundred and one. After that, it wasn't possible to fail. They had reached the finishing line. There was so much that had happened, Lusifer and Dian's feelings had been thrown up in the air constantly.

Dian doubted that Lusifer loved her. Lusifer saw that it didn't matter what he said. Dian didn't say anything, but Lusifer could tell that there had been too much trickery with her emotions. He decided to do the one thing, that would get Dian to believe in him again, he proposed to her.

Timmy came and said God was annoyed with him. Timmy missed God in his usual clothes.

"Tell God that the diamond clothes gain much more power if they are worn only on special occasions."

"Really?" said Timmy.

"That's how it works," said Dian.

Timmy ran along to tell God. He couldn't wait to have the good old God back again.

"I have made you a wedding dress," said Lusifer.

"Can I see it?"

Lusifer lay the dress on the bed in front of Dian, who was still in bed drinking coffee. She got up and held it in front of her, it was grey and purple with horizontal clouds, with a collar shaped like a cloud.

"It's lovely," said Dian. She gave him a silver ring with a blue stone. She put it on his finger and hung a silver jewel with a blue stone around his neck. Lusifer wondered if she knew he was going to propose.

"Sus couldn't keep his mouth shut; he was scared I would say no."

"Was there a chance you might?"

"Normally I would have said no, but not after what we have been through lately. We are getting married four months after the first time I saw you on the roof in Edinburgh."

"The fourteenth is a good date," said Lusifer. "All the black angels have been out on the meadows picking the bluebells of Scotland for hours. The whole table is full of them and the bells of Ireland."

"What are you gonna wear?"

"A black suit, white shirt and yellow shoes."

"Who have you invited?"

"Everyone in Falkland that we know."

"Lennie will be my maid of honour," said Dian.

"I know," said Lusifer. "I've already given her the dress I made for her, it's grey and pink with light grey clouds. Sus will be my best man."

"And he's gonna wear a black suit and emerald green pointed suede shoes?"

"He will. We have to go," said Lusifer and looked out the window. "They all stand by the gate waiting for us."

Dian drank the last of her coffee and put on the wedding dress. When they came outside Raven started to play the trumpet.

"Raven has just learned how to play," said Lusifer to Dian.

They resisted the urge to cover their ears. It was impossible to interpret which song he was playing; he had probably composed the piece himself.

"Let's run," said Lusifer, "maybe he'll stop playing."

Raven didn't, he flew while he played, he only stopped when he saw all the guests put their fingers in their ears.

When they were wed, Sus gave the first speech. He laid out broadly why Lusifer loved Dian.

"I'm gonna tell you why I love you," said Lusifer to Dian and got up. "You don't make a noise about trifles; you see when I'm tired and let me rest. I know you'll rescue me if you can, and until now you have managed to do so every time."

The blue hour came and lowered itself over the Hidden Place. Everyone was calm inside, they had reason to celebrate, after the hundred and first formula, nothing could go wrong. Dian looked at the guests chatting with each other, and the stars that eventually appeared in the sky. Orion's belt shone brighter than usual.

Who would have thought that the diamond clothes came from there? thought Dian.

She toasted with Timmy, the star people had made him a diamond coat and hat, Lusifer had given him black suede pointed shoes. Timmy raised his glass against Dian's, they didn't say anything, they just looked at Orion's belt.

"I hope Raven doesn't begin to play trumpet again," they heard Lusifer say.

91

Something was going on, Dian could feel it in her bones, she asked Lusifer if they were going down to the inner core of the earth again. He nodded.

"When?" asked Dian. Lusifer just looked at her.

"It's now, isn't it?" Lusifer nodded again.

Dian put her wings tightly around her and set her body in full spin. This time she didn't think, it went really fast. Lusifer landed at the same time as her.

"Did you use the number formula?" she asked.

"I multiplied it with a million."

"We went down in a split second?"

Lusifer laughed and said, "Ellie didn't know what hit her."

They stood and looked at the water Dian had cleansed the last time they were there. This time the water was full of star people. Dian didn't ask, she felt there was a time setting on the formula. She put the love chain around the water, then she took the DNA-chain in the water.

The DNA-chain went up in a spiral, all the way up to the Milky Way and took all the star people with it. Zodiak had been obsessed with power and fame, he wanted it to be his legacy, that he was a great ruler. Dian sent them home to Zodiak, so he could bring them back to life. She made an energy ball around the Milky Way, so none of them could leave again.

Jordi's water got a golden colour, fish swam around already, it was full of life.

"Darwin was right after all," said Dian. "It started with a fish."

"But who created the fish?" asked Lusifer.

This time Dian didn't fall asleep, she got to see the beautiful way up. The mountains, waterfalls and trees were one of the rainbow colours, then they flew into the next colour of the rainbow. They stopped and sat on one of the glass benches when they reached magenta. The mountains were dark red, almost purple, it was magical.

"Where was Jordi?" asked Dian.

"Jordi hid, he thought it was Zodiak who came to revenge all the star people."

"What happened?"

"The star people wanted to take over the earth, they decided to start by taking over the earth's inner core, but Jordi fooled them, he said if they were all in the water at the same time, they would get all the knowledge they needed to break you. They knew you were the only one who could stop them.

After they had heard what Jordi said, they all jumped into the water. Jordi did the same as I did with the scoundrels, he sent electricity through the water."

"So now everything falls back into place once more," said Dian.

"I believe so," said Lusifer, "anyway the star war is avoided."

They flew the rest of the way up and sat in front of the fire when they got home. They had just sunk into an armchair each when the door opened. It was Raven and Lukas.

"I heard it was just before we had a star war on our stairs," said Raven upset.

"That's right," said Lusifer. "The star people have always been our allies, but not any more obviously."

"I wonder what the next will be," said Raven. "What

happened in the inner core of the earth?"

Before Lusifer managed to tell, Sus came flying.

"Zodiak has found a loophole, he's on his way out."

Dian changed the energy ball into yellow and gold and intensified the field around the ball. It helped, Zodiak could never leave the Milky Way again.

Gyda came rushing through the door.

"God is captured!" she shouted.

"Where?" asked Lusifer.

"He went to try and reason with Zodiak."

Dian used the reverse formula. God was on his way to Zodiak.

"Don't go," she said to him.

God stayed at home. Soon after he came rushing through the door as well. Dian fetched a bottle of whisky and a bottle of brown rum for Raven. They toasted in silence, what they were toasting for, they didn't know, God only knew that the diamond clothes had lost their charm.

Zodiak contacted him soon after through his thoughts.

"They are furious because they can't leave the Milky Way," God said to Dian.

"Just let them be furious," said Dian.

Lusifer didn't say anything. After a while Dian asked him what he thought.

"Let's release them and see what happens. But not here, we need more space."

"Send them to my garden," said God.

Dian removed the energy ball, and soon after Zodiak and the star people came fumbling through the air.

God was full of excuses. Zodiak didn't bother to answer, he was too busy giving Dian the evil eye.

"You want to rule the world?" asked Lusifer.

"I do," Zodiak replied.

"The star people are welcome to settle anywhere in the world," said Lusifer, "no need to rule the world."

Zodiak sneered now, Lusifer could hardly understand what he was saying. Zodiak said he wanted power, honour and fame. The star people liked what Lusifer had said about them settling down wherever they wanted. They began to discuss where they wanted to live.

"We're gonna rule the world!" yelled Zodiak.

Most of the star people were gone in a blink of an eye. Only a couple of hundred stayed behind. Dian wanted to be sure that God was on her side before she did anything, so she asked him what he thought.

"I think you are right, and I'm wrong," said God and looked down. Zodiak and Dian stood looking at each other for several minutes, nobody said anything. Dian waited for Zodiak to do something, but he didn't.

Finally, she made a new energy ball around him, and sent him back to the Milky Way. She sealed the energy ball once more and sent four laying eights around as guards.

Dian understood what Timmy meant when he said that he missed God in his normal clothes. The diamond clothes had manipulated him, that's why God had gone to the Milky Way, and asked Dian to free the star people.

Dian and Lusifer had given away the clothes at the last minute, otherwise the clothes would have manipulated them too.

It had been impossible for Zodiak to imagine that Dian and Lusifer would give away such a beautiful gift.

If they hadn't given away the clothes, Zodiak would have managed to take over the world.

"It's on a hanging hair all the time," said Sus. "What's next?"

"Hard to say," said Lusifer. "There's two days left till the twenty-second of July when everything should calm down.

The gateway is closing, twenty-two is the double of eleven, maybe everything ends up being turned upside down, if we are lucky, we land on our feet."

"Let's fly where the wind takes us," said Sus. "I fly first, I have never flown first in wing with you two present."

The wind carried them to all the valleys evil had used as main arteries for their evil thoughts and wickedness. They flew in all the valleys where they hadn't been able to speak before, evil had heard everything.

Lusifer and Sus started singing "To Be by Your Side."

92

It was the twenty-second of July; Dian had said the last formula the night before. Then she had received the message that she shouldn't say any more formulas. Dian used the truth formula to see if they tricked her again, but something stopped her, she listened to her heart instead. It said that they were right, she couldn't even use the truth formula.

Sus showed up a little later and said that Dian had to save Lusifer, he was dying. Dian felt that it wasn't true. Sus begged on his knees that she had to do something, Lusifer had two seconds left to live. The formula was ready, it was HC 202 to the left, and 44458 to the right.

Dian said HC 2 before she felt it was wrong, she stopped herself by saying, "Fuck!"

Sus laughed before he collapsed, Dian didn't have to ask if it would have gone to hell if she hadn't stopped herself. She went to sleep; she couldn't stay awake any longer.

Lusifer showed up when Dian was almost asleep. They slept like two stones the rest of the night. The next morning was a heavy day to wake up to.

"Why are we so depressed?" asked Dian.

"I have lost Storm," said Lusifer.

"What happened?"

"He chose to go with Zodiak to the Milky Way, he has been Zodiak's spy."

Lusifer couldn't believe that he had lost his best friend. The only reason Dian had trusted Storm was because Lusifer had trusted him, she wondered if he still did, but she didn't ask.

"I've heard that Raven and Lukas started a company," she said instead.

"Guess what it's called?" asked Lusifer.

"It can only be one thing," Dian replied, "Rats & Toys."

"Raven makes the toys and Lukas is selling the rats as pets. He is keeping the gang of rats that performed for Dine."

"Where do they stay?"

"Lukas has an outbuilding they are using."

"I like how you have decorated here," said Dian.

"The wallpapers with the psychedelic patterns, and the armchairs with the iguanas are from Timorous Beasties. Josef Frank is responsible for the curtains."

"Teheran and Hawaii," said Dian impressed. She wasn't depressed anymore. The changes Lusifer had made worked on the nervous system straight away.

They decided to sit in the garden and have some peace and quiet. Soon after Raven and Lukas appeared, then Elwin and Lennie. They got invited to the pub later on, Elwin planned a meal on the first floor with white candles in the large silver candelabras and white damask tablecloths. Raven asked if he and Lukas were invited too.

"Of course," Elwin replied, "you are here now, I would never have invited Dian and Lusifer without you. There's only one thing," he said sternly to Raven. "Do not bring the trumpet."

Raven didn't answer, he just looked down at his purple suede shoes. Lusifer had given them to him when Raven returned as himself.

"Don't be sad," said Lennie, "you have a beautiful singing voice. It's more than can be said about Dian."

They all looked at Dian, then they burst out laughing, they had all heard Dian sing, when she thought she was alone.

"I heard about Storm," said Lennie to Lusifer when they stopped laughing.

"Sus and Markus are moving back to their childhood home, since Storm is gone."

"Everything is back where it started," said Lennie. "Sus and Medusa moved to the Hidden Place to look after Snowflake and Blackbird. Now that they are big enough to take care of themselves, Sus moves back to his old house."

"How was it to say formula number 222?" asked Elwin.

"I almost collapsed," said Dian, "the formula needed me to use a part of my brain that is only available when collapse is banging on the door. I was so fed up that it was just before I decided to lay down inside a hedgehog for the rest of my life."

"We heard that for the first time you couldn't listen to your heart, and not use the formula of truth. What did you do?"

"I could tell by looking at Lusifer's face that he wanted me to reason. I used logic, reason and emotion at the same time, Einstein calls that combination a bomb."

"Einstein is right," said Lusifer. "When you have used everything, then the only thing left is reason."

"Are you glad it is over?" asked Raven.

"I haven't understood it yet, when I do, I'll be over the moon."

"You will understand it tonight," said Elwin.

"Your best friends will celebrate with you, and that's exactly what you need."

93

God sat and moaned to Timmy day in and day out. "It could have gone so wrong he said constantly." Timmy was about to lose his marbles. He called out to Lusifer and said he had to come fast. Dian went too. She could see that Timmy was about to break, so she told him to pack his suitcase.

Lusifer talked to God while Dian took Timmy to Lukas and Dine. She asked Lukas if Timmy could stay with them for a while.

"Of course!" Lukas said with a smile. "He can stay in Lady and Mantle's room."

Timmy wore the diamond hat and the diamond coat.

"Shouldn't we send all the diamond clothes back to where they belong?" asked Dian.

"Love to! It was after God began to wear the diamond clothes that he changed."

"Come by more often," said Dine to Dian, "it's nice when somebody suddenly stands at your door."

"I agree," said Dian. "You know where we live too."

"If the radio isn't on too loud," said Lukas and grinned.

Lusifer failed to calm down God. Dian had to use the reverse formula on him. Timmy moved back to his house the very next day; he was overjoyed that God was himself again.

Dian and Lusifer went home and sat in the garden. The sun shone and hit Dian's sand-coloured hair and made it golden.

"You look like an angel," said Lusifer.

"Is that supposed to be a compliment?" asked Dian.
Lusifer didn't know what to say, he just laughed.
Raven came around the corner.
"What's so funny?" he asked.
"Dian wonder if it's a compliment to look like an angel."
Raven looked at his hands and feet and said, "Hell knows, I don't." Lusifer just laughed even more.

94

On Thursday the thirtieth of July, Dian sat and ate an ice cream outside the Village Shop in Whiting Bay. A pod of dolphins appeared from the water jumping up and down towards Lamlash, Dian knew some things were about to change fast.

It was a blue moon the day after, usually the blue moon appeared every second year. Dian dreamed the black angels showed her the secret entrance. When she woke up, she had orange clothes on, Lusifer wore turquoise clothes.

Dian understood that all the black angels were about to get a new colour.

Raven was pink, Sus green, Lukas blue, God yellow, Elwin red, Oak light blue, Purple purple, Midas black, Gyda grey, Eloise light grey, Lennie light green, Markus light pink, Angus light yellow and Flora golden.

The sky was bright blue, Dian decided to spend the rest of the day outdoors. She drove cross the island when she passed a glen with a mountainside where different patterns were revealed. It was two lily-shaped patterns where deciduous trees grew instead of spruce trees, they looked like stylized French lilies. Three lines went straight down the mountainside where the trees didn't grow.

Finally, there was another lily-shaped pattern that went all the way up to the mountain.

At the bottom of the glen, Sliddery Water went down to the firth. At one point Sliddery Water had been bloody red. Some

Vikings had decided to settle down in the glen, something the Hamilton clan completely disagreed with, they had surprised them while they slept. The clan wanted as much blood as possible, they had slaughtered the Vikings like cattle and thrown them into Sliddery Waters afterwards.

Dian let the lily-shaped forms and the lines get different colours. It was the same colours as the ones the black angels and druids got. The first lily was turquoise, blue and green. It was Lusifer, Sus and Lukas' colours.

The line was pink, purple and light pink. It was Raven, Purple and Markus' colours.

The other lily-shaped form turned orange, yellow and red. It was Dian, God and Elwin's colours.

The line was light blue, light green, golden and light yellow. It was Oak, Lennie, Flora and Angus' colours.

The last lily became grey, light grey and black. It was Gyda, Eloise and Midas' colours.

The line that turned into white was Jesus' colour.

Dian sent the lines and the lilies into the burn; they were floating out to the Firth of Clyde and yonder around Ailsa Craig. Then she sent the lines and the lilies off to the Ness of Brodgar.

The colours came together at 4.55 p.m. The first time they mixed was at 4.56. The colours went apart again, only to be mixed again at 4.57. The last time the colours mixed was at 4.58.

Everyone held each other's hands before being thrown into the air and sent to the Ness of Brodgar. They were sent up again, this time they lost all their colours.

The eternity symbol came from the Ness of Brodgar, that's why the black angels and druids had chosen to change their colours there. They didn't get their colours before Dian made time fall into place. She had a feeling the time would fall into its place on March the twenty-second, 2017.

Dian wrote down the names and colours of the black angels and the druids. She got the formula 63132-1. 63132 was sent to the left and 1 to the right.

The formula was sent around the first time at 08.58 on the twenty-second of March. Next was 09.00, the third 09.02, and the fourth time 09.04. Number nine stood for both on earth and in the sky. It could be turned around and become number six.

Number four stood for spring equinox, summer solstice, autumnal equinox and winter solstice. Dian first thought she had to wait until the summer solstice to send the second formula around, this time reversed from the way the first formula was passed around. She didn't, the formula could be sent around four times during the same day.

The formula gave the colours back to the world. The whole rainbow spectrum became a part of each living cell on earth and in heaven. The colours gave the druids and the black angels their original power back.

As usual, Dian hadn't been told anything in advance. Sus told her when it was all over, that the colours were just as important as faith hope and love.

Dian did so many formulas every day that the black angels couldn't tell her what it was all for. She just did it, but it was time for a change, it was time for her to live more in the real world.

95

Lusifer had just realised that Storm was the Devil. Keep your friends close, but keep the enemy closer, that's what he had done without realising it. Storm was originally from the Milky Way, he was Zodiak's son. None of them knew, not even God. Storm had kept it hidden from them.

Raven came along and Lusifer told him what he had realised.

"Your best friend, how do you feel?"

"I trusted him, but not the way I trust you, Dian and Sus, and that says something, doesn't it?"

"Storm has been too close to you," said Dian. "It's difficult to see who you have around, when they are so close."

"She's right," said Raven, "if you hang a picture on the wall, you always take a few steps backwards to see if it hangs straight. I think what really fooled you was that he is Sus' brother. You can't get your head around that they are brothers, something tells you they are the same."

"It's true," said Dian. "Look at you and Jesus, you are completely opposite, and you are brothers."

Lusifer had to sit down. He still couldn't believe that Storm had managed to fool him all these years.

"That man knows everything about me."

"He doesn't," said Raven. "He doesn't know what you are thinking about him right now."

"I have to start my life all over again."

"Nobody can start their life all over again," said Dian. "You need to understand something. You gave him the best of you for so long, the years ahead of you, he will get nothing."

"Dian's right," said Raven. "What you have already given him isn't something you need to forget, or the rubbish word forgive. Nope, my friend, all you need to do is live your life with people you know you can trust, and that's us."

"And you can trust me," said Sus. "He had been listening to what they were saying in the hall. We are here for you, and you are here for us."

"What happens now?" asked Dian.

"We have a concert to attend to, that's why I came by. Andrew and four boys are about to start their first gig in the square."

"I saw the billsticker," said Raven. "Release concert with the Kings of Fife on Saturday the fifteenth of August."

"There were once seven Pictish kings in Fife," said Dian.

"No time for a history lesson," said Sus, "the concert starts now."

"Five ten year old," said Lusifer and smiled. "The star trolls suddenly became ten years and teen stars."

"Did you do the same with Andrew and Blair?" asked Dian Sus.

"They would have lost all their friends otherwise."

They got ready to go, and managed to reach the square just in time to hear them play Scotland's national anthem.

Falk and Hauk both wore glasses with thick lenses. Falk hit on a tambourine and Hauk played acoustic guitar and moved his left hip. Falk wore a green jacket and Hauk a black shirt, both wore tight trousers that had been pulled all the way up under their arms.

The funniest was Scott playing bass, he had exactly the same weird dancing as the bassist in the Proclaimers. He held the bass under the armpit. Andrew played drums and Robin electric guitar. They played only the one song, but it was enough, they had copied the Proclaimers down to the smallest detail.

96

Dian sent love to the left and hatred to the right. She didn't know that it was the formula for creating balance in the world. All the sorrows that had been, and were in the world, were filtered through her continent by continent.

It would take a couple of hours until it was over at twelve o'clock. The black angels had never filtered all the sorrows of the world through a human before, they were worried about how Dian would handle it. They sent all the joys through her at the same time to preserve the balance.

God was worried, he talked to Dian after the clock had passed 23.45 and she had sent 23 to the left and 45 to the right. God saw all the feelings that went through her body and came out on the other side as neutral emotions, ready to be used again. He hoped she would make it through if he talked to her all night. Dian read his mind and said she was mentally fine, or as usual, she added, all she needed was a good night's sleep.

Dian slept for twelve hours. When she woke up Sus, Raven, God and Oak stood watching her.

Lusifer checked if she was okay. He drew a sigh of relief shortly afterwards; Dian was herself again. They had been watching her for five hours. She usually woke up at seven a.m. If Dian wasn't in balance, it meant that everything had failed.

When Lusifer told them she was balanced, they changed colours on their clothes to white shirts and pants with a yellow glow, it looked as if the sun was shining on them. The wings were yellow, golden and white, Oak and God also had wings now. Raven's hair had changed, it was long and smooth at the back and stood to all sides in front and on the sides.

"We want to hear a nice song before we leave," said Raven.

"Which one?" asked Dian.

"When an Old Cricketer Leaves the Crease."

Dian asked if they were going to die.

"For me, the song is about life," said God, "not death."

Dian put on the song on the record player in her bedroom, and Sus, Lusifer, Raven, God and Oak stood calmly and solemnly in a row in front of the window.

When the song was over, Raven said, "It's been a pleasure," then he disappeared.

Next out was Oak. "I lost my son, but I always had you."

God said that Dian was always welcome to come and visit him and have a biscuit and a cup of coffee.

Sus didn't know what to say, but he knew Dian understood so he just left.

"Five months and a week," said Lusifer when they were alone.

"It's over," said Dian, "is it really just five months and a week since the thirteenth of March?"

Lusifer nodded. "Maybe we'll have an ordinary day," he said and laughed.

97

"Tell it again," Scott said.

Robin, Falk, Hauk, Honey and Scott sat in Raven's bed. He had just woken up, his hair stood to all sides.

"What do you want to hear?" Raven asked sleepily.

"We want to hear when you swam naked in the holy druid river," said Scott.

"Life of Water," mumbled Raven and put his pillow behind him before he sat up.

"For the first time no one believed in Dian. When Dian asked if they were going to die, they had first become completely speechless, they thought it was so strange that she saw straight through them all the time.

It was God who saved them, he said for him the song was more about life than death, but they had said goodbye for good to Dian that day. There were no formulas that could help her either, the battle was lost. It was let us do or die, but there was nothing we could do."

"How did you know?" asked Falk.

"Zodiak used Jesus' thoughts and made him do what he couldn't."

"Because Dian had encapsulated Zodiak and Storm into the Milky Way," said Honey.

"That's right," said Raven. He tried to explain to the star trolls why Jesus was so weak. "Lusifer was on earth most of the time and God, Gyda and Jesus were mostly in the seventh heaven."

"Where were you?" asked Falk.

"I was with Lusifer."

"Why didn't Jesus fight?" asked Hauk.

"He was afraid of being hurt," Raven replied.

"In other words, he is a coward," said Hauk.

Raven didn't answer, he just looked down, he still felt tired.

They had all been so intent on dying. The last thing he had said to Dian before he left was: It's been a pleasure. Sus hadn't been able to say anything. Lusifer had stayed behind, he had the worst job, he had to hide the fact that they were going to die. He also had to hide that Dian was going to die.

Dian could tell they were nervous, but she didn't understand why. She suddenly understood what had happened the day before, when they kept telling her to go to Whiting Bay.

She brought a sheepskin so she could sit outside and read the newspaper and kill some time. She spent three hours in Whiting Bay. Finally, the black angels were satisfied, and Dian was able to go home again.

Eventually it dawned on her that she had been a decoy. The black angels knew that nothing was going to happen in Whiting Bay, but the one they wanted to expose didn't. Dian suddenly understood who it was they had exposed, that was why they were so sick and tired of everything. They were about to give up a battle that had been ongoing for more than three thousand years.

It wasn't something that broke them, but someone, and that was Jesus. Sus remembered the time Dian had said that she thought Jesus looked stupid in his white and light blue dress the first time she saw him.

Sus had begun to keep an eye on Jesus after that. Jesus had great difficulty connecting with anyone, he just hovered on the surface and relished that so many worshipped and loved him.

God and Gyda knew how weak Jesus was, but they refused to do something about it, it got worse when Lusifer returned, everything was just amplified, Jesus was jealous.

He started putting together a plan with Zodiak. The first thing Jesus wanted was to kill Dian, that's why he had been in Whiting Bay that day. He had picked up what the black angels were talking about.

"Tell us the rest of the story," said Falk.

Ravn looked at him and continued, "Dian went to the Water of Life, she was so sick and tired of everything that she didn't even look for Lusifer. The black angels were swimming further down the river. Dian swam underwater up the river. Suddenly she noticed that the river got deep and cloudy. It was plant arms that held her tight."

Raven looked at the five star trolls that were captivated by the story, he could still feel the plant arms around his body.

"Continue," said Robin.

"Dian saw that I was captured too, I had almost drowned. She used the reverse formula and got me loose.

The day before, Dian had seen a programme about a spider that could see far only when the light switched to green. She coloured the river water green.

Zodiak saw through Jesus' eyes what happened, he was furious. He had intended to send electricity into the river to kill us all at the same time, he just wanted to have some fun first. Zodiak had captured me and Dian, he had planned that Lusifer should arrive too late to save us. Zodiak had composed one scenario after the other with Storm and Jesus. The only colour that protected the black angels in the river was green. Zodiak was so furious that he was about to blow up. Storm reassured him and said that Jesus could still do great harm.

Zodiak didn't believe him, because everybody had seen the real Jesus. Suddenly they saw Dian rising up from the river.

She had her golden wings closely wrapped around her in a yellow spiral.

Zodiak got really nervous, and asked Storm what she intended to do.

Storm answered that they had to wait and see, they didn't get out anyway.

Dian lay a layer of silver and a layer of turquoise, and finally an invisibility bubble all around the Milky Way. On the outskirt she lay a huge hedgehog with all the spikes out. The hedgehog made it possible to enter the Milky Way, but it was impossible to get out again.

All the black angels lay in the river and watched Jesus disappear, none of them tried to stop him."

"Where are we going to live now?" Robin asked when Raven had finished the story.

"You know I'm a born father," Raven said and laughed.

They jumped on top of him laughing, until Raven asked for mercy.

98

It was an illuminating day on Arran. The ones who didn't need to be inside were sitting outside enjoying the sun or they went for a walk. It was the perfect day to spend outdoors, it was just before the autumn fastened its grip.

Lusifer had found the perfect spot for fly fishing.

"If it's uphill then we fly," said Dian, "I hate uphill."

"Fair enough!" said Lusifer. "We can walk down again."

They flew past a waterfall and through a forest to a lake that lay surrounded by spruce trees. Lusifer had brought two fly fishing rods and a basket full of food and drinks.

"I know you like a salmon fly fishing rod the best, but here it's only rainbow trout that bite, so I got two trout fly rods."

"That's fine," said Dian.

The best with fly fishing anyway was the sound of the line flying through the air. Lusifer felt the same, he threw the line again and again.

After a couple of hours, it started to get cold, Lusifer packed the picnic basket and disassembled the rod, put it in the holster and hung it over his shoulder.

It was quiet in the dark forest they walked through. The sun rays only managed to penetrate small parts of the branches and hit the ground.

"It's strange how quiet it is," said Dian, "not a gust of wind."

"Let's hope it's not the quiet before the storm," said Lusifer, he felt calm and uneasy at the same time.

99

Dian had interpreted the three dreams Lusifer had sent her. It had been an appetiser, a dinner and a dessert. The result was amazing. Black and red were off and blue was on. It meant that the Devil was put out of action, and calm lay ahead.

"Do you think I should pick up Jesus from the Milky Way?" asked Dian.

"You could try," Lusifer replied.

Dian went to the Milky Way, but she failed to get the right Jesus out. Zodiak had made so many versions that Dian needed help. She sent back the copy of Jesus and asked the little blue bird for help.

"Find the real Jesus," she said to the bird.

It flew inside the Milky Way and whispered in Jesus's ear that Dian would try to get him out. Jesus followed the little blue bird to the exit. He saw that Dian opened the aperture just long enough for him and the bird to escape.

Jesus had been invaded by Zodiak when he tried to kill all the black angels and Dian.

He could only blame himself for being cowardly and weak. Dian said she thought Jesus should go and visit God; she knew he would appreciate him coming.

For the first time in a long while Jesus was looking forward meeting God, he felt he had finally grown up.

100

Dian went to the Ormidale hotel, she didn't want to, but the black angels insisted, she had no choice. Dian ordered steak, chips, vegetables, sauce and mushrooms. She couldn't order beer and whisky since she was driving.

The bar was full of men in their sixties. They were loud and only interested in each other and the beer they drank. Dian suspected there was a match starting soon, they wanted to be on track.

On the top shelf of the bar stood forty-eight whisky bottles. They were divided into Highland malts, Islay malts, West Coast malts, Campbeltown malts, Arran malts, Orkney malts, and Lowland malts.

Later in the evening the greenhouse attached to the hotel would host a disco, it was something that had been a regular event since the '70s.

Dian felt completely invisible, it was actually quite nice, no one looked at her, and she could be alone amongst people. She began looking forward to a delicious meal.

It flooded in with gentlemen in their sixties. Dian would normally have been sitting by the bar, but it felt wrong since she was only drinking orange juice.

It was a strange night; the date was 09.11. The world had never changed so fast before, as it did at this point in time. Nothing happened that evening, and Dian had no idea why she had to be there.

101

"What are you listening to?" Lusifer asked Dian. They were sitting on the terrace, watching autumn draw near.

"The Waiter."

Lusifer picked up the album and looked at it. "Black Heart Procession," he said, "I like the name."

Dian had put grey stones inside Lusifer, Sus and Raven the day before, they were high and low and couldn't calm down. Death had almost overtaken them so many times, they were constantly on the edge.

They had been sleeping in her bed with a grey stone belt around their stomach. Dian had asked God if it was okay if she put the hedgehog and the bubble around them so they could have a good night's sleep. God replied that he and the rest of the black angels should be able to hold the fort while they slept.

The next morning Dian blew on the grey stone belts, and they became small stones that settled in Lusifer, Sus and Raven's bodies where they needed them the most.

She asked them why they had tricked her to go to Ormidale. They replied that it was the same that had happened in Whiting Bay, they were going to smoke out somebody, but it wasn't Jesus this time, it was Storm.

He had entered the little blue bird when Jesus left the Milky Way. Storm had placed little devils in the men at Ormidale. He used them to camouflage himself. Storm had managed to escape, but it wouldn't be for long.

When Dian came home, she saw that thousands of little devils had gathered in her garden. She sealed the house with the hedgehog, the bubble, turquoise, silver, and invisibility carpet. Raven, Lusifer and Sus made Dian's house electric, then they stood behind the little devils and shouted, "Attack!" All the little devils stormed the house at once and were killed by the electricity.

Raven, Lusifer and Sus were let in through a flap in the invisibility carpet. Dian had made sour cream porridge earlier that day, she served it with white sugar, cinnamon, butter and red currant juice. None of them said anything, after the meal they fell asleep on the sofas and armchairs.

The next morning when Dian woke up, she felt depressed. She rejected Lusifer for the first time, he had left without a word. There was too much going on. It was impossible to be on earth, and it was impossible to be with the black angels. Dian didn't know if her condition would go away or not, she went outside into the garden.

"What is she doing?" Raven asked Sus.

He had just landed next to Sus who was watching Dian in her garden.

"She is digging a big hole," said Sus.

"What do you think she's gonna use it for?" asked Raven.

"Dian promised Lusifer that she shouldn't shut herself inside the bubble again."

Raven nodded and said thoughtfully, "And now she intends to dig a hole in the garden so she can be alone?"

Sus nodded and said, "Looks like it."

They stood and watched Dian lie down in the hole she had dug, and the other Dian threw earth over her.

"That's why she made another Dian, I wondered a bit about that," said Sus.

"Does she have enough air down there?" asked Raven.

"I have no idea, but I hope she knows what she is doing."

"She really has to be desperate to be alone."

"It's not easy to escape Lusifer," said Sus.

At the same time Lusifer came flying. "What are you looking at?"

"We want to see how long Dian manages to be buried," said Sus. Lusifer looked down at the brown soil that was recently dug up.

"Do you mean to say that Dian has buried herself, and you are just watching?" Lusifer asked furiously.

"That's right," Sus replied, "she wants to be alone." A large load of soil buried the whole house.

"And there the other Dian got buried," Sus said.

Lusifer just stood and gaped, he didn't know what to say, he had to sit down for a while.

"I have heard the expression that one should go and dig oneself down," said Raven, "but I've never seen anyone do it before."

"Neither have I," said Sus.

"What shall we do?" asked Lusifer perplexed.

"We are gonna let her have some air," said Sus.

"Not a stupid idea," said Raven, "what doesn't one do to escape the first lover of the universe?"

Lusifer looked furiously at him, but Raven couldn't hold it in any longer, neither could Sus, they burst out laughing.

Lusifer was so angry that he flew home to God and Gyda to get some sympathy. He shouldn't have done that, both God and Gyda laughed when he told them what had happened. Lusifer went back to the garden again.

"Dian!" he shouted, "if you come out from the soil, you're allowed to hide inside the hedgehog and the bubble."

The soil covering the house disappeared, and Dian arose from the earth.

"I'm going to take a shower," she said to Lusifer, "and don't you muck up while I'm in the shower."

"Muck up," said Raven to Sus, and they cracked up laughing again.

Lusifer snuck inside and hid underneath the bed. He didn't dare to leave Dian alone in case one of the little devils had managed to hide too.

He had never in his life heard anything so stupid as someone digging themselves into a big hole in the ground. Lusifer had to laugh a little, Dian could still surprise him.

102

Dian and Raven went up to Glenashdale Falls.

"Glen means valley, and dal means valley," said Dian.

"And in between you have ash," said Raven, "someone named Glenashdale on purpose. We both know that evil has used the valleys as transport oars."

Dian crossed the first waterfall, the contrasts between the water and the reflection of the leaves hanging down was stronger than usual. By the next waterfall the shadows had grown stronger, it was a combination between a calm and unsettling nature. It was as if the surroundings had been disturbed too much.

"Here you have two valleys connected through two waterfalls," said Raven. "The area doesn't feel right somehow, you are right, it has been disturbed. Where evil has been, there is also a great force you can use. You can get rid of the past and only look to the future, it's harder than you think. That's why we are here, it's time to let go."

Dian drank coffee and watched the huge waterfall running down the mountainside. Behind her was a dark spruce forest, the sun was barely shining through. Dian finished her coffee before she did what she had come for.

Her past was burnt between the two waterfalls in Glenashdale. When she got up, the forest behind was even darker. The sun had disappeared behind a cloud.

There was still too much going on, but Dian felt okay again.

103

Dian drove to the horseshoe bench the day after the Blood Moon on the twenty-eighth of September. Half of the firth towards Ardrossan was bright blue, as was the cloudless sky. Close to Arran lay a thick fog that looked like cotton waves.

The next day Dian went around the island. The fog moved from village to village, the ground was steaming wet. Drops hung so heavily on the spiderwebs that they were dragged almost down to the ground. Except for where the fog was, the sky was blue, and the sun shone. The fog had transformed everything that had come up from the warm and steaming soil during the night.

The butterflies on the island were so full of all the nectar they had eaten that they just lay on the ground gasping. The Blood Moon had changed the earth in a way that reflected the nature and the animals.

Dian drove through Monamore glen, she had to drive over the last cattle grid at a particular time. She managed to, so she stopped the car and sat on top of a table by the road, resting her feet on the seat.

Lusifer, Sus and Raven joined her, none of them said anything. They looked at the Firth of Clyde in a distance and listened to the burn trickling behind them. The buzz of a bumblebee was the only other sound.

Dian had never seen Raven, Lusifer and Sus so calm before, she could hear their calm breathing. Suddenly she heard the beating of the wings of a raven flying high in the sky.

"What's going on?" asked Dian.

"Nothing is going on," replied Raven. "It's how it should be, you should be able to hear the wings of a raven high above."

"It's how it should be, but it's not?"

"It is hard to explain," said Sus. "We wanted to show you what was possible to hear if you want to. You can open your ears."

"Sounds in your ears reflect not only what happens on the outside, it also reflects what's going on inside of you. If you are listening to yourself or others," said Lusifer.

"It is made so simple," said Dian, "but all we do is complicate things."

"It's almost always someone else who complicates things for you," said Raven.

"The reason we survive being called the worst things all the time, is that we have each other," said Sus.

Dian decided to go to Machrie Moor. When she had parked the car and started to walk towards the Standing Stones, the time showed 4.58, she sent 4 to the left.

Purple showed up. He flew up on a mountain top. When she sent 58 to the right, it was herself who appeared. She flew up to the mountain top and stood next to Purple. On the way to the stones the same thing happened again twice.

When the clock showed 5.5, she sat and looked at the Standing Stone that stood in front of the moorland. Dian sent 5 to the right and 5 to the left.

It was a ceremony that appeared, but not between the black angels and the druids. It was between herself and Purple. Dian wore a white wedding dress and Purple a black suit. A reverend stood in the middle and consecrated them. Angus was Purple's best man, and Sus Dian's man of honour.

Lusifer came and sat beside her.

"You give the one you love a hard time," he said. "You two live in the same sphere, we don't."

Dian and Purple from the druid era appeared.

"When you managed all the formulas, you fixed everything that went wrong in the past as well," said Purple, "we can be with Hazel and Flora now."

Flora, Oak and Angus showed up.

"You know that everything is fine now," said Flora.

"I know," said Dian, "I have never been more happy."

Dian was left alone on Machrie Moor. It was almost seven o'clock in the evening, and the sun was on its way down. It was time to leave.

She arrived at the exact same place she had been at 4.58 just when the clock struck 6.58. Dian didn't quite know what it meant, but she thought it meant that she was in the right place at the right time.

On the way home she felt how tired she was.

"Buy yourself lot of snacks and watch a movie," said Raven, "and not nuts and raisins."

Dian did what Raven said, she stopped at the Co-op in Lamlash and bought all the snacks she could hold in her arms. When she came home, she tried to find a movie, but all she could find was a programme on Alba, about the Belted Galloway cow.

"Perfect," said Raven and fell asleep.

"All I want is to be completely brainless," said Sus.

"Count me in," said Dian.

Dian and Sus fell asleep in the middle of the programme, while Lusifer managed to stay awake until it was over.

The next day was the fifth of October. Storm and Jesus showed up now and then, they managed to lay something nasty here and there, it was activated as time went by. Dian put an end to everything that was suddenly activated.

Jesus had made himself a victim again, he moved in with God and Gyda. Timmy had moved out a long time ago, he couldn't take it anymore, Jesus was too much for him.

Dian saw that Lusifer was tired of not being able to talk to God alone, Jesus was there all the time, he thought he was such a good son, because he gave God and Gyda all his time and attention, but Jesus was just a pain in the ass.

Dian went home to God when she saw that he was alone in his workshop. She sat down on the bench; she didn't have to say anything.

God stroked his hand slowly through his hair and said, "It didn't turn out as I thought it would. Jesus is with me and Gyda all the time, he controls our lives with his presence. None of those we want to see are visiting anymore."

"Tell him to move out," said Dian.

God knew Dian was right. "I will," he said, and fell into heavy thoughts.

104

Lusifer said goodbye to Dian at Machrie Moor, but he couldn't leave straight away. He took Dian to the Hidden Place.

Dian knew their last hour had arrived. They didn't say anything. Lusifer lay her on the grass. This time he wanted to reshape them to two dark blue butterflies with gold on the wings.

They both had dark blue wings. The grass was dewy, and the drops hung large and heavy on the spider webs that were between the leaves of the old trees. The fog had moved from village to village over the recent days.

When the fog disappeared and the spiders spanned millions of nets, the butterflies arrived. No one had seen so many butterflies before. They were so heavy with nectar that they lay on the grass resting.

It wasn't as pleasurable between Dian and Lusifer this time, it was more sad. Time went faster and faster and soon it would be over. Dian looked closely at Lusifer and imprinted everything into her memory.

She asked to see him as a two-year-old. Lusifer gave her an image. He had dark curly hair and a round face with large blue grey eyes and a small red mouth. He looked at her in astonishment from the side.

Then Dian asked to see him as a ten-year-old. His hair was smooth and dark brown, Lusifer was serious and stood straight. The next age she wanted to see was when he was seventeen. Dian saw a Lusifer with black clothes and black straight hair to his shoulders, he was furious.

The next age was twenty-five. Lusifer was hard-working and

thoughtful. At thirty-five Lusifer sat on a rock in the wilderness and wept.

Forty-five was the age he was when she had met him this time. She saw a Lusifer who laughed pretty much all the time and was happy.

"Weren't you happy before we met?"

"It was a heavy matter we worked with; it seemed like it would never end. Do you want to decide the last song the Crow Choir should sing."

"The Mercy Seat."

"Why?"

"That's the first song you sang on Machrie Moor the first time I went there, but I think you should sing it on the Hidden Place this time."

"It will be good to sing it with certainty and not with rage as the last time," said Lusifer.

Lusifer stroked her hair. "You know the time we have together is soon gone?"

"Show me the two blue butterflies with gold on their wings," said Dian.

The day after Dian left Arran for good, it was the seventh of October. The adventure was over.

Back to reality, she thought.

Lusifer made himself invisible and stood next to Dian, who hung over the railing on the ferry and watched the island. She would just take this one last ferry ride over to the mainland, then the adventure would be over.

Dian put her hand on his.

Lusifer smiled, he should have realised that he couldn't hide from the best nutcracker in the universe.

It was a special moment when the Golden Apples of the Sun disappeared for good.